THE STOPOVER

PART ONE

A New Road

PETER THOMSON

A Signature Proof Publication, 2015

ISBN-13: 9781507768549
ISBN-10: 1507768540

FOR CHARLIE,

WILL AND EMILY

Born and brought up in St. Albans, UK and is
resident in France, where he lives with his wife
and an exceptionally enthusiastic mole; Peter Thomson
has been a merchant seafarer, soldier and businessman.
He is now an ardent gardener and novelist,
with two children and three grandchildren,
to whom this book is dedicated, and is a ready rebel to
join any cause against unfairness in society today.

The Stopover: A New Road is the first book in a
series of novels that introduces the small, agricultural
community of Bamptonville, Nebraska that lies off the
Interstate-80 freeway, somewhere between two
or three hour's drive west of Lincoln.

Should this town or any of its inhabitants or institutions
seem familiar to the reader the similarity is purely
coincidental. They are fictional, as is most of the story.

1

The crash of the judge's gavel ending his second marriage resonated in Greg Mitchell's head as he ran down the worn stone steps to get away from the courthouse and the injustice it served up to him this day; his mind crazed by confusion and disbelief.

At the bottom of the steps he stopped, turning back to look at the ancient building where, once again a contested divorce settlement had gone against him and upended his life. Greg glared at the iron studded oak door, regarding it now as a symbol of injustice. His jaw hung slack, quivering to match the trembling through his body at the court's arbitrary unfairness.

His wife's philandering made him the innocent party, yet she had won the case and that justified him hating not only her, but also the court for its unjust decision. With a growl of contempt, he scrunched up the court order and hurled it at the door; facing it in a pugnacious attitude, one of challenge, while his thoughts struggled to make sense of the court's findings.

The successful recruitment business he had built over the last five years was no longer his - wrested from him by the rap of a judicial gavel. The business belonged to her father, a family concern. Greg had no proprietary share; yet he had built it up from nothing, relying on the promise that one day it would be his. Until now he had depended upon Bailey's for his status in the business community and as the means to support his wife's lavish social round. Without Bailey's Recruitment he had nothing. No career! No home! No purpose and no income. His main reason for contesting the divorce was to retain his senior position in the company with the promise of succession to the top-job, given to him verbally soon after his marriage to the owner's daughter; all of which was now lost without leave to appeal the judgment.

His wife's expensive tastes ensured there were no joint savings and their few marital belongings were to be sold and shared between himself and Victoria, his newest ex-wife. He didn't overly care about these marital leftovers or even losing Victoria as a spouse; they shared little in common and had mostly lived their own lives. The loss of his involvement in the business caused him the deepest hurt and he resented that more than the loss of a wife or a marital home.

Fortunately there was no alimony to pay. He had come out of the proceedings emotionally scarred, but with some money in the bank, largely due to a generous redundancy package.

He gazed at the forbidding façade of that gray stone and unsympathetic building with an increasing sense of dry-mouthed loathing. In that instant the building became Greg's personal enemy, barring him from the happiness of a prosperous future. Thoughts of what might come next released a new and unfamiliar emotion inside him; the numbing sensation of fear for his immediate future. He was thirty-five years old.

Where could he go from here?

How could he pick himself up after this loss?

What could he do now?

His life revolved around Bailey's. The time was right for his ideas and success quickly followed their implementation. Under his direction, the tiny company rose from nothing to a position where people mentioned its name in the same breath as they spoke of Adecco and Randstad - the major international recruitment companies operating within the UK.

Two things motivated Greg in his business lifetime; his personal wellbeing and making money, for which he possessed a proven talent. He held scant need for personal friends or fellowship, being perfectly content with his own company. Both of his ex-wives complained he never let them get close to him, not really close so that they could be as one together. That was true. His first love was always the challenge of the business adventure of the moment; it captured his heart and soul leaving little of him for his wives. He could never understand their demands to spend valuable time with them in useless and unproductive domesticity and pointless socializing, taking him and his energies away from the paramount task of growing the business.

Greg stood still at the foot of the cold, stone steps feeling drained, angry and forsaken with yet another unfamiliar sensation washing over him. For the first time in his adult life Greg Mitchell experienced pangs of loneliness. There had always been somebody dutifully following behind to do his bidding at the click of his fingers. The awareness and concern of being totally alone swept over him to his surprise and dismay.

Everybody he knew was either a business or casual acquaintance. With no family or close friends to call upon for solace or even a place to stay for a few days, he must now look after every detail of his daily life himself. He thought back to the times when he rushed about the country, oblivious to everything except sourcing new business under the maxim, 'When you've done the deal, what's the point of relationships?' He knew the point of it now when he wished for somebody to turn to for comfort in this moment of intense distress. The realization frightened him. Greg rubbed his hand across his forehead and its receding hairline as the chill dread of emptiness coursed through his veins.

Greg walked away from the courthouse towards the High Street, struggling to come to terms with his situation; while his inner voice reminded him, 'You're on your own again. You'll be forty in only five years time. You have no wife, no family, no friends and with nowhere to go. All you have is a little cash in the bank. Could you settle for working for somebody else in an ordinary job?'

Greg shuddered, knowing it would never be enough. He believed his ill fortune was all down to this place and this day's events. Everything would come to rights again in a few days time. He'd be back to normal, building up another business venture in need of his abilities. What he needed was a break to turn his back on this upset.

"That's what I'll do!" He hollered at the next passerby, who jumped from the pavement into the road in shocked bewilderment. "I'm free now, of everything, I'll take a long break and start again. There'll be no holding back Greg Mitchell!"

There was nothing and no one to keep him here. He needed to get away and find himself and the more he thought of it, the more the idea appealed and gave him some small and instant relief from the anguish causing his hands to shake and his stomach churn. Various ideas for a holiday flowed through his head in quick succession. He settled on America where, in more affluent times, he found the pace of life and lifestyle agreeable. He decided to drive across the vastness of the USA from the East to West and back again.

Greg noticed the café on the other side of the road when a couple stood up to leave the small, seated area set out on the pavement. He felt the need for coffee and hurried across the street to occupy the vacated table. To his delight he found the café offered free wi-fi Internet access. With increasing excitement he opened his laptop and brought up the USA on Google maps. Names of cities and towns he might visit emerged from his laptop and the immediate problem of his divorce faded as he threw himself wholeheartedly into the task of planning his route.

Thirty minutes later, the coffee lay cold and untouched on the tablecloth beside him. He sat back in his chair with a clap of his hands and a huge grin on his face.

"Job Done!" He announced to nobody in particular, Greg had found his ideal route for his holiday and decided to travel along the Interstate-80 from New Jersey to California and back to Florida on the Interstate-10. The more he thought about it, the greater became its appeal. The route took him through places he had wished to visit at some time and others whose names he'd only heard of. It would be good to put some first-hand images and experiences to those names.

Three days later, Greg listened carefully to the Hertz rental clerk at the airport in Newark, NJ as he gave him directions to the freeway system and the Interstate-80.

2

Greg Mitchell snarled in frustration as he swung the wheel of the 5-Series and drove into yet another side street. "Where is this blasted Main Street?"

He beat the steering wheel and licked the dryness from his lips as they spread into a thin smile when he noticed a traffic light ahead.

"There you are!" he growled.

He pressed hard on the accelerator and the powerful BMW lurched forwards. For the tenth time he read from the typed paper lying on the passenger seat.

"Turn north from Charmain Street into Main Street and Melody Inn Motel is four blocks down on the west side."

He tapped the wheel in irritation as his eyes scanned the buildings for a street name.

"North! West! Don't they know left or right in this country?"

He released another gasp of exasperation when the light changed to red the instant before he reached it. Greg braked slightly, glancing swiftly to the left, with no oncoming traffic he stepped on the accelerator to swing right into Main Street.

The car was immediately bathed in a shaft of bright sunlight coming from between two buildings opposite that burned into Greg's eyes.

"What the hell?" He shouted as he jerked backwards, shielding his eyes from the dazzling glare as his foot stamped on the brake. The car swerved to the left. He heard a cry, followed by a heavy bump on the bonnet. A flash of blue passed the windscreen – like a large bundle of laundry.

"Shit," Greg yelled and scrambled out of the car. He caught sight of a boy in the road shuffling away from the car. A shock of chestnut hair fell across the youth's forehead, but not enough to hide the fear blazing from his bulging, almond eyes. Angry irritation replaced Greg's frustration. He pointed an accusing finger at the boy on the road as he scrabbled away on his back, dragging his left leg beneath him.

"What the bloody hell do you think you're playing at running across me like that? You could've got yourself killed, and God knows what damage you've done to my car?"

Turning to the car, Greg ignored the boy, striding to the front of the Beemer to inspect it for damage. The boy's mouth moved in speech, but the strident wail of a siren drowned his voice.

The police car skidded to a halt across the forepart of the BMW. A middle-aged deputy sheriff followed his blue shirted stomach out of the car, slapped a wide-brimmed hat on his head and walked over to the boy. Greg rushed towards the policeman.

"Officer I was turning right and this foolish boy"

"Stand back, Stand back." The officer shouted at Greg.

The deputy turned to face Greg, his left thumb hooked into his leather belt, his right hand hovering above the heavy service revolver holstered on the belt. Greg froze and the officer turned his attention to the boy.

"Are you hurt bad son?"

The boy shook his head in response, rising to a sitting position on the ground; pale, panting and looking frightened.

"Do we need to get you to a hospital or a doctor or somethin'?"

"No sir, thank you sir, I'm okay. I do need to get going sir."

The boy's mouth continued to open and close after speaking, gulping air like a fish out of water.

"Well you stand up and show me you're all right or you're going nowhere's 'cept to the emergency room."

The boy's face paled and the corners of his mouth twitched as he tried to hide the painful shock of the accident.

The teen staggered to his feet under the scrutiny of the deputy. The boy slapped his left side in an effort to show he wasn't badly injured and forced a quivering smile as he replied.

"See sir, I'm okay. It's just a scratch. I'll be good in an hour.

Can I go now please?"

The deputy grunted, then snapped. "You, wait right there."

"But sir" The boy protested, but was stopped in mid sentence by another bark from the deputy.

"I said wait!"

The deputy studied Greg quizzically as he took out a notebook and the stub of a pencil, licking it with a slow deliberation to add another blue line to his tongue. Greg hadn't seen an indelible pencil since his elementary school days twenty-five years earlier.

Greg was boiling inside, but controlled his feelings and stood quiet and still as the deputy took his time getting himself organized. Greg noticed the increasing anguish of the boy as he looked down the street every few seconds. It intrigued Greg because this was the direction in which the boy was running when they collided. His attention was brought back to the incident by a brusque question from the officer.

"I take it from your accent you're not from these parts!" It was a statement more than a question.

"No. I'm English."

"Your first time in the US of A?" The deputy's eyebrows rose.

"No, I've been a few times. On business." Greg felt the need to justify his maneuver. "And I know it's okay to turn right on a red light."

"Only when it's clear." Greg noted the mocking tone in the lawman's voice, prompting him to press his case.

"It was clear! There was no traffic coming from the left before I made the turn."

The smile on the deputy's lips flattened into a sneer. He spoke as a teacher might address a child.

"That's from the south and it was not clear from the north. I saw it all from the other side of the road. This kid was already crossing from the north when you made your turn – that's to your right."

"I didn't see him. The way was clear from the left. I mean the south." Greg was rattled, but reined in his feelings, for he knew he could be at least facing a traffic charge.

The deputy pushed back his hat to scratch with his podgy fingers among the sweat drops on his forehead to reveal the dark patches on his shirt below his armpit. The officer gritted his teeth and pointed at the traffic light swinging slightly in the breeze overhead.

"Well now, let me put you to rights here and now. You can turn right on a red only if your way is clear; that line there and that sign there says you have to stop first."

He pointed to a white line under the car, then to a sign hanging above the sidewalk. Greg's eyes followed the directions and felt a leaden lump come into his stomach, a lump that became heavier as the deputy continued.

"You didn't stop. You went over the line like you was turning right, then when you crossed it, you swung the wheel the other way - like you was trying to hit the kid."

The boy stood lopsided with his weight on his right leg, open mouthed and anxious to get away. Greg's mouth ran dry. He knew the deputy was right and that he was in trouble, yet the boy seemed shaken, but otherwise unhurt and eager to be on his way.

"Okay Sheriff, I take your point, but there's no harm done here. You can see the boy's fine. He just told us he is. I can just say I'm sorry, can't I, and let's leave it at that?"

"I'll be the judge of that." The deputy snapped.

He walked around the car making entries in his notebook and then pointed his pencil stub at the youth.

"What's your name boy?"

"Jesse White sir," Greg saw the boy shivering with the onset of shock and interrupted the deputy's questioning.

"Officer I've a blanket in the car and it looks like he could use it."

"I'll be the judge of that too! You stand where you are." Greg felt chastened, but remained standing silently by the car while the officer spoke to the boy.

"You'll be at the Community College?"

"Yes sir, Junior High." The deputy looked sideways at the boy with his eyebrows raised.

"Junior High?" The man's eyes took in the small and undeveloped frame of this smooth faced kid and sniffled. "You sure you're not a freshman. You don't look a day over ninth grade to me. And what's your big hurry? I saw you rush out into the road in front of this car."

Greg heaved a slow sigh of relief. Perhaps things wouldn't be so bad for him after all.

"I have an appointment at the grocery store sir, and I'm late already. Can I go sir? Please."

"You sure you're not hurt any?"

"No sir, just shaken up a bit. Maybe a bruise or two, I reckon."

The deputy nodded. "Very good, move along. I know where to find you if I need you for a statement."

Greg watched the boy limping away as fast as he was able, then turned to face the officer. The blue clad policeman stood an inch from him. A slight breeze brought more dust along with a fearful smell. Greg exhaled and grimaced.

"What on earth is that?"

"What is what?"

"That awful smell?"

The policeman's lips twisted into a downward grin. "Oh that, we call that Noble's Breath. It comes from the chicken farms on the north side. There's a few of 'em up there."

Greg covered his face with a handkerchief and mumbled through it.

"How'd the people put up with that stench every day? Isn't anybody doing anything about it?"

The deputy's eyes lifted to settle on Greg with a wry smile and he inhaled deeply.

"It's the manure heaps. The Nebraska Rockies – some folks call 'em. These farms give work to a lot of families round here."

He took another deep breath and added, "You get not to notice it after a while." Then the smile faded. He held out his hand and barked. "ID?"

Greg took his passport from his back pocket, handing it grudgingly to the deputy, acutely aware of the eyes of the passers by in Main Street and the scowls of drivers as they maneuvered awkwardly around his obstruction. Greg shuffled his feet in discomfort and asked.

"Do we have to do this here?"

The lawman continued to study the passport and didn't look up as he replied.

"We can always go to the office. I got you a'ready for a hundred an' twenty dollars and thirty days jail as it is. And I always get inspired in the office."

Greg bit his tongue to stifle the outburst that sprang to his lips.

"What brings you to Bamptonville Mr. Mitchell?" The deputy squinted at Greg although the sun was at his back.

Greg shielded his eyes from the strong setting sunshine and shrugged. "I'm just passing through and picked it out as a stopover for the night."

"Is that so now? Where've you come from today?"

"Iowa City."

The lawman whistled. "That's four hundred maybe four hundred and fifty miles from here. You been drivin' all day?"

Greg saw the trap and nodded his affirmation, hoping the officer would pass over it, but he didn't.

"You must be real tired after all that drivin'."

"Not really, it's a good comfortable car and the drive was mostly on the Interstate Highway."

The lawman said nothing, but licked his pencil prior to writing something else in his notebook. To break the silence, Greg added.

"I'm looking for the Melody Inn, I'm booked in for the night. They said they'd keep the room for me until five."

The deputy looked at his watch. "Melody Inn eh? It's ten after five right now, but I wouldn't let that worry you, they're never full. Not these days and they can always find a room for wheeler-dealers like you just passing through."

The officer spoke as if making an accusation, but his eyes remained on the pages of Greg's passport.

"It says here you're Gregory Vernon Mitchell, Trader, age thirty-five. What do you trade in Mr. Mitchell?"

"Anything at all - commodities mostly." Greg replied, coming onto the balls of his feet, sensing he was coming under attack.

He saw his reply increased the officer's interest in him and his doings, prompting Greg to add, "anything legal that is."

The deputy appeared to smile as he handed back the passport. "I'm curious about you Mr. Mitchell. Tell me. What's an English businessman doing in the little plains town of Bamptonville? What commodities are you trading here? Are you like other out of State wheeler-dealers that stop over in the Melody Inn with no wife alongside? That's what I want to know?"

A spasm of concern passed through Greg as he understood the deputy's implication and opened his arms in an attitude of good behavior.

"Aw come on officer. I'm on a trip. For a break..."

The deputy stopped him by raising a hand. "I need to inspect your car. Stand aside."

Greg stood back, knowing it was futile to argue. The accusing eyes of other drivers on him as they drove slowly past made him more uncomfortable and increased his irritation. The officer pointed to the sidewalk. "Stand over there, where I can watch you."

Greg sauntered onto the sidewalk, kept his cool with difficulty and waited impatiently while the officer rummaged inside his car.

Sharp stabbing pains ran down Jess's left leg. He tried not to show his hurt as he hurried as fast as he could manage to McKendrick's General Store. The storekeeper was bringing in the last of the goods he displayed on the sidewalk prior to shutting the shop for the night.

"Mr. McKendrick. Mr. McKendrick," Jess bawled, "I'm sorry I'm late. I got held up by the deputy sheriff."

The storekeeper put down the bucket of mops he carried and wiped his hands on the apron tied around his waist. His eyes looked tired and sad as he shook his head.

"Sorry Jess. Rules is Rules. I said I was hiring at five…" He stopped to look at his fob watch. "Not twenty after. The job's gone."

"But Mr. McKendrick I need that job real bad. I've got bills to pay."

The elderly shopkeeper heard the tears in the boy's voice and guessed they were not far behind in his eyes.

"I'm sorry Jess. I told you I wanted to help you and I really did. If you'd been here at five, you'd have got the job. But you weren't and it's gone to Ricky Horowitz. I'm sorry, but business is business; and that means five o'clock is five o'clock, not twenty after."

The shopkeeper picked up the bucket, went inside and closed the door behind him. Jess stood outside, his mouth agape with dismay as the man turned the sign on the window to 'CLOSED' prior to pulling down the shade behind it.

Jess stood rooted to the spot looking at that closed door. It represented so many things to him and his situation. He couldn't think beyond this moment. His mind whirled over and over again what the storekeeper had said - the job would've been his if he got here on time and his troubles would be over. But he hadn't and the job went to Ricky Horowitz, leaving him with no other acceptable remedy to solve his financial problem.

A girl's voice called out from the other side of the street, snapping him out of his stupor.

"Jess, Jess, over here." The girl stood outside Harry's Place, the bar come diner where they met and shared a Coke on most days after school.

He turned around and waved. The road was clear and he made his way across the street to meet her.

The deputy was opening everything in the car that would open, even examining the trim for likely concealment places. Greg nibbled his lip to curb his impatience, shifting his weight from one foot to the next. The officer was finishing up in the back seat.

Greg's papers and objects from the glove compartments were strewn over the front seat. He couldn't stand it any longer and was about to say something when the girl's voice shouting for Jess diverted his attention.

A teenage girl with long blonde hair tied back wearing a white, below the knee frock that would have been fashionable in the 1950's waving and calling from outside a diner.

He looked to where she was calling and saw Jess get into the road and stumble across, half dragging his left leg behind him with his head bowed and the boy's whole manner one of dejection.

Something else must have happened. Something important. Greg recognized once again the fear in the boy's eyes about being kept back when he lay in the road.

Greg decided he wanted to know what problem might be upsetting this kid. Something else stirred inside and it made him uncomfortable. It was the raw twinge of guilt. He knew that whatever misfortune had befallen that boy then he, Greg Mitchell, was its likely cause.

The deputy slammed closed the trunk and came around the car brushing his hands together.

"Have you seen what you wanted to see officer?" Greg could not keep a touch of contempt out of his tone and the policeman picked it up. He pushed back his hat to show a broad, furrowed forehead dripping with sweat runs.

"For now I have."

"Don't you want to see my driver's license? You haven't asked for it yet." The layer of contempt in Greg's tone thickened.

"I don't need to. This is a rental car. I've seen the papers and they would've checked your license so I don't need to. But if you insist your highness." The officer made a mocking bow.

Greg held his breath to control his temper before asking another question.

"So what now officer? And what was that all about." Greg waved towards the car.

The deputy stuck his thumbs in his belt, shifting it around his waist to make him more comfortable as he replied.

"I'll answer your second question first. In this year of our Lord 2007 we've got for the first time in Bamptonville something of a drug problem. The kids, the ethnics and other good people we're finding with cannabis and illegal substances and we don't like it. Crime's up too. So we go after the dealers that bring it in here."

Greg shrugged, but felt another stab of concern shaft through his body.

"What does that have to do with me?"

"What it has to do with you Mr. Limey wheeler dealer, is that every time we get someone like you through here on your own, a trader, in a big plush car, stayin' one night at the Melody Inn we find drugs on the street soon after. That's what this is about."

Greg closed his eyes as he realized the man wasn't just picking on him for no reason. He cleared his throat. "Sheriff I apologize for my attitude. I thought you were just picking on me. I'm not into drugs and I will cooperate fully with you."

A broad grin flitted across the deputy's face.

"That's nice. That's real nice. At this time you're up for traffic violations. If that kid, Jesse White, prefers charges you'll be seein' Judge Denman in the morning. Don't leave town without checkin' in first with me. Got it?"

Greg watched the deputy drive away, and looked around the town from where he stood. He saw mostly frame buildings with paint cracked by hot summer sunshine and freezing winters, now faded and peeling with age. Except for the asphalt roads and electricity this could be the town as it was when the first settlers came and built it out of the plains a century ago.

Greg couldn't help thinking about John Wayne and expected him to ride in on his horse at any moment. Even some of the side street buildings retained the old boardwalks outside. One night here would be enough for him.

He got in the car. His mind immediately threw up the image of that kid: hurt, defeated and dragging his injured leg across the street to meet his girl. The kid bothered him, not only because he might press charges, but also for other reasons he could not fully determine or even understand.

He started the car, drove to the Melody Inn and checked in.

3

Greg was unimpressed with the room. It was like the town, past its best with plain, old furnishings to match the fading, stained and nauseous green paint on the walls. A short stretch of threadbare carpet with more cigarette burns than weave design completed the appointments.

The late afternoon heat was oppressive. Greg switched on the elderly, window type air conditioner to obtain some relief from the temperature, but as a trade-off for its ear shattering noise.

In irritation, he slapped the machine with the back of his hand growling. "I've heard quieter Jumbo jets taking off."

After showering, he dressed in fresh, clean clothes and made his way back onto the sidewalk heading for Harry's Place. According to the wispy motel clerk, this was the nearest place in walking distance where he could buy a proper meal if he didn't want burgers or fried chicken.

"How far to the next best place for a decent meal?" Greg had asked.

The clerk jerked a thumb behind him. "You'll have to drive south on Main to the Truck Stop, where it joins the Interstate."

Greg gasped in disbelief. "You mean you can drive directly from here to the I-80 without diverting through the suburbs?"

"Yessir. You sure can."

"Then what's the 'Diversion to Main Street' sign doing there when you come off the Interstate?"

The clerk scratched his temple in indecision.

"I couldn't say. Nobody knows why that old sign's still there."

Greg grunted, the information did nothing to improve his poor mood.

He stormed out of the building onto the sidewalk just as a zephyr blew more dust into his face along with the acrid stench of rotting chicken manure. The late afternoon heat struck him the instant he stepped outside to bring on sweating under his armpits and around his crotch. "Why the hell did I bother to shower," he snarled under his breath?

Harry's Place was fitted out in a traditional mid-last century style and decorated garishly in vivid prime colors. There was a bar at the far end separated by a foyer from the dining area at the opposite end. It was pure 1950's kitsch, but lacked the waitresses on roller skates skidding around to Bill Haley, 'Rockin' around the Clock' or Elvis, 'Returning to Sender'.

Greg stood there, looking around to take in the scene. Several high school kids clustered around the jukebox in the foyer, twitching and gyrating to Justin Timberlake's latest release. The teens regarded him cooly as he came into the foyer from the street and then promptly ignored him.

Half a dozen redneck laborers sat at the bar. They paused from sucking on bottles of Coors to glare at him long enough until the bottle in their hands reached their lips again. Several diners sat at tables, singles and couples. He saw Jess White slumped over a table at the far corner of the dining area being lectured by his girlfriend.

A small, worried looking man with a balding head, his remaining hair blackened with pomade, distracted Greg by greeting him anxiously.

"Table Sir?"

Greg smiled. "You must be Harry?"

The man chuckled agreeably.

"Not me. Harry's my great grandfather and he's long gone. I'm Merv."

"Well thank you Merv, I'll be dining a bit later but I just wanted to catch up with a twosome I can see sitting over there."

Greg felt Merv's eyes on him as he walked all the way to the back of the dining area where Jess sat, face in hands, resting on the table - like he was sleeping. The girl hadn't noticed Greg approach and he heard some of what she was saying.

"…for the sake of your immortal soul you must hold onto

your values and resist temptation. That's the road to damnation. However bad your problem the Lord will..."

She stopped mid-sentence to glower at Greg when she noticed him standing beside their table.

Greg adopted what he thought was a suitably apologetic stance, taking her silence as his cue to address them politely.

"Good evening. Sorry to disturb you. I need a word with your boyfriend here, if it's no trouble?"

"He's not my boyfriend," she snapped, with heavy emphasis on the negative. Greg guessed she was older than Jess, but he looked younger than eleventh grade, so they might be the same age. Greg went into conciliation mode.

"Pardon me for my error ... Miss?"

"Johnson. Melissa Johnson, and I'm Jess's friend and counselor."

Jess looked up. Greg noticed the boy's sickly gray pallor and the dark shadows under his eyes. The boy was obviously still in pain. Greg replied to Melissa, keeping his eyes fixed on Jess.

"Well I'm glad we got that cleared up Miss; if you don't mind, I would like to speak to Jess."

The boy sat back with his eyes flickering uncertainly between Melissa and Greg. Her jaw dropped with sudden comprehension. She pointed an accusing finger at Greg.

"You're the man that knocked him down!" It was a statement, spoken in a low, venomous tone of voice.

"I'm afraid that's right Miss. It was an accident."

She went on the attack.

"You know you cost him a job by making him late? A job he so badly needed for his money problems?"

"No Miss, I didn't know that, but I suspected there was something important going on by the way he wanted to get away from the deputy; and the downcast way he walked over the street when you called him."

"Well I just hope you're satisfied. You've put him in the way of temptation and the Devil now. Are you a devil's angel mister?"

Greg smiled wryly. This was unbelievable. As she spoke, Greg watched Jess who silently watched both him and Melissa alternately.

Greg chuckled and replied.

"I might have been a Hell's Angel in my biking days Miss, but I've not had contact with any devil lately, and why I was at the junction at the same time as your boy friend here is due to that useless diversion sign to Main Street down at the I-80."

"It's been there for years." She snapped haughtily. "Everybody knows it. And I told you, he's not my boyfriend."

Greg smirked good-naturedly.

"This is my first time here Miss and if you'll excuse me for saying so; people generally follow road signs when they meet up with them. I don't know anything about losing your boyfriend any job. As things stand, the deputy sheriff says he can press charges against me for the incident, so a judge can decide the right and wrong of it all in open court." Greg instinctively didn't care for Melissa and deliberately stressed the word 'boyfriend' to irritate her."

Melissa snorted, making as if to go on the attack, but Jess cried out "No, that ain't right. It was me that was wrong. It's my fault it happened. I ran out in front of the car. I'll go tell the sheriff and put it right."

Greg stood back a pace to watch as the boy laid the palms of his hands on the table, pushing himself upright. He saw the pain radiating from the boy's face as he slowly rose to stand shakily by the chair.

Melissa screeched.

"What are you doing Jess White? Sit down, before you fall down."

Jess shook his head in silent reply and limped towards the door, dragging his left leg.

Greg stopped him.

"Hold on there. You need attention for that leg. Where's the nearest doctor?"

Melissa shrieked more loudly than before, attracting the

attention of the other diners in the room.

"He's got no money for doctor's. He ain't got money for dinners much less doctor's bills."

This startled Greg. On impulse, he caught hold of Jess's arm.

"What's she mean? Is she saying you've no money for food? Aren't you getting proper meals?"

Thinking over the incident later, Greg's concern for somebody else surprised him, but at that instant in the diner, nothing was more important to him than getting this boy's problems fixed.

The teen shook himself free of Greg's hand to address the girl.

"Leave it Melissa?" He turned to Greg. "Yes I get meals."

Melissa stamped her foot.

"No you don't. Your dinner tonight was half a Coke; shared with me. And you don't have money for doctors, but don't worry; you don't need it. Trust in the Lord. He will provide for you."

Greg's impatience showed in the sharpness of his response to the girl.

"Thank you Miss; I get the picture. He's no money for doctor's bills. I do, and I want his leg fixed. Maybe the Lord sent me, okay?"

She looked daggers at Greg as she swept her things into a large, cloth handbag.

"I have to go. I'm late. I have to meet my boyfriend at the ballpark. Just remember Jesse White; you have to hold onto your moral values to save your immortal soul."

"Amen to that." Greg couldn't resist the parting shot as she hurried out into the street.

Jess lowered himself awkwardly into the chair with a sigh of relief.

"Don't mind Melissa. She means well, and she's about the only real friend I got around here."

"That's sad Jess White; by the way I'm Greg Mitchell. I'm on holiday here."

"Holiday?"

"You call it vacation."

The boy smiled. "I knew that really. I'll get down to the sheriff's office and tell him there'll be no charges."

The youth's unexpected generosity humbled Greg, at the same time he felt uncomfortable with the boy's decision.

"Why ever would you want to do that? The deputy said he saw the whole thing. He's plainly standing with you on this if you file charges. Don't get me wrong. I'm not asking you to sue me, but you could get enough in damages out of me to settle your immediate money worries."

Jess smiled again.

"Nah! Not like that. It wouldn't be right. I was running late for an interview at the store. I just rushed across Charmain without looking or thinking where I was going. It was as much my fault as yours. I don't want to take you for your money mister."

A searing pang of emotion passed through Greg. The boy's integrity and sincerity moved something inside him. Greg stood up with a determination to take control of this situation.

"Oh yes you do young man. You need my cash right now to pay for a doctor to examine and fix that leg. What is more, I will stand no arguments. Where's the nearest doctor's office?"

Jess exhaled as if in surrender.

"Two blocks south." He jerked a thumb in that direction, reminding Greg of the motel clerk.

Greg stood on the boy's injured side, his arm around Jess's waist, taking as much of his weight as possible to make the walk to Doctor Finch's office more comfortable for the boy.

The white haired doctor spoke to them through a luxuriant white mustache. Jess stripped to his shorts and laid on the couch for the doc's examination. Greg gasped in surprise when he saw the extent of the injury, the young flesh already marked with angry, black, blue and deep red bruising from the hip to the knee.

"Lucky nothing's broken." The doctor announced. Jess winced as Doc Finch gently probed the bone structure.

Greg drew nearer to get a closer look and asked.

"Shouldn't he be in hospital doctor?"

The doctor's smile was repeated in his baggy eyes.

"Yup. Maybe he should, but I happen to know he ain't got no insurance and this ain't bad enough to admit him to hospital without."

Greg didn't understand.

"Insurance doctor, what's that got to do with it? Doesn't everybody have health care here when it's needed?"

"Nope, not everybody. We have a pay system for health care here in the US of A and it's expensive. Folks that can't afford insurance like Jesse White's family, don't have it and they have to rely on charity when things go wrong; that is unless it's life threatening, then they get hospital treatment – some."

"Well if he needs it doctor, I'll pay for it. I'm the reason he's hurt like he is."

"That's mighty noble of you mister, but you don't know what you're getting yourself into so my advice to you is to stay out of it. I'll fix him up and he can rest up at the schoolhouse for a couple of days. I'll need to see him again if the pain gets worse or if the leg gets infected. Lucky the skin's not broken."

"Okay Doc. Thanks for your help, is there anything else?"

"I'm prescribing painkillers and a sleeping pill for a couple of nights. Sleep and rest is what he needs. The dressings should be changed every day with ointment put on the damaged area. They'll do that for him in the school sick bay. I've given him an injection to hold off infection, just in case. He's lucky, could've been a whole lot worse. I'll file a report for the sheriff's office. It's the law."

Greg paid the doctor while Jess dressed after which they left the office heading for the pharmacy.

"If you have no objections Jess, I'd be happy to do the dressings for you starting tomorrow. Then you wouldn't need to worry about the cost of getting that done or lose class time and bothering the sick bay at school. I can buy the bits and pieces we'll need at the pharmacy. It'll be mostly ointment and bandage to keep the mess off your clothes."

The boy's big almond eyes dampened as he asked.

"That's very kind of you Mr. Mitchell. You don't have to do all that. I'm sure I'll get by at the school sick bay. The nurse'll do it for me free of charge. So don't worry."

"No arguments Mr. White, I'll do it. I insist."

Jess smiled, a small, uncertain smile before asking.

"Are you stopping over then?"

Greg noticed some color coming back into the teen's face and hoped this was a sign of an early recovery.

"I have to, the Sheriff won't let me leave."

The boy's mouth dropped open.

"I'll fix that..."

Greg put his hand on the boy's shoulder, passing the sleeping pill and painkillers to him.

"Not tonight you'll not. You go back into Harry's Place. Get us a table for dinner. I'll see you in there after I take these packages back to the motel."

4

Harry's was quiet except for the rednecks sat drinking in the bar area. Merv was pleased to see Greg come back and had given Jess a pleasant, private table on the west side. He led Greg over and handed them menus before leaving them alone to make their choices.

Greg watched Jess over the top of the menu folder. The boy played with his menu as if he was not really interested in ordering a meal.

"When did you last eat a proper meal Jess?"

"Lunchtime, I guess."

"Do you mind telling me what you had for your lunch?"

Jess looked sheepish.

"Aw! I wasn't really hungry. I had an apple."

"An apple?" Greg sighed, dropping his menu onto the table. He thought quickly.

"I have a problem Jess. And you can help me if you will?"

"Yes sir." The boy replied without hesitation.

Greg pursed his lips and paused, as if pondering how to express his problem.

"You see, I've come in from Iowa City today and I'm very hungry. I want clam chowder with crackers to start, rib eye beef and a baked potato with sour cream and chives to follow and to finish up with pecan pie and coffee. But I can't eat alone; that's my problem. Would you do me the favor of eating the same meal with me? I'd be so obliged?"

Jess gasped. "Of course I'll help, but I couldn't pay for any of that and I doubt I could eat it all anyway."

Greg smiled and patted the boy's arm. "Don't you worry about paying for the meal. I'll take care of the bill and you don't have to eat it all. Just as much as you want will do. It's just so's I'm not eating alone."

Merv was delighted with the order and fussed around their table. Jess became ravenous when the food arrived and Greg noticed with satisfaction that the boy cleared his plates without any difficulty.

Over coffee they chatted.

"Tell me about yourself?" Greg invited, asking the question casually to avoid alarming the boy.

Jess sighed, reluctant to speak, but after a moment of initial hesitation opened up and told Greg he came from a family of small farmers in the south of the State. His father grew half an acre of melons and alfalfa on the rest of the farm for drying as a cash crop. "Money's always tight." He said quietly, lowering his eyes as if in shame.

"So how come you're at school here and not somewhere closer, where you can live at home with your family?"

Jess smiled.

"There's no proper high school near where I live, not one where I can go home every night. This is the best for miles. We got some help for me to come up here, but the boom everywhere else hasn't reached us here yet." Jess halted to sigh, an aura of sadness dropped over him as he continued his explanation. "Times are hard for my folks and now they can't afford to keep me here anymore; not now the help's stopped as well."

"You mean you'll not be able to finish high school? You won't graduate?"

"That's right. Besides, my Pa needs me to help him on the farm, he keeps tellin' us all he ain't gettin' any younger and the chores ain't gettin' any lighter."

"So what was the point of sending you here in the first place?"

Jess shrugged and fiddled with a salt pot.

"My folks just thought we might get one of us educated some."

Greg scratched his head over a furrowed brow.

"I don't understand. If you can come here and go through, what is it, two or three grades of high school?"

"It's four grades to graduation, ninth to twelfth," Jess corrected, "and I'll be finishing eleventh grade at the end of this semester."

Greg opened his hands in front of him in an attitude of mild despair.

"That makes no sense. You've all made sacrifices to give you three years of high school education and you're not going to finish it. That's like running a race and giving up in the last ten yards. It's madness!"

Jess responded with a lopsided smile.

"It might be crazy, but it's a fact. I have to go outside the schoolhouse into lodgings for the senior year. That makes it even more expensive. We can't possibly manage that cost without help."

Greg could not grasp the logic of what he was being told.

"If it's the same here as back home where I come from; it means if you fail to finish high school and don't graduate, then it's the same as if you never went in the first place – that's as far as a career or employment prospects are concerned. Is it the same here?"

Jess nibbled his lower lip before replying and Greg was pleased to see deeper, healthier color coming into the boy's cheeks.

"Pretty much." Jess fiddled vigorously with the salt pot and wouldn't meet Greg's eyes as the man continued to press his point.

"If you knew you couldn't finish the course here, why the hell didn't you go to a less costly school nearer to home where you wouldn't have these lodging and other expenses? Even if it's not so good as here, at least you'd be able to finish the course, graduate and have a qualification to show for it."

Jess smiled. He seemed more relaxed and Greg was pleased to realize the boy's physical pain must be easing.

"It'd be the same wherever I went. The schoolin's free, but there'd still be extra costs for my family they can't afford to pay. We had help for me to come here from our neighbor, Colonel Stewart. He said I should go to high school. He believed good folk shouldn't be held back 'cos they ain't got no money. He said the key to getting out of poverty is education. He didn't have any kin at home and he put up all of the extra expenses for me."

"He was right, and still is; so what went wrong with Colonel Stewart? Why'd he stop his contributions?"

Jess looked away. This was intensely personal, yet he felt at ease with this stranger and it lightened his sense of loss to talk about the colonel and his schooling problems. In a way he owed it to Greg to explain his haste in running across the road the way he did and causing the accident. He became solemn when he replied.

"He died last Easter. His kin came from the east coast and sold his property. Old Colonel Stewart hadn't made any provision for me in his will or written anything down anywhere. He just paid his part of the bill as it came in each semester. He didn't expect to die and his kin didn't want to carry on the arrangement."

"That's a great shame," Greg spoke with genuine sympathy. "Is that what was behind the urgency to get this grocery store job today?"

The question made Jess uncomfortable again and he shuffled on his seat, looking away. Greg said nothing. The pressure of silence suddenly got to the boy and he blurted out:

"No, that's for my outstanding expenses for this semester."

Greg felt he was getting in deeper than he should, but was intrigued and persisted.

"You mean your allowances don't cover all your costs, you still have to work to cover them. How are you supposed to do that when you're at school all day?"

Jess's face had now turned beetroot red with embarrassment and he shuffled around and stammered.

"I'd rather not say if you don't mind."

"Okay, I'm cool with that. I suppose that was what all that hell fire and damnation stuff Melissa was preaching was all about?"

Jess replied with a single nod of his head and Greg took a stab in the dark.

"Would these outstanding bills be for food and things?"

Jess looked down at his feet, nodding his agreement.

Greg inhaled deeply as he succumbed to an immediate and alien impulse to help this young person to settle his debts.

"So that's what the job was for, well it just might be your lucky day after all."

Jess's head spun upwards and his gaze fixed on Greg's face. The unspoken question hung on the boy's lips 'What do you mean?'

It had been a big meal and Greg sat back in his bench, easing his belt a notch for added comfort.

"That's better," he exclaimed, "well I plan to stick around here for a while and do some trading to cover my expenses. That's what I do, trading. I'll need a part-time assistant. Would you be interested? It can pay well with bonuses."

Jess sat bolt upright, instantly alert.

"What sort of trading?"

Now Greg fiddled with the salt pot. He knew without Jess saying anything that he had aroused the boy's interest.

"Oh this and that, commodities, goods, things like that. Nothing illegal. Just plain, honest trading. I'll need somebody to help me with research. We can talk about it tomorrow if you like. ...You can use a computer?"

"Yes sir and I'd like to work for you, that's as long as I can do the jobs you want that is. And if it's honest work?"

Greg was delighted to see Jess come alive. His eyes gleamed now as they shone with the hope Greg had given him.

"Good, you're hired. What time do you finish up at the Community College tomorrow?"

"About half four, quarter to five."

"Okay, meet me in my motel room, it's…"

Greg pulled a key from his pocket and looked at the black plastic tab.

"…it's one-twenty-six. Check in with the clerk when you go in, we can talk through the details then."

Jess nodded but the smile disappeared from his face and it clouded with doubt. Greg wondered why that should be? The evening had suddenly cooled for no apparent reason.

He didn't understand the cause of the change in the boy's attitude since they had been getting on so well, but he decided not to pursue the matter. Greg slapped his chest and said,

"Okay, we've wined and dined, albeit without wine, now what do people do after dinner in Bamptonville to finish off their evenings?" Greg smiled agreeably and put his hand over the saucer holding the bill that had appeared on the table.

Jess remained dour and answered noncommittally. "Mostly watch TV or go to the movies."

"There's a movie house here?"

"The Capitol! It's got two theaters."

"Let's go!" Greg said ebulliently and stood up. Jess shrank back into his seat with indecision written all over his face.

"What's up? Something wrong with that idea?" Greg asked across the table.

Jess shook his head slowly. "I don't know sir. We don't know each other and you've been very kind. I don't want you to get any wrong ideas about me."

"Ideas, what ideas?"

Jess swallowed and his face colored red again. He looked away from Greg's searching eyes as he explained.

"Well sir, excuse me sir, but the job you spoke about is in your motel room and now it seems you're asking me out on a date. I just wanted you to know, I'm not like that."

"Not like what?" Greg spoke softly.

Jess looked away in embarrassment and spoke through his hand that covered his mouth.

"I'm not like Kyler and the others who do things like that for Felix Gleitner…" Jess stopped mid-sentence as if he'd said too much and now regretted it.

Greg was bursting to probe further but held back. He perceived the need for prudence and an old saying came to mind 'slowly, slowly catchee monkee.' But things were falling into place for Greg. Melissa's advice that he'd overheard and her threats of damnation made more sense now.

Greg assumed that somebody must have approached Jess, or even involved him in some unsavory means of paying his way at the Community College. He shook away these thoughts from his head and rested both hands on the table as he leaned across and spoke with an affable firmness.

"Jess, you're right. You don't know me from Adam. I could be anybody after anything from you. You're right to question me and my intentions. I wish to assure you that it is your company at the cinema I wish for tonight and not the use of your body or anything else afterwards. I hope that is clear. Okay?"

Jess became instantly relaxed and gave Greg a beaming smile, restoring the evening's amicable ambiance.

"Thank you sir. I'm so glad it's not like that! Can I still have that job please?"

"You can, providing you're at my motel room on the stroke of five and not a second later." He put his finger in the air dogmatically, like a politician. Jess laughed. It was the first time he had laughed easily and it sounded fresh and free of anxiety; like a mountain stream running over rocks.

They both enjoyed the movie and Greg hailed a taxi when they left the theater. Greg dropped Jess off at the schoolhouse entrance. He poked his head through the taxi window that Greg had rolled down.

"Thank you Mr. Mitchell, ...for everything."

"It's my pleasure Mr. White and I'll see you tomorrow at five."

"Not a second later," Jess said. Leaving a peal of light, happy laughter behind him as he climbed the steps as fast as his leg would allow and disappeared into the schoolhouse.

5

Back in his motel room, Greg showered again to remove the lingering stench of Noble's Breath merging with the clamminess of his skin before climbing into bed. It had been quite a day and its many emotions and sensations denied him rest. 'Could it still be the same day since I left Iowa City – it seems so much longer.'

Once settled under the comforter his thoughts drifted to Jess and his problems. The teen's immediate financial needs appeared to be pressing. The deputy had told the boy he could lay charges against him. No doubt that would solve his immediate money worries, yet this youngster had passed up that chance on the grounds that 'it was not right.' Such selflessness in adversity was an uncharacteristically humbling experience for Greg to contemplate or witness even. The remembrance made him sit up in bed with a chill sweat dampening his neck.

'Dammit, the accident bruised him a bit, but it was a gift from the gods for him to settle his money problems by laying charges. Why the hell didn't he go for it? That deputy was one hundred percent on his side. Why would he pass it up just because it 'was not the right thing to do'? There'd be no easier money for him after losing his chance of a job, but he didn't take it; he just let it go. The kid thought it through, reasoned it out and let it pass and all the time with a leg that'll keep him awake at nights and out of the football team for a while. That's scary.'

Greg shook his head in bewilderment, failing to understand how anybody could choose against going for easy money purely on a personal interpretation of right or wrong in the particular circumstances. If Greg had been the injured party he would have seized the opportunity to sue even before the deputy mentioned it. 'Me, me, me! That's the norm in today's world.'

Then along comes this boy with a dilemma: pressing money

worries on one hand and old fashioned moral values on the other - and he chose to follow the moral pathway and go against the accepted norm.

"But why'd he do that?" Greg half shouted out his question to the darkened room and hammered the bed clothes with his fists in his frustration.

To Greg, that spelled a depth of character that was more than unusual, it was strangely attractive; admirable even. It was also worrying and some advice from when he was starting out in business came to the front of his mind. 'Beware of an honest man; an honest man can't be bought and will always do the right thing because it's against his nature to do otherwise.'

"Is that it?" Greg asked himself. "Is it as simple as that! He let it go because he's honest? Surely not!" Greg failed to come up with an answer that satisfied him and hammered his fists into the comforter either side of him again to ease his irritation.

But that was not Jess's only characteristic striking Greg as odd that night. The sudden change in the boy's mood from cheerful contentment to dour withdrawal, almost fright, when he mentioned going on to the cinema together. The teen's genial disposition had swung across to the opposite extreme in a second. To be followed immediately by the youth's bold assertion that this was not a date; thus ensuring Greg entertained no misunderstanding about how far the boy was prepared go with him. 'What was that all about? Does that mean men have propositioned him for sexual favors? And who were these boys he mentioned working for this Felix character that he doesn't want to work for, and then clammed up as soon as he mentioned the man's name – like he'd said more than he should have done? Then there was that girl's preaching and her question whether he was a devil's angel. Could that be to do with this Felix grooming the boy to sell sexual favors? Jess was embarrassed when I asked and wouldn't say how he was supposed to get by financially without an income from home or work. It seems pretty obvious he had no other choices. Was he about to go down the Felix route to get by?'

These unsavory thoughts brought a bad taste into Greg's

mouth, but his mind raced on. 'I reckon he's being targeted by this Felix. He must be, even if Jess won't say. After all, he's a good-looking kid, with a nice body and an agreeable personality to match'.

The fact that Jess appeared to be holding out against any such approaches to him by making clear at the outset that amorous possibilities were not available was another of the boy's characteristics Greg found endearing.

'Holey moley! Have I stumbled into a vice operation using school kids here in this hick town? Shit, that's not only unbelievable; it's sinister, and evil. Could Jess be mixed up in it already? ...Possibly, but if he was he wouldn't need the store job to get by.' Greg's reasoning was plausible; even so, it left him with a persistent, nagging doubt. He scratched his chin as he pondered the possibility that Jess was already involved with Felix. 'But even so he could be or was about to be involved that way. The boy said, 'he don't want to do those things' and made that pretty clear to me before we went to the movies. But he didn't get the store job, and was slumped in defeat when I caught up with him being preached at by that girl.' A twisted smile came to Greg's lips along with a burning sensation in his gut that always arrived when he faced a challenge. He lay back in the bed, rolling onto his side to settle for sleep, punching the pillow and speaking into its foam rubber softness.

"Perhaps I got here just in time? It's been a while since you did anything worthwhile for anybody other than yourself Greg Mitchell; perhaps it's because you never found a deserving case before, or you never knew before now what it was like to have nothing and nobody fighting your corner with you."

He punched the pillow again, telling it with determined emphasis.

"You will go to the ball Cinderella. Let's see if we can get you set-up to finish high school and possibly even go on to college. And, understand this Jesse White; if you were thinking you had no other choice to settle your bills except by doing what this Felix character lines up for you. Think again! It wasn't my car that knocked you down today - it was another option."

Greg Mitchell had forged a bond and a commitment without knowing why or what was involved and upon that decision dropped off into an uneasy sleep.

Jess didn't notice the pain in his leg as he limped into the schoolhouse and shuffled his way slowly up the stairs to his dormitory. He was too occupied with thinking over the events of the day: the accident, losing the store job and then meeting Mr. Mitchell. It seemed they had already become like friends. He also held the promise of a job: that hope brought him intense relief from his anxiety over settling his semester dues.

He wondered what might come of working for this strange man and hoped he was serious about trading here. He'd heard that Brits often start out with well-meaning intentions, but tend to drop out before things are finished. Jess had taken more than his fair share of knocks and tumbles since he'd been at the high school in Bamptonville. He'd best not raise his hopes too high or too soon, and see how things developed at their meeting tomorrow.

Jess instinctively liked Mr. Mitchell; he was an interesting man and fun to be with – generous too.

"Start small," Jess said to nobody. "If I can just get the three-hundred and twenty bucks I need to cover my expenses here before the end of the term, that will be more than good enough for me."

Jess understood that the reality of his financial situation meant leaving school and going home to work on the farm with his Pa at the end of this semester; but it was unthinkable for him to arrive home with a hefty bill for school dues; one his folks couldn't pay. He breathed a sigh of relief over the thought that this job with Greg could settle that debt for him. Jess held his hands across his over filled stomach as he climbed to the second landing and turned into his dormitory gleefully mumbling.

"And I won't have to go with Felix Gleitner after all."

After losing the job at McKendrick's, and while he was half

listening to Melissa's preaching, Jess had racked his brains to find another way to settle that bill before school closed at year end in five weeks' time.

When the day opened he had only two possible avenues for income to settle the debt – McKendrick's Stores or Felix Gleitner. And now Mr. McKendrick had given the job to Ricky Horowitz, which left Felix Gleitner as the only possible source of income. It made Jess feel physically sick just to think that he had no other choices.

In Harry's, after the accident, he lay slumped across the table, psyching himself up to the inevitability that he'd have to tell Felix he'd work for him. That very thought added mental anguish to his physical distress. He recited multiplication tables, silently, in his head to shut out what Melissa was saying, and then, as if by magic, Mr. Mitchell had appeared at the table, offering him a better option.

Jess smiled. 'It could be that he was sent by God. Like he told Melissa?'

The thought comforted Jess as he limped into the dormitory, but stopped abruptly just inside the door. Something was wrong. It was too quiet, too dark. Most of the overhead lights were out. The long dormitory housed twenty boys, each in their own bed spaces partitioned by six feet high stud-walls for privacy, but without doors and open to the central aisle running the length of the dorm.

He glanced into the nearest spaces. The occupants were all in their beds, unrecognizable mounds beneath their comforters. The individual bed lights were turned out as if they were all asleep. It was never like that. There was always banter and laughter and joshing until after midnight. It was too early for them all to be turned in and asleep. 'Something's wrong! But what is it?'

Jess's space was near the far end. He saw the overhead lights were switched off at that end with only those at the entrance lighted. With a lump in his throat and butterflies in his stomach he crept on into the increasing gloom towards his own space.

The fear that something odd was happening here and not

knowing what it was hammered away at him as he moved further into the dorm. He believed that whatever it was must be to do with him.

Jess had regularly suffered from bullying at school because he came from a poor, out of town family and was a ready-made target for his better-off peers. It mostly took the form of name-calling, taunts and ostracism; Jess had got used to that as much as one could. This was altogether different, and he stole forwards with short steps, his heart in his mouth.

Jess expected something to happen each time one foot went in front of the other, but all remained silent and still by the time he reached his bed space, where he sighed with relief. He hadn't realized he'd been holding his breath. He switched on the bunk light and began to undress.

He'd got down to his jeans and wife-beater undershirt when they appeared, as if from nowhere. Three seniors walked into his space blocking him inside. Kyler, Leon and Billie-Joe, the three principal goons in Felix Gleitner's vice ring stood there leering at him, creating an aura of menace.

Jess's heart raced. He picked up his shirt from the bed, holding it in front of him instinctively for protection, and waited with his heart pounding with fear for whatever was to come. Kyler spoke, mocking and unfriendly.

"So tell me sodbuster. How's your day been goin'?"

Jess's lips quivered as he replied.

"I don't understand what you mean. What are you doing here? What do you want?"

Jess realized none of his roommates would help him. He was on his own and scared. Possibly the smell of fear escaped from him and Kyler and his thugs picked it up for they moved further inside, closer to him.

Kyler sat on the bed. Leon stood beside him, tapping a short, round wooden bar slowly into the palm of his hand; each move ending in a loud slap of wood on flesh, heightening the atmosphere of intimidation.

"We been hearin' stories about our poor l'il sodbuster, him

with no new clothes, no cell phone, no money even to pay his semester dues. Then we heard how he didn't get the job at the store today." Leon and Billie-Joe offered their false sympathies in mocking tones.

"Now ain't that a shame."

"Ahhh! Tough luck, sodbuster. What you gonna do now?"

Kyler raised his hand and they fell silent, slavishly paying attention to their leader who spoke to them as if Jess wasn't there.

"Now that was the job to make everythin' come out right for him. Now we're talkin' here about that same little sodbuster who shouldn't even be here in Bamptonville at all, no sir, not at all. And he should be home digging up all them turnips on the farmstead where he belongs. Look at him guys, our very own schoolhouse joke. He'd rather run grocery store chores fer pennies than workin' fer good money with Felix, and be one of us, with new clothes, a new cell phone, could be a car and no debts. I said no debts, sodbuster. Now what sort o' person in his right mind makes choices like that?"

Kyler looked around at his crew and they laughed, as if on cue.

Jess didn't know why Kyler spoke about him that way, his body shook in fear and hoped his voice didn't show when he spoke.

"That's right. Mr. McKendrick gave the job to Ricky Horowitz. What's it to you?"

"Now that's not nice. Here we all are, out of the kindness of our hearts tryin' to help the poor li'l sodbuster get over his problems and he gets all uppity on us. That's plain not nice."

Leon leaned forward.

"Seems they got diff'rent manners to us in sodbuster land. I reckon we gotta teach him some o' ours." He smashed the rod loudly into his hand for emphasis making Jess wince involuntarily. They laughed at his discomfort.

"Well now, think we might have to do jus' that. This homespun straw-sucker who don't even have the price of his own Coke down at Harry's and thinks he's so much better'n us who's workin' fer honest pay with Felix. Can you b'lieve it. A chicken-wrangler, better'n us?"

The others laughed loudly, a harsh and heartless sound. As their laughter died away Leon hurled a taunt to encourage more derisive laughter. "D'you know why they never make pockets in turnip-cruncher's coveralls – 'cos they never got nothin' to put in 'em, that's why."

"I don't think I'm any better'n you," Jess asserted with a determination to hold his ground. "I just don't wanna do what you guys do for Felix. That's all."

"But Felix wants you for next semester. He'll go settle your dues right now just for your li'l old promise to go work for him next semester. That's all. A walk in the park"

"But I don't want to do any o'that stuff."

"But you ain't got no other choice." Spittle flew from Kyler's mouth into Jess's face as he shouted. "How else you gonna make out here. Price o' melons bein' what they are."

They laughed at this jibe at his family's poverty and it stung Jess. His mind raced on. He could take the money. Nobody else was aware he wasn't coming back next semester. He could agree, take the money, settle his debts and run out. The notion was attractive and it was the easy option for him to take. But he recalled a line of Shakespeare that had resonated with him one time when he'd been home, talking about this and that with Colonel Stewart and he had quoted the line to him.

'Shit, what's Shakespeare doing here,' he thought in near panic as the seniors crowded in on him. His adrenalin flowed and the line came clearly to mind. 'Unto thine own self, be true!' That's what he had to do, he had to be like that, true to himself: no lies, no deceit, no running out. He faced his tormentors with added strength.

"That's where you're wrong. I do have another choice. I expect I'll be workin' for a trader; startin' tomorrow."

"Oooh," they scorned in unison, "the shit-shoveler's got hisself a trader in tow."

They were crowding around him now. Kyler pulled the shirt out of Jess's hands, tossing it disdainfully on the bed like it was so much garbage.

"Well Felix thinks you're just a bit scared. He thinks you really want to join his team; his remuda fer next year, and all you need is a bit of encouragement to get started. He's asked us, your friends, to help you get over that small problem of shyness."

Jess looked quickly from one to the other, retrieving his shirt from the bed to hold in front of him again as a token of protection.

Kyler stuck his finger in Jess's waistband, expanding and letting it go so that the elastic smacked into Jess's stomach as it recoiled.

"Felix thinks we can do you a big favor tonight by lettin' you know what it's like; so you'll have nothin' to be scared about when you get under the lights in a studio or into a cab with a trucker or a motel room, back seat of a car, or in the woods with a salesman."

Jess came over cold and his breathing quickened.

"I told you already, I don't want to do what you guys do. I don't want to work for Felix."

"But you need his money," Kyler crooned, salivating with excitement.

Jess tried to back away but came hard up against his wardrobe. He was trapped. He thought of shouting, but all the others in the dormitory were already awake and listening, keeping quiet and to themselves; no doubt warned off by Kyler about interfering. They would be no help to him.

"What you gonna do?"

Kyler wiped his lips with the back of his hand.

"We're gonna get you started little sodbuster, that's what we gonna do and we gonna do it right now."

"Wha...t do you mean?" Jess's eyes rolled in fear.

"Well Leon here's gonna put his dick in your mouth a bit and then I'm gonna put mine up your butt a bit, real gentle like, just so's you know what it's like and there's nothing to be scared of. Felix says to call it trainin'. It's gonna happen, chicken, you can cooperate or we can do it the rough way and that hurts – a lot!"

Kyler looked at the others, who laughed through closed teeth, and then turned to Jess and asked. "What's it gonna be, moonshiner?"

Jess's defences imploded, and he fought back tears. He could struggle, but without help would get nowhere, the end result would be the same except his leg would be more damaged. His brain urged 'get it over and done with and get 'em out of here.' Adrenalin streamed strongly through Jess's veins by now, bringing him coolness, confidence and ideas.

"Just one time?" Jess asked with a thin smile.

Kyler reeled back in surprise and spoke to his crew.

"See! The sodbuster really wants to do it after all. Yes, just one time."

"Okay, stand back while I get ready."

They stood back while Jess slowly took down his jeans. Leon and Kyler unzipped their flies. Kyler turned to Billie-Joe and said, "Get the jelly."

Leon's cry distracted them.

"Holy shit! Just look at that leg!"

He pointed to Jess's leg with a wavering finger.

Jess had removed his jeans and the dim glow of the bed light revealed the angry extent of his injuries; there was now a sickening touch of yellow adding to the color mix.

The seniors gaped in awe, backing away as if Jess was diseased.

"What the hell happened to you?" Kyler cried.

Jess's anguish diminished and could see they were not invincible. They obviously hadn't heard about his accident. He laughed at them, addressing them flippantly.

"I was learning bull fightin' over at Noble's ranch and one of 'em got me."

"You're puttin' me on!"

Jess had control and stepped towards them with a fierce

determination, his face hardening.

"I guess I am, but you get this through your heads. I'll not work for Felix Gleitner, not this semester or next semester or any semester. I don't do those things he wants me to do. I don't do 'em with anybody and that includes you three. I can't stop you doing what you say you're gonna do tonight 'cos I'm not strong enough to fight y'all. But understand this. If you do go through with what you're sayin'? I'll get each and every one of you afterwards. I'll get you sometime when you're not expectin' it. I won't kill you, but I will hurt you – a lot. That's not a threat. It's a promise. So go ahead. Do what you came to do. I won't stop you, just expect what happens to you afterwards, you won't know when or where, and you won't see me when it happens, but you will hear me. Laughin'! Laughin' louder than you can scream. So go ahead. Get it done."

"You're bluffin'," Kyler said with false bravado as he backed away from Jess. Leon smashed the rod onto his palm in front of Jess's face. This time the boy did not flinch, and as he moved slowly towards his tormentors they backed away from him, his injured leg and the promise he made them; and then they were gone.

It was over.

Jess fell onto the bed feeling sick, shaking with reaction as the adrenalin dissipated from his system. The overhead lights came on in the lower part of the dormitory. Jess's bed space filled with people and noise as they got out of bed to come around to his space.

"You all right Jess", they chorused.

Jess lay there trembling hiding his face beneath his hand and said.

"I need to think. Leave me alone."

He rolled onto his side and with one violent retch emptied his stomach onto the floor.

6

Greg slept poorly; waking each time he turned in bed, which seemed like every few minutes. He supposed it was just the hardness of the mattress and the strangeness of his surroundings, together with the ever-present stench of decaying chicken manure that was responsible for his restlessness.

Once awake he considered his discomfiture justified him following his usual morning ritual of mouthing a string of groans and obscenities at his image in the shaving mirror. More so this morning since the air conditioner had ceased to function during the night and the shower delivered water no warmer than tepid. In spite of these irritations, today was different.

His mind filled with ideas - good and pleasant ideas - ideas that brought with them a sense of purpose. So instead of directing his customary torrent of abuse at a luckless mirror, Greg chuckled his way through his misfortunes in rare good humor. While he brushed shaving foam over his face he made a mental list of all he needed to get done before meeting Jess later that evening.

He stopped mid-shave while he considered his plans for Jess. The notion of working with the boy so he could settle his debt gave Greg something of a buzz. During his shave, he summarized his usual daily routine when he had worked at Bailey's. He would get up in the mornings, get out, make money, bank it, make or confirm appointments for the next day then go to bed to bring on tomorrow so he could get up, get out and make more money.

It was his regular routine, almost automatic and definitely unexciting. He got through his days that way with fewer distractions. Today would be different. It would be a working day for him once again; but one working for himself, not Bailey's. He was a free agent now, the idea of being his own boss in his own enterprise, whatever that might be appealed considerably. He moved more swiftly, more purposefully and stopped shaving to address his image in the mirror. 'You don't need a holiday, what you need is the challenge of wholesome work to stretch your wits.' And his immediate challenge was to find something profitable in which to engage his talents, thus filling the gap in Jess's finances left by the demise of his benefactor.

The commitment he had muttered into his pillow last night came to mind, Greg brandished his shaver at his reflection. "Let me see what else I can do for you Jesse White besides running you down in the road."

Greg felt good about the decision as he continued dressing, but couldn't fathom why it should give him such a lift.

He stopped to consider the implications of what he was undertaking. Nothing in his career to date had been more important to him than success, an imperative that remained strong with him. Whatever business he engaged in on Jess's behalf could affect the boy's life for all time and should be carefully considered, since he could not contemplate its failure. This was a sobering thought, one that presented not only a challenge, but also a commitment to ensure its success; for however long it took or whatever difficulties he might face.

Greg grinned as he buttoned up his shirt; he relished challenges. The outcome would be so much more personally satisfying than a note read out in a dreary board meeting that stated whether or not 'we had attained or failed' to achieve the targets for that month. This had been the reality of his business life until recently and he had thrived on attending these meetings to announce that he had exceeded the targets they imposed on him yet again. Greg shook his head with misgiving as his mind's eye looked in on these past meetings. He viewed them through different lenses now.

Of themselves, those meetings had no significance whatsoever in the wider world beyond that board room - not in the real world. Their importance existed only around that table.

And what was the purpose of those meetings, what did they achieve?

This was a moment of revelation for Greg. The answer arrived instantaneously and his lips moved to mouth a reply, but his voice gave it no sound; leaving his opinion unsaid and silently running through his brain.

Words! They were nothing but words. Corporate words, the same clichés uttered automatically and mindlessly at the correct moment as part of a regular, mechanical process. A routine practice that meant either there was more or less money in the bank at the end of the period than was projected at the last meeting.

"There's got to be more purpose to business than that!" His outburst echoed from the walls proclaiming the emptiness of the room: an echo that called attention to the emptiness of his life to date in a destructive and chilling parallel. Greg rubbed warmth into the goose bumps on his arms while he reflected on his past and the acclaim he had enjoyed at those useless board meetings when he ran Bailey's.

"Whatever did I achieve there that was worth a damn? What did I ever do to benefit anybody other than to earn the fickle admiration of lesser beings sat around that boardroom table when they learned by how much more my efforts had enriched them? What about those poor sods I took advantage of, my competitors or adversaries? Some I ruined, others I put out of business and to even more I handed out change, anguish, hardship and reduced circumstances; and for what? For the applause and platitudes of those that were not the equal in worth or character of those I deposed. The Bailey's lot was superior to those unfortunates only by the sum of the wealth that I created at the expense of those I trod down and who were powerless to come back at me."

This was a telling moment for Greg; one that gave him shivers. He rubbed warmth into his upper arms as he pondered the implications of his self-imposed appointment as Jess's benefactor.

Success in whatever he did in Bamptonville could mean Jess staying at school with the chance to graduate and make something of his life. Failure, or his early withdrawal from the project he set up would consign the boy to a life of perpetual poverty, as suffered by his family.

Greg tucked his shirt into his waistband and returned to the bathroom to brush his hair. He counseled his reflection in the mirror.

"Can you honestly and truthfully commit yourself to that Mitchell? Even if it means staying here much longer than you intended and with that stink of rotting manure."

Greg smiled thinly. "Yes, I can - and more than that, I will. And didn't the deputy say you get not to notice the stink after a few days?"

Greg made a cup of instant coffee and switched on the TV to pick up the local news while he finished dressing. It was mostly political, as the primaries were already in full swing for the Presidential election in the coming November.

Most pundits were arguing whether McCain's choice of Sarah Palin as his running mate was an advantage - because she was a woman - or another disadvantage along with his age.

Greg had seen blocks of Post-It notes printed up with George W. Bush 'howlers' on them and cracked. "The way that woman is going she'll have her own block printed up before she even gets elected." Greg paused with his fingers on the 'Off" switch while the newsreader recounted Sarah's latest wisdom. "If God don't want us to shoot the animals, he shouldn't've made 'em outta meat!"

Greg muttered through a chuckle "That says it all, even if she has a point." He switched to radio and soon after wished he hadn't. It played an old Ricky Skaggs country music number that stuck in his head for most of the rest of the morning.

The motel clerk had Greg's bill made ready to settle when Greg entered the reception area.

"Moving on Mr. Mitchell?" he asked, showing a mouthful of yellowed teeth.

"That's what I want to talk to you about. I would like to stay longer. That is if the sheriff allows me to?"

"How long for sir? Another day, a week perhaps?"

"No I was thinking of a month or two, perhaps longer. I'm

planning on doing a little business here. Can we discuss long term rates?"

The clerk sprang back around the counter and opened his register. "We sure can sir."

The clerk's hunched and obsequious manner brought the Charles Dickens character – Uriah Heep – to Greg's mind. He dislodged the image with a violent shake of his head.

"Do you also have a bigger room, one that's a bit more private?"

"We do Sir, if you need more privacy then one-ninety-six is the suite for you; it's right at the end of the block. You'll not get disturbed there at all."

"And what about broadband Internet access, do you have wi-fi here yet?"

The blank stare on the clerk's face answered Greg's question and so he explained carefully.

"I'll need a fast internet connection if I'm to work from here. If you don't have it connected by cable I'll need to buy in a satellite connection. Will that be okay?"

"We can come to an agreement on that, I'm sure we can, but it will all be down to your own expense mind?"

"Good! That's not a problem."

"But afore you go an' buy it in Mr. Mitchell, let me tell you we have Internet here a'ready. Feel free to use it at cost just any times you like sir, that's when it ain't in use fer the motel mind?"

The clerk rushed into the office to open his Internet connection. Greg didn't know whether to laugh or cry when he heard the almost forgotten chirping of a dial-up connection - an everyday sound from the last century.

"That's okay, thank you." Greg wanted to let the clerk down gently. "I'll make some enquiries about the satellite and will confirm the room after I've seen the deputy sheriff. He did tell me to get out of town when I last saw him yesterday."

"That'd be Grant Bronsky who said that to you. I'll have a word with him Mr. Mitchell. I know him well. We're kinda like good friends."

"Oh! Thanks for that, and for your time."

Greg looked at his watch and muttered. "Ten past eight, it's too early to call Dean Halburton in Boston."

He stood thinking and the clerk interrupted his thoughts.

"If you're looking fer breakfast Mr. Mitchell I'd recommend Ma Tooley's pancakes and she's just across the street from here, a bit to the north. That's to the left to you Mr. Mitchell."

The idea sounded good. Greg thanked the clerk, stepped outside with a big breakfast in mind and immediately became convulsed in choking. He'd thought when he looked out of the window this morning that it seemed to be an overcast and dull day, but a fresh breeze had picked up clouds of foul smelling, acrid tasting dust that obscured the sunlight, but without diminishing its heat.

Greg half dropped to his knees, bringing out his handkerchief to cover his nose and mouth. He felt sweat running down his brow and his spine. The sensation robbed him of his appetite and he made his way slowly down to the sheriff's office with his face covered over like an old time bank robber.

Relief came as he entered the office. He shook the dust from his shoulders and wiped his face clean with his handkerchief.

An elegant, middle-aged man wearing a gray woolen suit, opened to show a multi-colored waistcoat, covering an ample stomach crossed with a heavy gold chain greeted him cheerfully.

"You must be new in town? It's bad today, we call it Noble's Breath."

Greg looked into the man's gray, all-seeing eyes below his greased black hair with its central widow's peak.

"I was told that Noble's Breath was the smell of the chicken manure?"

The man laughed and held out his hand. "It's the same thing. I'm Sheriff Donovan. What can I do for you?"

Greg took the hand, but thought on what the man had said.

"Good morning sheriff. I'm Greg Mitchell, do you mean that

out there; that what's blowing down the street and blocking the sun is CHICKEN MANURE?"

Donovan chuckled "Every bit of it. It's from the piles next the farms up north. Today's a bad day."

The sheriff walked behind a desk and pulled a file from a drawer to read from. "I see from this file you've already met Deputy Bronsky, Mr. Mitchell?"

Greg hadn't noted the deputy's name from yesterday.

"I met a deputy when I got into town yesterday. I had an accident and bumped into a young fellow following the diversion to Main Street."

Greg's voice hardened at the mention of the road sign. Donovan dropped the file onto the desk. "That was Bronsky, he's been out to see young Jess White this mornin'" Greg interrupted.

"How is he sheriff, the boy I mean? Did he sleep well? Is he okay?"

The sheriff's face softened.

"Thank you for askin' Mr. Mitchell. I heard from Doc Finch about your concern for the kid's well-bein' and how you looked after him yesterday."

The sheriff rubbed the end of his nose with his knuckle. "Bronsky says the boy won't press charges against you. Now if you choose not to press charges against him we can let it all drop with a caution to exercise more care and attention. That'll go for you both."

This bewildered Greg.

"Why? Why ever would I wish to press charges?"

Donovan shrugged.

"So Judge Denman can decide who's right and who's wrong. Bronsky says it's too close to call."

Greg waved his arms negatively across his body. "No! No charges, the deputy told me to leave town after checking in with him first, but I want to stay a while. I'd like to do some business here, if I may?"

The sheriff's expression hardened at the mention of business, he narrowed his eyes and spoke in a low, slow monotone.

"What kind o' business would that be, Mr. Mitchell?"

"Buying and selling really, anything, goods commodities, anything that's legal."

"And why would you want to be doin' that in Bamptonville? We're a small town of three-thousand or more souls and mostly live by grace of agriculture and God's goodness to us. We're sixty-three miles from Larksville; that's the nearest city of any size and all around us are townships of a hundred or so souls and villages of up to no more'n thousand. Now why would you want to spend your time here when you could do so much better for yourself somewhere's else? Somewhere where there's more folks around to buy what you're gonna be sellin'?"

Greg's lips formed a hard, straight line; his jaw jutted forwards.

"Because, yesterday I met Jess White. A youngster from a poor background whose family has struggled to get him through three years of high school and find they can't afford the final year. He's holding on to his values and trying to find work to help pay his way. I think there are others who would have him do things for money that would solve his problem, but those things would offend society, his family and the boy himself. I can help him do it a better way, more'n that, I want to. I reckon I owe him."

The sheriff's face remained expressionless throughout Greg's emotional speech, but his eyebrows twitched at the inference of possible corruption of the boy's morals by others.

"You know that for a fact Mr. Mitchell, about the coercion you mentioned that is?"

"No sir, I don't. It's just what I've picked up from loose talk, but I never met a more deserving case than Jess White and I'm ready to help him as best I can."

"How do you plan to do that? Won't you get bored hereabouts? Won't you want to move on before you've got the job done? There's a full year to go before Jesse White graduates at the end o' twelfth grade."

Greg scratched his head. "I've been thinking about that. It's no problem for me to stay in Bamptonville. I'm free of all commitments right now. I came on this trip to relax after my divorce. You asked me how I'm going to do it for Jess? I don't exactly know - yet. I thought I'd set up a charitable trust or something that would give him work, paid work, to let him pay his own way. I'd sponsor him through the trust if it didn't make enough or if I had to move on. But I need to talk to my lawyer in Boston and he don't get into his office before eight-thirty of a morning."

Donovan glanced up at the wall clock and pointed to an empty desk.

"It's after eight-thirty right now. You can use that phone over there if you wish."

"Thank you Sheriff that's very kind of you."

Greg sat at the desk and put through the call. He noticed the sheriff remained in earshot while he waited for the connection to make.

"Everly Peabody, Good Morning."

Greg recognized the fresh, youthful voice of the receptionist.

"Hello Adele, it's Greg Mitchell, you did some work for me recently"

"Oh yes, I remember. Hello Mr. Mitchell, how are you? Are you back here now?"

"I'm in Nebraska, Adele, calling from the sheriff's office"

She interrupted. "Oh dear, are you in trouble?"

Greg smiled; she had left off the final word, 'again'.

"In a way I am Adele, I need to speak to Dean is he in?"

"Just a minute Greg."

Vivaldi's Four Seasons played on hold for a few seconds before the over elocuted, New England voice of Dean Halburton came on the line.

"Greg! Dean! Adele says you're in trouble in Nebraska - where the hell is that exactly?"

Greg grinned. "It's South of the Dakotas, West of Iowa and northwest of Missouri."

Greg heard sucking noises before Dean came back on the line

"I don't know any of those places you mentioned. Never been to any of them."

"Don't worry Dean, they're nowhere near Martha's Vineyard."

"Ahh! Now I know where that is." The lawyer brightened and asked. "What appears to be the trouble?"

Greg gave him a run down of his recent happenings and what he intended to do in Bamptonville. Dean listened carefully and Greg knew from the echo he had been put on a speakerphone; but he didn't know who else was listening to him. Greg finished by asking.

"That visa you got for me to do business here, will it let me trade like I want to do, or even start a company or a charitable trust? I might want to make a few bucks for myself while I'm at it."

"I'll need to check it out and get the information to you through Adele, we can use email or fax. We'll need to check the local State laws for possible objections. Will you be working only in Nebraska?"

"Good question, you should check out the neighboring States on each side. I've a mind to start small, buying and selling through Ebay, and maybe some bulk commodities or whatever else comes up. You know me."

"Yes Greg, we do know you. Okay, until you get an email, give me a fax number, one where I can reach you confidentially."

Greg looked up. "Sheriff, my lawyer needs a confidential fax number to contact me; can you further oblige me please?"

The lawman smiled and dropped his card with the fax number in front of Greg, who noted for his own reference; 'Donovan's hearing must be particularly acute'.

Greg relayed the number.

"Thanks Dean, I think that's all for now, love to everybody, I'll be in touch..."

"Greg, Greg, don't go. Stay on the line, we have a problem."

"Problem? What problem?"

"I just pulled up your account Greg. Your account with us that is, and I see there's an imbalance. You see; there's money still in it that belongs to you, and that's just plumb not right. It's not the way we work at all, dear me no. It should all be ours by now."

The belly laugh in his earpiece told Greg the call was over. He hung up, thanked the sheriff again and prepared to leave.

"I'm staying at the Melody Inn if you need me Sheriff and I'll be operating from there. Jess will help me in the evenings, for pay. We'll get things set up properly and I'll keep you informed."

The sheriff took Greg's hand in farewell and passed over a slip of paper.

"Appreciated Mr. Mitchell. I've written here some names of folks hereabouts you might care to introduce yourself to, along with their numbers; you can say I said for you to call. The first on the list is Bill Courtley, our town's bank manager, you'll need to set up an account and he's a good man to have on your side. So is Mayor Denton, Harvey Denton. You'll find him at the Town Hall most days before noon. Ross Noble is next on the list. He's our most prominent citizen and you'd be advised to call and make an appointment to pay your respects without delay; and you should let him know what you're doing and why. Also Judge Denman, you'll meet him in the Hapsburg Hotel where he takes an aperitif before lunch most days from ten-thirty, exceptin' when court's in session that is. It's okay to go up and introduce yourself at the bar. You'll do yourself no harm at all buyin' him a drink to make his acquaintance."

Greg got the picture, thanked the sheriff again and walked out into the choking dust and heat of the street.

7

Greg greeted people warmly as he passed them on the sidewalk, although they mostly regarded him with hostile, suspicious eyes, responding to his greeting with silence or more rarely with a curt nod. He put it down to the 'Noble Breath' getting them down and walked on taking in the town, looking at what was for sale in the shops. More particularly he noted the prices of those items he and Jess might trade with the prospect of profit, as a start to building a bank of market intelligence for their forthcoming trading operations. Telling himself. Trading needs planning! You can't plan properly unless you know what people are buying and how much they will pay.

He strolled confidently along the side streets and ambled down the back of Main Street. The air seemed cleaner at the back of the buildings and he realized he was walking behind the fast food outlets on Main Street; looking into their back yards as he passed. The numbers of plastic drums lying out back of each business fired his curiosity and he wondered what they were for?

At the back of the 'Fryway' burger outlet one drum oozed a dark liquid from a crack at the neck that congealed into a crust on the drum. Curiosity got the better of him. Greg looked left and right; there was nobody around and he walked in to have a closer look. He inspected the seepage, smelled it, poked it with a finger and rubbed it on his thumb, identifying the substance as spent cooking oil and his brain shifted into overdrive.

If nobody was collecting this stuff, the quantity waiting for disposal suggested there was a problem and that advocated a potential business opportunity. A buzz of excitement passed through Greg. This could be the small business venture he needed to fund Jess through high school next year.

Greg had acquired some first-hand knowledge of this business, having previously invested in a small start-up plant in

Florida collecting waste cooking oil and converting it into bio-diesel. The process was not difficult, time consuming or costly to set up or run; and not at all dangerous as long as reasonable care was taken when using the chemicals the process required. Greg experienced a buzz of excitement, this was an idea to work on and perhaps mention to the mayor when he introduced himself later that day.

He walked along a few more streets, looking into the backyards of food outlets mentally marking down even more drums of waste oil waiting for disposal. It all added strength to his perception that if nobody was already processing this oil; here was a business opportunity ripe for exploitation. He wrote in his notebook. 'Check bio-diesel from cooking oil, process, regulations and equipment- US Rules.'

His next stop was to introduce himself to the local bank manager. He whistled the tune of the Ricky Skaggs number he'd heard that morning as he walked to the Commercial and Farmer's Bank on Main Street.

Bill Courtley was not only expecting him, but lost no time applauding him on his proposed benevolence for the benefit of Jess White. It seemed that Bamptonville was no different from any other small town where everybody knew everything about everyone else – at least amongst the top echelon of the local society. Greg made a mental note not to delay meeting the others on the sheriff's list.

He set up an account at the bank by drawing a cheque on his bank in London, talked about transferring funds and enquired into ongoing local investment opportunities. The manager promised to keep him informed when suitable openings arose.

"See me any time Mr. Mitchell, a prior appointment will not be necessary, not for you, sir. Come at any time!"

"Thank you very much Mr. Courtley. Perhaps you can recommend a local accountant. I'll be working on a diverse range of business opportunities and possibly setting up a charitable trust. He'll need to be somebody who can work with my Boston lawyers, Everly Peabody. Does anybody come to mind fitting that requirement?"

The banker wrote a name and contact information on a Post-It note and passed it over.

"There's nobody at that level in Bamptonville I could suggest Mr. Mitchell. But I'm sure you'll find Bill Elbury to your liking. He's in Larksville, that's sixty-three miles due north of here."

Everything was pointing him towards Larksville; he needed to get out there to check the place out. But before that, he needed to pay his respects to the mayor, the judge and Mr. Noble.

Greg encountered the mayor rushing down the steps of the Town Hall and attempted to introduce himself.

"Delighted to meet you Mr. Mitchell. I've been hearing good things about you since you came to town. Do come and see me when I've got more time to give you. My apologies, I have to rush off for a meeting."

Greg waited until the mayor was hurrying away towards Main Street before following him down the steps into the street at a more sedate pace.

"Just the judge and Mr. Noble." He grimaced, looking at his wristwatch. "Nine twenty, another hour before the judge gets to his watering hole. I'd best try Mr. Noble next.

Greg had bought a 'Pay as You Go' cell phone when he started out on this trip. He consulted the sheriff's paper and pressed Ross Noble's number into the keypad.

A crisp, businesslike voice came into his ear. "This is Ross Noble."

It was the voice of a man used to exercising authority and Greg decided to proceed with courteous caution.

"Good Morning Mr. Noble. I'm Greg Mitchell. We haven't met. I've just arrived in town and will be here for a while. I'd like to come out and pay my respects, as a matter of courtesy, sir."

The voice lost none of its crispness.

"Thank you Mr. Mitchell. That's mighty neighborly of you.

The sheriff told me you might call. I believe you've some ideas for setting up a local business and I'd sure like to hear them."

"Thank you Mr. Noble, when could I call? I'll put myself at your disposal sir."

Greg heard the pages of a diary rustle in the background

"You say you'll be here for some time Mr. Mitchell?"

"Yes sir."

"I have to go away for a few days. Let me see now, today's Tuesday, can you come over next Monday morning, say about ten. I'll be able to give you a good hour then?"

"Thank you sir, I'll be there; until next Monday morning at ten. Have a good trip."

"Thank you. Mr. Mitchell. You have yourself a good day."

Greg regarded his phone thoughtfully after Noble had rung off and reflected. "There's no doubt who's running the show around here."

Greg formed the impression that anything he wished to do here would need the approval of this man for the simple reason that nobody else in town would likely help him without it. This had been a valuable call.

"Next stop, the judge!" Greg slapped his side with determination and strode off to inspect the wares for sale in the shops and wrote copious notes in his notebook to fill the time until he met the judge. Greg waited in the street until his watch read ten thirty-five when he walked into the chintzy lounge of the Hapsburg Hotel on lower Main Street.

An overly thin man in breeches and laced up riding boots stood at the bar with one foot on the rail and a large glass of iced beverage in his hand.

Greg waited for two minutes until the glass was a third full before going over to address the man at the bar.

"Excuse me sir, but would you be Judge Denman?"

The man stood bolt upright, he twisted his neatly trimmed ginger mustache and regarded Greg severely.

"And who would want to know," he bellowed?

"Pardon me your honor, but I'm new in town and plan to

stay for a while; I just wish to pay my respects to you. I'm Greg Mitchell. May I buy you a drink sir?"

"No! You may not!" The judge bawled like a bull that couldn't find its cow. He put his hands on his hips and faced Greg squarely on.

"You'll be the English driver that ran down one of our junior citizens."

It was an accusation and the hard eyes that bored deep into Greg made him feel ashamed.

"I'm afraid there was an accident"

The judge wagged a finger at him and interrupted.

"Accident be damned. I'd have given you a week in jail and a hundred and twenty dollar fine if you'd come up before me this morning."

The stern face held Greg's and once more those eyes bored deeply into him as if reading his soul.

"Yes your honor, Deputy Bronsky said it would be about a hundred and twenty dollars."

"Did he, be damned? Never mind Bronsky." The judge waved a hand above his head and then drained his glass; banging it loudly on the counter top. The barman sidled over, holding himself ready to attend his honor's pleasure. The judge wiped his mouth on a pocket-handkerchief and wagged his finger at Greg again.

"I've also been hearin' how you took care of the youngster and how you're gonna be doing somethin' to help him pay his way at school. Would that be right?"

"That's right sir. I was impressed with the boy's integrity and sincerity. I'm presently in a position to help him and wish to do so."

"Good man!" The judge slapped the counter with the flat of his hand and the sound echoed from the papered walls yellowed by decades of tobacco smoke and rattled the old photographs of long gone citizens hanging there.

"Good Man, no, I'm not giving you seven days jail. Do you know what I'm going to do?"

"What's that sir?" Greg was confused, but anxious to hear

what the judge held in store for him.

"No Sir, I'm going to buy you a drink instead." The judge slapped the counter with his hand again as if he had pronounced sentence with a gavel.

"That's very kind of you sir," Greg was overawed and not a little relieved.

The judge beckoned to the waiting barman.

"Adam, another for me and one for Mr…Mr?"

"Mitchell sir."

"That's what I meant to say. One for Mr. Mitchell."

The judge turned to Greg. "Little pre-lunch cocktail I invented, you'll love it. I call it Gin and Tonic with a Twist."

The barman expertly poured the drinks, adding ice and a slice of lemon to the glasses before placing them in front of the men.

"Your health Mr. Mitchell."

"Skin off your nose, your honor."

The judge laughed and Greg was emboldened to ask. "If you don't mind me asking sir, what's the twist, in the drink I mean. What did you invent?"

"Twice as much gin to tonic, that's the twist." The judge bellowed and burst out laughing.

They got on well and supped three drinks together before Greg excused himself.

"Good luck to you, young fella. Come and see me if you need my help. You know where you can find me."

Greg staggered out into the midday sun, glad to find the wind had dropped and the dust settling. He wondered if he was in a fit state to drive to Larksville after drinking with the judge on an empty stomach and decided to try a plate of Ma Tooley's pancakes; with a large jug of coffee before setting out on the drive. Things were going well for him so far.

Ma's ample bosoms rocked with laughter when Greg told her about the judge.

"Judge Denman's a good man to be your friend. He's got a

farm on the west side of town and he owns the Flyway Burger joint. He's only here days when he's not in court."

"This town doesn't have a courthouse?" Greg asked in surprise.'

Ma's bosoms rattled again as she chuckled while topping up his coffee mug.

"We do, if you count the lounge in the Hapsburg Hotel, otherwise Larksville's the nearest."

Greg finished, paid for his meal and with Ma's raucous farewell ringing in his ears walked over to the motel to collect his car for the drive to Larksville. It had been a fruitful morning in which he had learned much about the town and its people. He tapped his inside pocket where he safeguarded the sheriff's paper.

"And I've got the names and introductions right here to the men who run it."

8

Jess passed a restless night and welcomed the arrival of daybreak. The courage that came with the adrenalin rush facing Kyler last night had long since evaporated with fear creeping in to take its place.

Every creak or noise of the building during the night scared him into sitting bolt upright in bed and shaking at the thought that Kyler and his thugs were returning to torment him. It would be so unlike them to give up on him so easily.

He lay wide-awake when dawn broke and decided to get himself through the bathroom before the rest of the dormitory rose. Anxious to avoid any repercussions from last night, he planned keeping a low profile during the day to stay clear of Kyler and his crew.

He rubbed the soreness in his leg. It was still stiff and painful when he walked. He limped down to the cafeteria to get himself an early breakfast. The attendant stood wide-eyed with surprise and checked the clock on the wall as Jess walked up to the counter.

"We don't get to see you down here at this time o' the mornin'. Is there a fire out there or somethin'?" She delivered her question with a good-natured smile.

Jess shrugged and mumbled. "Need to get an early start today."

He took breakfast alone at a corner table and was nearly through his meal when a bunch of rowdy students crowded into the room. Jess glanced up anxiously to see if Kyler was with them. He exhaled in relief when it turned out to be a bunch of high-spirited freshmen. The uneasiness was enough to take away his appetite for the remainder of his food. He dumped his garbage in the trashcan, stacked his plates and left hurriedly, to hide away and wait for the bell to mark the start of the school day proper.

At morning break he went to his dormitory instead of leaving the building for the yard with his classmates; just to make sure he stayed clear of Kyler. Jess didn't want to give the bully any chance to come back at him and worried what mischief they might have planned for him for later?

Looking out of the window his heart missed a beat when he spotted Felix Gleitner's old blue Buick draw up to the school gate and Kyler Reeves sauntering across the yard towards it.

Jess pulled back from the window so he couldn't be seen; watching them with his heart in his mouth. Felix rarely came to the school to avoid drawing attention to himself. It had to be something important to make him do so today, and Jess guessed he was that reason.

Felix shifted across to the passenger side, wound down the window and scowled. He knew from the expression on Kyler's face and his stance, arms open and ready to deliver some fatuous excuse that the operation had gone badly last night.

"What happened," he bawled and Kyler flinched?

"It weren't no good Felix. We went to do it, just like you said. We got him stripped down an' all. Shit! You should see the state o' his leg. It's got more colors than a goddamn rainbow."

"What leg? What colors? What the hell you spiffin' about? Tell me what the fuck happened? I cain't hang around here all day."

Felix looked nervously around him to see if they were being overheard. Kyler bent down to whisper in Felix's ear.

"He's been in a rumble. A Limey ran him down off Charmain and he's hurt pretty bad. The Limey's payin' his doctor bills an all, but that leg's got more colors than Joseph's coat so help me. Jess'll be no good fer you in pictures fer a coupla weeks at least"

"Shit an' double shit." Felix nibbled his knuckle while he thought.

"You an' the others, you did the business or didn't ya?"

"No Felix! Be reasonable fer Chrissake. Not when we saw that leg we didn't. He told us to go right ahead when he knew he had no choice, but he still said he don't want doin' none o' that stuff like we do, an' besides, the Limey's fixin' him up with paid work. Jess said he'll make enough to cover his bills and don't need no other sort o' work. D'ya want us to do anythin'. I'm talkin' about the Brit guy?"

"No! Nada." Felix bellowed. " I'll tell you what and when if there's somethin' to do. You say he's gettin' moolah from this Brit?"

"S'right Felix. Ever'body's talkin' about it."

"How much's he givin' Jess an' how often?"

Kyler shrugged and grimaced. "Dunno, 'nough for him to stay at school next sem'ster."

"Is that so?" Felix stroked his chin while he considered that implication. He came to a decision and looked sharply at Kyler.

"That's not good news, but we got ourselves another problem now. Charlie Vaughn from In-Between Films is coming over at the weekend. He's settin' up a studio outside Lincoln fer a session. He's got Duggie Bishop comin' down fer a Beauty and the Beast filmin' this weekend. I promised him Jess White fer the beauty when I talked to him. If what you say is right an' Jess's gone an' signed up with this Limey blow-in we ain't got us no beauty no more!"

Kyler whistled softly.

"Whew! Duggie Bishop; is that the ex-con truck driver that's three 'undred pounds plus of tattoos and mean muscle?"

"That's the beast, but like I said, I'm stuck fer a beauty if Jess don't do it. You got any ideas?"

Kyler looked doubtful and while Felix pondered, spoke with slow deliberation.

"You know I ain't no Jess lover, but that's a real tall order for a first time out Felix? The only things touchin' his ass since he come out o' diapers is his shorts an' toilet paper. How you plannin' to get Jess to do all that 'beauty' stuff with someone like the Beast o' Babel? You should see how timid-like he is in the showers. It'll be as much as you c'n do to get him t' undress down to butt naked

– that's with folks watchin'. An' yer still expectin' him do that beauty routine with Duggie Bishop? Impossible I'd say."

"You leave that to me. There's always ways and means. You hunnerd percent sure this Limey's fundin' him through twelfth grade?"

"That's the word goin' 'round. You sure you don't want us to do somethin'?"

"Could be. Maybe I will. I dunno yet. I heard Jess's got a school bill he cain't pay. That right?"

"'Bout three 'undred or more. The guy that paid his bills went an' died on him."

The worry lines left Felix's forehead for the first time and a thin, sinister smile crept over his lips.

"Okay, that ain't all bad news. I'll call Charlie Vaughn an' tell him it's on fer this Sunday. Some o' you better stand by fer action this weekend; just in case Jess goes sick or somethin'."

Kyler reeled backwards.

"Not me! No way! Not with Duggie Bishop, the Beast o' Babel. Not in a million! That guy's so big and mean and he's not just rigged like a mule he acts like one too. Count me out. I don't need none o' that grief."

"You'll do as you're frackin' told." Felix snapped. "Just be ready. Leave Jess alone. In fact, try bein' nice t' him. Just tell him I wanna see him tonight, after school's out. I'll be waitin' just down the road under the tree. Tell him t' come get in the car. Tell him it'll be all right. He can get out anytime he wants. Now get goin'. I got calls to make."

Felix drove off and Jess jumped back further from the window when Kyler turned to look his way with his eyes scanning the windows of Jess's dormitory. The boy felt a cold hand clutch at his heart. Kyler's brief search confirmed him as the subject of the conversation with Felix; in that instant it seemed that thousands of butterflies took off at once in his stomach. He came over physically sick and rushed to the bathroom.

That's where Kyler found him.

"Hiya pornstar, I've been lookin' fer you," Kyler's friendliness didn't fool Jess who shrank back against the white tiled wall.

"Why? What do you want?"

"I just wanted to apologize fer last night. I just talked to Felix. Seems we got the wrong idea. He wants to talk to you, to put things right between you two."

Jess shook his head with vigor.

"Not necessary."

"But Felix insists. He says he'll wait fer you tonight after school; down from the gates. Just get in the car; Felix said it'd be okay. No need fer you to get scared or nothin'."

Jess shook his head from left to right and back again to give his words emphasis. "I've nothin' to say to Felix, besides I'm doing things tonight."

"It'll only take a minute, no more'n that. He just wants to talk to you and maybe apologize too for the misunderstandin'. He says you got him all wrong. Tonight! After school's out! Outside the gates! Be there! See you later, sodbuster."

Kyler left with a cheery wave and Jess rushed back into the booth to throw up again.

Felix parked outside Harry's Place and walked purposefully into the bar area. Four unshaven rednecks wearing yesterday's clothes were already sat with their butts overlapping the stools and sucking on the first beers of the day.

They dropped the bottles from their mouths to greet Felix with a hollow cheer.

"You guys live in here?" He asked.

"Just about Felix. Gotta have somethin' t' do all day; no work an' all."

It was the largest, longest haired redneck that spoke. Felix remembered the man's name was Dwight something or other; they were not well acquainted. Dwight's lips tightened, his eyes glinting while the other three watched with vacant expressions and mostly empty bottles in their hands.

"Now you wouldn't have a li'l ol' anythin' on you to make the day pass a bit more agreeable, would you now Felix?"

Merv appeared behind the bar and Felix ordered an ice and slice. The rednecks mouths turned down in disgust at his order, but said nothing and watched in silence as Merv left to prepare the soft drink.

Felix dropped two twists of white paper on the bar counter. Dean's huge, hairy backed hand closed over them and he nodded his thanks.

"That's mighty kind of you Felix, much appreciated." The others nodded their appreciation. "If there's somethin' companionable we can do fer you anytime. Just say the word."

Merv placed the soft drink on the counter and Felix raised it to the rednecks.

"That's mighty comfortin' to know. I can count on yer help when I get me a problem. Here's to y'all."

Greg walked out of Ma Tooley's to find the sun streaming out from behind the clouds, bathing the town in a golden sheen. The substantial meal Ma had forced onto him sat as a comforting lump in his stomach, mellowing the drinks taken with the judge down to a warming glow and fostering good impressions of Bamptonville and what he would try to achieve here.

He chose to walk to the motel by the back route to check again on the numbers of waste oil containers. Greg needed to be certain he wasn't mistaken about the quantities of waste oil before he went ahead with his bio-diesel enterprise. He decided to take a closer look in the yards this time.

Greg was encouraged to find his hopes substantiated; there was a lot of waste cooking oil lying around in Bamptonville. If there was as much again to be gleaned from Larksville and the neighboring villages, there was an opportunity here promising a larger return on his investment than he needed to fund Jess through high school.

Just before he turned right into Greener Street, a trio of high-spirited, giggling youths rushed around the corner and almost bumped into him. They quieted down immediately they recognized Greg; who saw expressions of guilt break out over their faces. They ran on past him without speaking. Greg stopped to watch them and wondered what mischief had they been up to before resuming his walk to the motel office?

Greener ran up into Main. The motel rooms and car park were on Greener with only the office and reception building facing onto Main.

He was about to cross the entrance to the car park when a rusted, white Toyota pick-up blaring out a Dixie tune on its horn sped out into the road from the motel car park entrance and narrowly missed hitting him. Greg was startled, but instinctively jumped backwards onto the sidewalk out of the path of the vehicle. The Toyota speeded out of the car park without stopping at the road or showing consideration for any other road users who might have been passing.

"Bloody idiots." Greg was angry.

He caught sight of the grinning face in the driver's seat and recognized him as one of the rednecks he'd seen at the bar in Harry's Place last night. Greg's first impulse was to go after him and give the man a piece of his mind, but he shrugged it off as a pointless exercise, consoling himself by muttering: "Where there's no sense, there's no reason." With a determined stride, he walked the back way into the reception area to firm up his ongoing arrangements at the motel.

The motel clerk rubbed his hands together greedily when Greg confirmed he'd be staying for an unlimited, but lengthy period of at least a month and agreed a monthly rate.

"I'm going into Larksville today to arrange satellite Internet for my room, like we discussed." The clerk looked doubtful and Greg put him at his ease by adding. "Don't worry. It will all be at my own expense. I need to get going, could you take my things down to the new room please. I'll be back before five tonight."

"It'll see to it m'self an' it'll be my pleasure Mr. Mitchell." The clerk continued rubbing his hands together, reminding Greg once more of the Dicken's character and expecting him to say, 'ever so humble sir,' at any moment.

Greg stopped on his way out and turned back to the clerk who stood watching and rubbing his hands together.

"Was there something else Mr. Mitchell?"

Greg pulled the lobe of his ear while he thought how best to express what he wanted to say without causing undue speculation or curiosity.

"Ye-es, I'm expecting a visitor tonight at five. Jess White, the kid I knocked down yesterday. He'll be working for me in the evenings. If I'm delayed and you've shifted my belongings by then will you let him into one-ninety-six and ask him to wait there for me?"

"No problem Mr. Mitchell."

"Thank You," Greg watched the clerk for a reaction, but there was none and he left the office for his room to get himself ready for the drive to Larksville.

9

Greg quickly showered in his old room and changed his clothes. After packing his things into suitcases, he took an overnight bag with his valuables and laptop out the back way to his car.

The air was still, but heavy enough for perspiration to form along his spine and under his arms. He stood to sniff the air, thankful it was free of Noble Breath this morning; or was he already becoming used to its presence?

He started the BMW and revved the engine to boost the air-con, sighing with appreciation when he felt its cooling blast swiftly evaporate the discomforting humidity. A perfectly straight road led to Larksville; even so he set the address for Bill Elbury into his GPS before setting off.

The route north gave him sight of the massive extent of the chicken broiler industry centered on Bamptonville with its row upon row of windowless, wooden chicken sheds. There were too many to count, running on both sides of the road for four or more miles out of town.

The sheds behind the front row facing onto the road were obscured from view by towering mounds of decaying manure, surrounding each shed like earthwork constructions around military ammunition dumps.

The stench returned and became so strong that even the air-con failed to filter out its noxious presence. Greg grimaced as the back of his mouth dried under the onslaught of the heavy, ammonium laced odor. He was looking at one of the rotting piles close to the road and wondering why nobody did anything about them – when it happened.

The right front tire blew out with the sound of an exploding landmine. The car slewed out of control, swerving immediately towards the deep ditch on the near side of the road. Greg stood on the brake and fought to control the car's direction. The ABS kicked in and prevented skidding. Fortunately he had both hands on the wheel at the time of the blowout. The wheel became like a live thing as he wrestled with it to bring the heavy car under control away from the ditch; finally coming to a stop on the other side of the tarmac road.

It had been a close thing. Greg leaned across the wheel breathing deeply; he was shaking and sweating, and yet felt cold. He switched off the engine to sit for a few moments to recover his composure before getting out of the car. One glance into the ditch, eight feet deep with straight sides revealed the good luck that brought him unscathed out of the ordeal. Opposing pangs of fear and joy of relief swept through his body that trembled in aftershock.

Greg looked into the ditch knowing he would likely be dead had the car crashed into that dried out dyke at the speed he was traveling. Once his breathing steadied, his reason returned to pose the question, why did the tire blow out?

He examined the carriageway, but saw no debris on the road likely to cause the tire to rupture. This was the latest model in the five-series range with the odometer registering less than six-thousand miles traveled since it came out of the factory in Bavaria. In spite of a lack of supporting evidence, Greg stood at the side of the road trying to convince himself it was an accident.

A farm tractor and trailer came up from behind and he waited in the middle of the road for it to arrive, expecting some offer of help or a word of sympathy from its operator. The driver sucked a straw under a straw hat and with a blank expression, merely nodding at Greg and glancing at the car as he drove past without stopping or speaking.

Damn neighborly, Greg thought as he hauled the spare from the trunk and prepared to change the wheel.

He rolled the punctured wheel onto the road, gritting his teeth with dismay when he saw a four-inch square area of tire had apparently perished and caused the burst, the breach had then spread around the wall of the tire. Greg examined the rupture closely, recoiling from the burning-in-the nose smell and the watering of his eyes.

He stood up abruptly. The cold fear of shock and upset became the colder fear of resolute anger as his brain assimilated the evidence he had uncovered and tried to make sense of it.

Acid had caused the tire to fail. But, he'd been nowhere to collect acid on a tiny, square area of the inner wall of one tire. That could only mean it was a deliberate act that placed it on the tire. Someone wanted him out of the way and was prepared to go as far as engineering a fatal accident to accomplish this. Greg's heart raced, he suddenly felt extremely cold and rubbed his arms to restore their warmth.

"So it wasn't an accident after all!" He spoke aloud, to nobody and then asked himself.

But why? Why would anybody want me out of the way? Whose way am I in?

His brain argued Move on, get out of here. Get back on the road to San Francisco – that's where you were heading for.

The warning made perfect sense, but something else snapped inside his brain.

"No! I'm no hero, but I'm staying to do what I said I'd do and I want to find out who did this and why. I'll run away from ex-wives and courtrooms, but not from cowards with murder or mayhem in mind."

Greg heaved the spent wheel into the trunk, wiped his hands on a cloth and with a gnawing doubt in his stomach about the good will of the people of Bamptonville resumed his journey.

He tapped the paper in his pocket with the names of the prominent people the sheriff had given him, surmising as he drove.

"If they know what I'm about it's a fair chance that everybody else in town knows." He racked his brains to recall what he had told Bronsky, the sheriff, the judge and the bank manager.

"All I told them was I was going to do business here and help Jess White with his problems. Now either someone doesn't want me here doing business or they don't want Jess White getting any help?"

He drove on more slowly, pondering who might have done the deed? The car had been parked in the open-air overnight. The car park wasn't closed or guarded. Anybody could have come in under cover of darkness and sabotaged the tire. He realized that if the miscreant had struck at night, the acid would have done its work overnight and he'd have met with a flat tire to deal with before he set off this afternoon.

He tapped the steering wheel with his fingers and said aloud

"That means the car was attacked just before I left this afternoon."

The memory of the trio of youths came instantly to mind. There was something about the way those high school boys shut up and ran on past him that was suspicious and didn't add up to Greg. They hadn't expected to see him, and panicked like rats caught in a grain sack when they came unexpectedly face-to-face around the corner.

They could easily smuggle acid out from the school labs. He remembered his own school days and working with chemicals. He vividly recalled the time when his nose came too near to a bottle of sulfuric acid. It didn't smell of anything, but it made his eyes water and gave him the burning-in-the nose sensation he'd suffered from the tire today. He beat the wheel with the palms of his hands in frustration.

"But why? Why would they do it? Are they jealous of Jess White? Don't they want him to get ahead? Surely they can't have anything against me?"

He became very calm and still when an answer came to him that carried with it a germ of truth and another pang of fear.

"Somebody put them up to it! But who and why?"

Greg reckoned Jess might know. Somehow he had to question the boy tonight without telling him about the blow out, and to do it casually.

"I'll probe it with Jess tonight."

Greg decided not to say anything about the accident to anybody in Bamptonville in case somebody mentioned it to him, and give him a lead as to who was behind the assault on the car.

Greg drove on and felt a slight shudder on the wheel when the speed reached fifty miles per hour and made a mental note to get the wheel balanced that afternoon.

Larksville was a small town and home to around five-thousand people. From a mile outside he could already see it was totally different than Bamptonville. It was altogether more vibrant with well-maintained buildings that were either modern or modernized. There seemed a greater sense of purpose about the place and, on stopping to check directions, found the people were welcoming and friendly. He was agreeably surprised to find the town had a Hertz rental sub-office and headed for it.

The clerk took over Greg's car and listened to his story with grave concern.

"I'm sorry about your misfortune Mr. Mitchell. Leave the car with me. I'll get it fixed up good and that wheel balanced. I'll lend you another car for your business here and if we can't get it done for you today we'll drive out to Bamptonville with the car tomorrow. Sorry you've been inconvenienced."

Greg noticed the clerk looked askance at the ruptured tire but did not comment on it and so he asked.

"I would like to know why the tire blew. Will you be running tests on it?"

"We will certainly examine it closely Mr. Mitchell and if it throws up anything suspicious we'll have to pass it on to the police for them to run forensic tests."

The deep sincerity with which the clerk made that statement reassured Greg. It was half past one when he set off to find Bill Elbury's office above a hardware store in a plain street two back from Main.

From the way Bill Courtley, the bank manager at Bamptonville, had recommended Bill Elbury as his best choice for an accountant, Greg expected a high-powered State grandee in a sumptuous office and wearing formal dress.

Bill Elbury was nothing like that. He did his own reception work and was crammed into a single office crowded with books, papers, files, tennis gear and rhythm guitars that filled every available space including most of the well worn carpet.

"Excuse me. Would you by chance be Bill Elbury?" Greg addressed the tall man in a check shirt and faded jeans as he tapped on the open glazed door and stepped inside.

"Just like it says on the door," the man replied with an engaging smile. Greg noticed the keen intelligence behind the eyes of this thirty-year-old man who was thinning on top and thickening in the waist, much the same as himself.

"I'm Greg Mitchell. Bill Courtley…"

Greg got no further. Elbury grasped Greg's hand in a firm shake and led him to a chair.

"I guessed you must be. I've had calls from Bill and from a Dean Halburton about you." A quizzical expression prompted Elbury to answer Greg's question before he asked it. "Apparently, you told Courtley I'd have to work with him if you signed up with me as your accountant, and he called Halburton who called me. Sit down please Mr. Mitchell."

Greg grunted and sat in the chair facing the cluttered desk, noting that Elbury remained standing, crossing his arms over his chest in an attitude of defense.

"Now tell me this Mr. Mitchell. Bill Courtley said you were staying in Bamptonville a while and wanted to do some business." Elbury stabbed a finger at a paper on his desk, slowly turning it around so he could read. "Trading is what he said."

"That's right Mr. Elbury. I plan to do a bit of buying and selling."

Elbury nodded and held up two fingers.

"Two questions; why does a big shot Boston law firm call me and guarantee my fees for a bit of horse trading? Second, why do it in Bamptonville? If you're serious about doing business here you should be here, in Larksville; we've even got Broadband Internet."

"I'm delighted to hear that. To answer your first question,

Dean Halburton called you because I pay him to do things like that. In my time, I've done a fair amount of serious business in the States. I'm between projects now and this is a sideline. Why Bamptonville? Because I want to work from there."

Elbury threw up his hands in resignation.

"It doesn't make any sense."

"It makes sense enough to me, the question is do you want to help me or not?"

"I'm not sure Mr. Mitchell. I want to know exactly what I'll be getting mixed up in. After all, I don't know you from Sharitarish's nephew." Greg's eyebrows rose and Elbury added for clarification. "Famous Pawnee Indian Chief from hereabouts."

Greg nodded and smiled.

"But you have references on me from Dean Halburton, aren't they enough for you?" Greg looked around the room with some disdain; an unspoken comment that said, it looked like Elbury could do with the business.

The accountant paced behind the desk touching his lips with his cradled fingertips.

"I might not have much, but what I've got is a solid and sound reputation and that's worth more to me than any big bucks you're going to bring me. Unless you tell me what all this is about, in your own words and in my time, I'll not take you on."

This first meeting was going badly and Greg shuffled in his seat, stretching his brain to find exactly the right words. Elbury stood behind the desk, silently watching and waiting for his reply.

"This is difficult Mr. Elbury. You see I've found this area to be a very tight community and one where confidentiality extends to any number of people in the community."

Elbury threw back his head and cut in.

"I find that offensive Mr. Mitchell."

Greg held up his hands.

"Sorry! No offense intended, but I've got to be assured that what I say to you stays inside these four walls."

"You have my word on my discretion Mr. Mitchell." Elbury

held out his hand again which Greg took in his. As if to add drama to the moment the lights went out and several buzzers sounded. Greg looked at Elbury for explanation as he moved about the room switching off machines and silencing the buzzers.

"Drat, it's a power outage. Happens all the time 'specially in high summer and deep winter. Power Company can't keep up demand. You'd better get used to it – particularly if you're staying in Bamptonville. The small townships and villages get worst hit of all."

Elbury pulled up the blind allowing enough natural light to enter through the window to continue their conversation. He sat down behind his desk, took a legal pad from his drawer, a pen from his pocket and said.

"I do believe you were going to share a confidence with me Mr. Mitchell."

Greg talked through his experiences from the time he arrived in Bamptonville until the present moment. As an after-thought he added the tire incident and finished by saying.

"You see Mr. Elbury, it seems someone either doesn't want me to do business here or they don't want Jess White to get the help I think he deserves."

Elbury scribbled some notes on his pad.

"That's a very serious allegation, but the tire will speak for itself. I'll check on that with Hertz and get back to you."

Greg crossed his legs and forced a wry smile,

"You're taking me on then?"

"Almost; just one more question. Why is it so important to you that this particular kid gets educated?"

Greg wasn't happy with the question; he caught his breath and recrossed his legs, thinking deeply. He trusted this lanky, unkempt accountant and decided to reply by baring his soul.

"I was born with two abilities Mr. Elbury. To make money and think only of myself. I don't think I've done a single worthwhile thing for others before now in my adult life unless it profited me to do it. It's the way I am and it's cost me two marriages and every friend I might otherwise have kept. When I came up against this boy's sincerity and values. This may sound corny, but I was humbled Mr. Elbury. I can't remember the last time I felt like that. Maybe I never have before? Jess White became a worthwhile project, an investment if you want to call it that, but for his profit, not mine. I can help him and I will."

Bill Elbury looked away from the fierce determination on Greg's face and scratched behind his ear.

"Trouble is there's going to be a lot more Jess White's around and very soon. The so-called economic boom of the last few years is about to implode. Enron is only the beginning."

"Are you saying that what happened at Enron is not an isolated case?"

"That's what I think. Enron's just the signpost to what must happen in the near future. I believe it's a much more widely spread financial malaise. The whole banking industry is way over-leveraged on doubtful domestic property deals and the bubble is bound to burst. At best we're heading for recession; at worst depression. Believe me, it will happen, and soon."

Greg chuckled and slapped his knee.

"Come on, you're scaremongering. It can't be that bad. We've had the biggest economic boom since the world war."

"Founded on lies and deceit Mr. Mitchell. You mark my words and if you have any sensitive stocks I'd advise you move them into something more stable and less exciting like utilities."

"Does that now mean you're taking me on?"

Elbury stood up and reached with his hand across the desk for Greg to shake again.

"It does and the first thing is for you to understand this. I don't take shit from anybody, least of all from clients and I speak my mind, whenever and however I feel the need. Got that Mr. Mitchell?"

Greg liked the man's direct style and his confidence in Elbury doubled.

"I wouldn't have it any other way Mr. Elbury."

"Good, and that's another thing; from now on I'm Bill, what do I call you?"

"How about Greg?"

Elbury removed a stack of files from the desk.

"Okay Greg, let's get down to business. I understand you're starting off with some light Internet and local trading along with young Jess to begin with?"

"That's correct, but I'd like to cover my own expenses as well; so I'll need to seek out some bigger one-off trades. I also want to get started on this bio-diesel plant."

Elbury pointed his pencil at Greg.

"You know about that business do you?"

Greg nodded. "Yes, I invested in a bio-diesel from waste oil business in Florida a couple of years back. I heard it took off and they're quite big now. I can draw on their knowledge and expertise. They owe me."

Elbury smacked his lips together and said.

"Talk to the local mayor, we can run off some stats from the Internet before you go back. Harvey Denton's a good sort. He's up for re-election later this year. The waste oil in Bamptonville is a problem. It goes to landfill and down drains, it's a headache for him. If you can make a good diesel oil alternative for fifty cents when it's two-eighty a gallon at the pump and take away a pressing problem, he'll go for it and give you what help he can. He needs to keep his costs down and has to run some expensive school buses. Fuel's his biggest outlay. Do him a deal and he'll bite your hand off, as long as you can do the business?"

The phone rang and interrupted them.

"It's for you," Elbury handed over the instrument.

"Hertz here Mr. Mitchell. I've been on to Regional Head Office and they want the damaged wheel returned to St. Louis for forensic examination. They're sending out a replacement car, but it won't be here until tomorrow afternoon. They want me to keep your car meanwhile and lend you my best car, but I'm afraid I don't have any exec cars or limos; only the wedding car."

"That's Okay, don't worry, I'll keep the car you've loaned me until I can collect the BMW. I'll be coming back tomorrow afternoon so I'll collect it tomorrow and return your loan car at the same time."

"Thank you Mr. Mitchell, for your understanding and cooperation."

Greg gave Bill the gist of the conversation.

The accountant slapped his hands on the desk.

"Okay, leave me the contacts with that firm in Florida you talked about, then let me show you around Larksville and get some of your chores done."

They walked around the town, picking up prices of goods and papers with information. Greg signed up for a satellite connection. Bill's firm nod assured the supplier he'll get paid, in consequence, the technician would be out first thing the next morning to make the installation. Greg was introduced to a few other people. Bill looked like he would continue, but at three forty-five Greg said he'd best be heading back to Bamptonville, but would be back tomorrow to pick up his car.

He bought a window air-con unit in good condition from a pre-owned warehouse and got the price down to twenty-five dollars. He'd seen one similar on sale in Bamptonville marked up at eighty-five and it looked more worn than this one. It could be a good first trade for Jess and it would go in the car. Greg stroked his chin as he stuffed it onto the back seat of the borrowed Geo Prizm.

He said his goodbyes to Bill Elbury with a handshake, turning away as he said see you tomorrow. But Bill pulled him back and whispered.

"I don't like the sound of that tire blowout and neither does Hertz. Just keep your eyes open and watch out, just in case some crazy is out to refight the War of Independence. I'll make a few discreet enquiries on the grapevine." He slapped Greg's back with a loud and cheerful, "See you tomorrow."

10

A mixture of emotions worked through Greg as he drove the borrowed Prizm along the straight, dusty road to Bamptonville. He pulled the visor around to shield his eyes from the sun's sideways glare and gripped the steering wheel so tightly, his knuckles stood out as white, bony mounds.

He was glad to be active again and working at something worthwhile and excited also by the prospect of having Jess work with him. But underlying these positive sentiments lay fears and doubts about the tire incident. It was a direct and personal threat against him demanding swift resolution; but where should he start?

"Who would do such a thing? Whose toes am I treading on here? Who could be against me helping Jess?"

He considered that line of possibility. "Could it be Melissa? The youths he'd seen – Jess's own schoolmates? Who?"

"Who else knew I was going to Larksville this afternoon? Who else did I tell?"

Greg drove mechanically while his brain raced seeking answers. With his mind thus occupied, Greg made a speedier return journey and hadn't noticed anything outside the vehicle until he approached the first of the chicken sheds. Neither had he consciously noted the police car heading towards Larksville, until it swung in behind him, sounding its siren for him to stop.

He pulled over and watched in his rear view mirror as the sheriff heaved himself out of the police car and walked towards him clutching a paper.

Greg sat still with his hands on the wheel. From his time in Florida, he remembered this was what one had to do when pulled over. Sheriff Donovan indicated Greg should wind his window down and then thrust his stubbly chin into the car.

"No harm done to you then? Bad place for a blowout. Was the

car badly damaged?"

The question surprised and alarmed Greg, instantly raising the question, 'how the hell did he know about that?'

Greg felt sick at the idea of the sheriff's possible involvement in perpetrating his misfortune, but decided to play along and treat the matter as casually as he could until he had gathered more facts. Greg's heart beat quickened in response to the adrenalin coursing through him.

"I was lucky, Sheriff; no harm done to me or the car." The lawman's eyes remained fixed on him, wanting more. Greg swallowed and lightly waved his hand in the air.

"Hertz reckon it's a faulty tire. Sometimes happens, they said."

The sheriff nodded in apparent satisfaction, smiling as he passed a folded sheet of paper through the window.

"This came in for you an hour ago. Looks important. Thought I'd ride out to meet you coming back."

"Thank you sheriff that's really nice of you."

Greg took the paper and ran his eyes swiftly over the page. It was from Dean Halburton in Boston.

Greg,

1. If you told the INS when you arrived you came for business and pleasure you're legal on your B1/B2 visa. If you didn't, then hotfoot it to Canada, Bahamas or Mexico for next weekend and tell them you're here for business and pleasure when you come back in on the following Monday.

BUT! Don't start anything big without consulting me and Bill Elbury. BTW I've talked with Elbury.

2. I've also talked to Wayne Fisher in Florida. His business is growing and he's making bio-diesel plants for sale. For some reason he's grateful to you. Perhaps it's to do with you putting up the capital and your support to give him a start (Ha! Ha!).

He's also concerned about the amount of your money he has growing in his accounts. (This is a bad habit of yours). He'll help you all he can. Call him! BUT CALL ME BEFORE YOU DO ANYTHING BIGTIME!

DEAN

The message brought Greg some relief from his anxiety and he grinned, folding the paper and stuffing it into his inside pocket. The sheriff's head still poked through the car window, his eyebrows raised high, as if waiting to be told something else he needed to hear.

Greg nodded. "I'm legal sheriff. I told the immigration officer when I came in at Newark I'd be doing some deals."

"I'm pleased to hear it Mr. Mitchell," The sheriff pulled out of the window and added just before he walked back to his car. "And it looks like you've got the help you need to get on with what you're plannin' Mr. Mitchell and good luck to you sir."

The sheriff gave a toot on his siren as he passed Greg on his way back into town. Greg sat for a while in the car just clutching the wheel. An unpleasant thought had entered his head.

Sheriff Donovan knew I was going to Larksville today. But how could he know about the blow out? Surely to goodness Donovan can't be so openly mixed up in anything going on that I could be getting myself in the way of. Did I tell him I'd be back tonight at this time, making it a fair assumption he could meet me on the road?

Greg fought to control his inner emotions and subdue the compulsion he felt to challenge the youths and the sheriff when he got back into town.

"Baby steps. Baby steps." He whispered as he started the engine and drove more slowly into Bamptonville. Greg parked in his new space outside one-ninety-six at the motel, got out and looked around. He saw nobody.

"I must keep my wits about me and my eyes and ears open. Somebody out there doesn't like me or what I'm doing here." Next he wondered about Jess.

"Could it be because there's something I'm not aware of about the boy? And whoever put acid on the tire doesn't want him being helped? And who is this person anyway? Is it more than one? What the hell am I getting myself into here?" Greg spoke out loud as he heaved the air-con unit out of the back seat, stopping suddenly with the unit balanced half in and half out of the car.

'Mitchell you know nothing about this boy and you're in danger of making a damn fool of yourself and possibly getting yourself killed.' The sobering thought made him think a little deeper and whisper out loud.

"Why do you think Jess is such a loner? It makes no sense! Why has he only got one friend and why is it the preacher Melissa? Maybe she's scaring others away with her religious fervor? If so, why does he put up with it? Why? Why? Why? Questions with no ready answers."

The air-con unit slipped slightly from the car seat and he took a firmer hold on it musing

"And according to Melissa, he's in danger of losing his immortal soul? What' was all that about? Is there a darker side to Jess I've not noticed yet?"

Greg shook his head and looked at his watch. It was fifteen minutes to five and he had things to do before Jess arrived.

"Too many questions, but what I need are some answers," He groaned as he heaved the heavy unit the rest of the way out of the car manhandling it onto the bench outside his room before he went inside to get ready for Jess.

For the last hour of the day Jess sat nearest the door. He kept one eye on the large, round clock above the whiteboard behind the teacher's desk. He became increasingly jumpy, his arms and legs twitched with excitement as the hands of the clock clicked towards the half hour when the bell would sound to end the formal school day.

With five minutes to go he slowly gathered his books and papers together, secreting them in his bag, and with one minute still to go sat poised with his muscles tensed ready to run out of the room on the first ring of the bell.

"I must get out of school and to the motel before Kyler gets to me. I don't want to meet Felix," he told himself to bolster his resolve and sat shivering with nerves in the last seconds before the bell.

Jess was up and out of the room as the first stroke of the bell echoed around the classroom. He ran along the corridor, pushing his way past the students that poured out of classrooms further along the corridor.

He ran down the stairs, breathing a sigh of relief when he got to the main school entrance and still there was no sign of Kyler. He slowed his pace and walked at a less noticeable speed – half walk and half trot. There had been a shower of rain in the afternoon and the agreeable freshness of the soil coming through the open doors wafted into his nostrils. His spirits rose. He had got away with it.

A dark silhouette came across the doorway causing Jess to focus his eyes against the brighter light behind and his heart sank. Kyler and Leon strutted in from outside and stood slouching in the doorway, leering at him. Kyler spoke first.

"In a hurry to meet Felix, turnip cruncher? That's good. Felix'll like that."

Jess's stomach churned and his chest heaved. Stars appeared, floating in front of his eyes. His haste had been all for nothing. They were waiting for him. He shook his head, but said nothing and walked out of the doorway, Kyler and Leon falling in step close beside him. The three of them walked down the steps towards the gateway. Leon kept his clenched fist in the small of Jess's back as a reminder of what Jess could expect if he tried making his escape. Nobody spoke.

"Jess! Jess! Where are you going with those people?"

Melissa's shrill voice carried across the yard on the breeze and the urgency in her tone made people turn to look at her. Before Jess could respond Kyler's hand came heavily onto his back and he snarled,

"Ignore her and walk on."

"Jess! Jess White! Don't you walk away from me? Get away from those people they're no good. Jess!"

Jess ignored her and walked through the gates with his escort, they turned right and thirty yards along the road the unwashed blue Buick waited for him.

The passenger door opened when they were five yards from

the car. Felix must have been watching them in the mirror.

"Get in," Kyler barked. Strong hands gripped Jess and twisted him inside. The door closed. Jess looked ahead. His chest heaved. His breathing fast, his body shivering and his jaw slack with fear.

"Hello Jess, nice o' you t' come." With sinking spirits the boy heard the sickly sweet tones of Felix Gleitner and slowly turned to face him. The man sat in the middle of the bench seat close to Jess. The boy's first instinct was to shift further away, but the unyielding steel of the closed door stopped him.

"Now then Jess, there ain't nothin' to be scared of. I just wanna word, that's all."

"What...what sort of word? What do you want from me?"

"Well that's surely not a nice way to say hello, is it now. We're friends after all." Felix placed his hand lightly on the boy's shoulder.

Jess shook his head vigorously, blurting out.

"No we're not! I don't want us to be friends. I don't wanna be one of your *remuda* and do those things those guys do for you. I told you all this last month; last time we met like this."

Jess was agitated, shaking his head to give his words emphasis. Slowly he caught his breath and watched as Felix slowly unwrapped a Hershey bar.

"Well Jess, I think you've got the wrong idea. I've changed my mind about you after last night and I want to apologize for that, most sincerely. I thought you really wanted to take over from Kyler when he leaves at the end of this semester. I know you ain't done nothing like it before and maybe you just needed a li'l bit of encouragement to get you over your nerves. So help me, I got it and you all wrong and I'm sorry."

Jess believed Felix because these were the words he wanted to hear, they gave him the relief he craved. Felix watched Jess out of the corner of his eye and saw the boy begin to relax. He smiled thinly and pulled the last of the wrapping paper from the chocolate bar with a theatrical gesture and grinned.

"But before we talk about any o' that stuff; let's see what we can do workin' together on this Hershey bar."

Felix broke the bar in two and held out half to Jess. The boy held back, confused. He was not expecting this and was psyched up for a war of wills and words with Felix.

"Go on take it, it won't bite, neither will I." Felix laughed and Jess caught the reek of stale tobacco on the man's breath and breathed out through his nose to clear the nauseating stench from his nostrils.

"Thank you," he muttered politely as he took the chocolate.

"That's much better," Felix purred, sitting heavily back into his seat munching candy. Jess took a bite. The familiar, yet rarely sampled, sweet taste of the confectionery brought comfort to Jess, loosening his guard a little.

After a couple of minutes, Felix rolled up the wrapping paper between the palms of his hand and made sucking noises as he ran his tongue over his teeth. He tossed the paper onto the floor of the car and slapped the seat beside him.

"Right then Jess White, tell me what it is you're up to?"

The question bewildered Jess who sat upright, sucking the last piece of his chocolate. He swallowed quickly, wiped his mouth on the back of his hand and said.

"Pardon. I don't understand. I'm not up to anything."

"Well now you're sayin' you're not comin' to work for me, so just what are you gonna do for money to get you by?"

"I hope to be working for Mr. Mitchell. He's new in town and going to start trading here. I'll be his assistant."

Felix Gleitner guffawed raucously in Jess's face. The boy turned away to avoid the stench of the man's breath.

"Is that what he told you?"

"Yes he did and I believe him."

"He's English ain't he?"

"Yeah, but what's that got to do with anything?"

"Well now, I happen to know he's over here on a visa that lets him stay in the US for six months - only fer six months: an' my guess is he's been here for one o' them months a'ready. So ask yerself this question. What're you gonna do fer money when he moves on - as he gotta do by, say, September time - that's if he don't go sooner?"

These words hit Jess like a deluge of iced water. Once more his world fell apart and he sagged in the seat. Jess had heard about visas. He didn't want this to be true and challenged Felix.

"How do you know all this Mr. Gleitner?"

Felix sensed by Jess's soft tones his message had gone to the boy's heart.

"Jus' let's say I got friends in high places. Tell me this Jess, did he promise to set you up to pay your way through school, doing trades an' all."

Jess nodded and Felix chuckled again and leaned across to put his arm on the boy's shoulder in a confidential gesture.

"Let me ask you this Jess. This man knows he can only stay for another five months at most. Why do you reckon he's making plans with you for after that time?"

Jess did not answer, but shook his head slowly. Felix pressed his point of view.

"What's in it fer him? Ask yourself that question? Why should he hook hisself up with a young, good lookin' kid like you. What d'you think Jess?"

"I don't know." Jess's voice sounded flat and very quiet, his mind in turmoil looking for the answer he wanted to find, but which escaped him.

"The deputy who saw the rumble at Charmain said it looked like he swerved the car towards you when he bumped you; like he wanted to make sure he knocked you - not bad, but just enough"

"Enough for what?" Jess spun on Felix and pushed the man's arm away from his shoulder.

"Hey, take it easy; I'm yer friend here. I didn't set this up. I'm just tellin' you how things are and what I think." Felix tapped his nose with his finger. "And what other folks tell me."

Jess's eyes flicked backwards and forwards as he tried to make sense of all of this.

"What others?" Jess's brow creased as he strained to find the lies in the argument. Felix tapped his nose again.

"Important people in town Jess; people who know about this and I cain't tell ya who they are."

Felix sat quietly to wait for Jess to speak, allowing silence to build and exert its pressure of tension.

"Why? Why would he do a thing like that?"

Felix stifled the exhilaration that swept over him and replied in a serious voice.

"Why does any unmarried man his age want to set hisself up cozy with a youngster?"

The full impact of these words fell on Jess like a ton weight.

"You, you mean? No … No … it's not like that"

Felix chuckled. "I suppose he told you that too, did he? Ask yourself this, why should he help you and what do you know about him?"

Jess sat quiet and miserable in his seat. He couldn't believe Greg was tricking him. He didn't want to accept it, but Felix's argument was strong. He had no counter arguments.

"What do I do?" Jess didn't realize he'd spoken out loud. Felix put his fingertips on Jess's shoulder again.

"What you have to do is take care o' yourself. Go work fer him, but watch out for come-ons. Know what I mean? Work fer him as long as he's here. Take his money and move on."

Jess was near to tears and it sounded in his voice.

"Where to? Where do I move on to afterwards?"

Felix brushed imaginary crumbs from his lap. He looked ahead through the car windscreen.

"That's a big problem Jess. I won't be able to help you by then. I have to get fixed up with somebody else. There's a kid from upstate that's interested…"

"But I already told you, I don't want to do those things."

Felix chuckled again and once more brushed his lap with the back of his fingers.

"Not that. I got other things in mind fer you now, but I need you or somebody fer next weekend."

"Wh...at other things? Anyway, I can't do next weekend, I'll be working for Mr. Mitchell."

"It shouldn't take long, you could still do both if you arrange it right. We can get this done on Sunday afternoon."

"Yeah, but, what would I have to do?"

"Nothing risky. It's photographs; studio shots; poses and that sort o' thing. It's fer an online magazine back east. Nobody'll see 'em here."

"What just poses, like photographs? Is that all you want me for? There won't be no sex or shady stuff like that will there?"

Felix sucked air noisily through his mouth and shook his head; he knew he had Jess taking his bait and said lightly.

"Nah, none of that stuff. That's fer the *remuda*. This is diff'rent. It's classy work, art studies. There'll be a coupla nude shots o' course, but it's all top line an' proper. I really would've liked you for this job Jess. Pay's good, but" Felix sighed deeply.

"But what?" Jess grasped Felix's elbow.

"I'll have t'get somebody else. But if you change yer mind, I'll hold off fer yer answer 'til Friday. This is a new connection an' more'n a bit important to me fer future business."

Felix paused to suck his teeth and gripped Jess by the shoulder. "If you could do this fer me I'd go as far as to settle your bill at school straight away - no strings attached. I want to help you Jess. I mean really help you, not groom you like that Limey. But you gotta do your bit and help me get that new contract so I can help you."

"What? All of it! I mean You'd pay all my semester dues?"

Felix waved his hands airily above his head in a magnanimous gesture and smirked.

"Yeah, all of it, ev'ry last red cent, why not. How about that?"

"But...why would you do that for me?"

Felix tapped the boy's knee with his fingers.

"Well Jess, let me put it t'yer like this. Apart from gettin' that new contract fer me, let's just say I gotta a soft spot fer yer. I know it's not been easy fer yer here and I respect you for not wanting to do what Kyler and the others do fer spending money. I could've got you more reg'lar an' better payin' work doin' that sort o' thing. But you don't want to do it an' I respect you for that. Mind you, your mother wouldn't want to know yer doin' this studio job either, but at least you'll be able to look her straight in the eye afterwards an' tell her no lies."

Felix watched Jess who sat staring ahead through the windscreen, nervously rubbing his hands together in his lap. Felix put his hand on Jess's knee and squeezed.

"You know Jess. I just want to help you and I wanna be yer friend. Yer'll need to make yer mind up an' give me yer decision before Friday; I cain't hold the job no longer. You can tell Kyler yer decision. Now where do you want me to drop you off?"

"Are you saying you'll do all this for me Mr. Gleitner if I do just this one photo shoot for you this coming Sunday? And if I don't then there'll be no chance for me doing the same afterwards and you won't pay my semester dues?"

"That's exactly right Jess. That's the way it has to be. I'm an honorable person. A businessman, and this is business. I need someone this Sunday and if it ain't gonna be you I gotta get someone else. Now you wouldn't expect me to drop 'em later just 'cos yer've changed your mind down the line, would you now?"

Jess didn't reply and sat quietly in his seat. Felix started the car and asked.

"Where did you say you wanted me to drop you off?"

"Melody Inn please," Jess spoke as if his mind was somewhere else. He had a lot to think about.

11

Conflicting thoughts hammered away in Jess's mind as he walked uneasily across the sidewalk towards the motel.

It had all seemed too good to be true meeting Greg the way he had; losing the job at McKendrick's through a bump with this complete stranger's car who had then sought him out with an offer of another job to make it all come right. Life was never like that for Jess. Felix's syrupy allegation that Greg had his own dark reasons for what he was doing laid deeper foundations of doubt about Greg's true intentions that grew more plausible each time the boy ran it through his mind.

It hurt Jess considerably to consider Greg might be helping him only for his own lustful purposes. But what Felix had said made practical sense. 'Of course it's right, don't let him fool you. No man would go out of his way to help a perfect stranger unless there was something in it for him.'

The notion that this was just another elaborate and novel way for a man to approach him for sexual favors upset Jess. He didn't want to believe Greg was grooming him for sex, and preferred to suppose the man's offer of help was honest and genuine. Even so, Felix's words gnawed away at him. The evidence was there, plain for all to see.

The expiry of Greg's visa would prove it, just like Felix had said. He'd given Greg a lot of thought during the day, raising him high as somebody to look up to. It came hard to convince himself that Greg was just the same as other men who had approached him for sex. Men like Felix, who wanted him only for what they could take from him.

The idea sickened him and he 'hawked' into the road to clear out the acrid taste from his mouth. Jess both needed and wanted Greg to be genuine. For that reason he resisted the urge to turn around and go back to the schoolhouse; deciding to keep his appointment with Greg and check out for himself whether or not

Felix had told him the truth.

Jess pushed open the door and walked into the motel reception area. The clerk looked up from his desk and asked through a wide mouthed yawn.

"Are you Jess White?"

"Uh-Huh," Jess responded to his name mechanically and without further elaboration.

The clerk looked him up and down and then waved towards the back door. "He's waitin' fer you in one-ninety-six, go through there, down the decking, it's last on the left."

Jess nodded and walked through the door at the back of the building onto the covered verandah. The decking stretched the length of the building from the office, separating the ten rooms from their allotted parking spaces.

Jess twitched with unease, wrestling with his dilemma as he walked slowly towards Greg's room. Like a recording on continuous play, the substance of his conversation with Felix ran through his head over and over again, the same question as every time before. Was Felix right or was Greg the real deal? One of them was wrong, but which one?

'Why should Greg break his journey here, put up money and spend his time here just to help me? He doesn't even know me, and why IS he here on his own?'

A cold shiver ran through his body from his knees to his chest when he again considered the unwelcome presumption that Greg was deceiving him; the expiry of the man's visa in late summer added weight to this growing probability.

Jess didn't want Felix to be in the right. He was always happiest when Felix was the bad guy, but if he was right. It made Greg even worse than Felix in Jess's eyes.

How do I check that out with him? Jess had no idea where to begin and he couldn't ask anybody else, but if it was right then it proved Greg was a phony. That also meant the job and everything Greg had promised was nothing more than barefaced lies. And, there'll be no money to pay the school dues!

Jess's mind, although overwhelmed by the conjecture of Greg's duplicity, now concentrated on the practical issues. If there was no proper work with Greg, his only chance of earning enough in the next month to clear his debt was working for Felix next Sunday on this studio photo session. There were no other options and he was back to when he was sitting at the table in Harry's with Melissa before Greg came over and introduced himself.

He tossed his head to rid himself of these thoughts and rubbed sweat from his neck as he walked along the decking, reading the cabin numbers. The hope in his heart that Greg might prove to be genuine, and have an explanation for the visa problem carried him onwards; one-hundred-six, one-sixteen, one-twenty-six. "Why does this place number its rooms this way? They've only got ten rooms, not hundreds?"

The uncertainty in the reality of his situation dragged Jess's concentration back to his major problem and that he'd better psyche himself up for the photo shoot on Sunday – just in case. The thought frightened and revolted him, but Felix had assured him there would be no funny stuff.

Maybe it won't be as bad as I imagine? Felix said it was for one time only and promised to settle my debt at the Community College afterwards if I did it for him; and that's what all of this is about.

He wasn't sure he could undress and parade himself naked in front of a bunch of men he'd never seen before and that part of the operation brought him out in a cold sweat. Even so, the shoot would be over quickly and, in that instant developed into a more attractive lifeline for him while he swirled in a sea of doubt washing over Greg and what might be the man's true intentions. Jess felt less anxious as his mind dwelt on a more agreeable prospect.

'Could be by next Monday I won't have no debt!' He walked on with more spring in his step. …One-forty-six, one-fifty-six, one-sixty-six…

He remembered something else that Felix had said in the car: Work with Greg, take his money, but watch out for any moves from him. "One-seventy-six, one-eighty-six – here it is".

Jess stopped to glance at the air-con unit sitting on the bench outside the door. Doubts assailed him once more. Should I knock or get out of here while I have the chance? His mouth and throat became dry. He swallowed three or four times and after taking a deep breath and squaring his shoulders, Jess knocked loudly on the door of one-ninety-six.

Greg had been watching the clock, becoming more anxious as five pm arrived and passed without sight or sound of Jess. He brushed aside the alien contemplation that the boy would not be coming. He busied himself half-filling the bathroom sink with cold water and emptying into it the contents of two ice-cube trays. Greg had just put two hand towels to soak in the bowl when he heard Jess's knock on the door.

He brightened immediately, wiped his hands on a dry towel and rushed to open the door, greeting the boy with a broad smile.

"Hi, I thought you weren't coming? Come in, come in. How's the leg today?"

Jess stood with his head lowered, held to one side, unsmiling, as if something was wrong.

"Are you Okay Jess? Greg asked with concern, putting his hand on the boy's shoulder?

Jess shuffled his feet, looking to one side and spoke in a flat monotone.

"Uh-Huh. I got held up. Leg's a bit stiff, but okay, thanks."

Greg waited for more, but Jess remained silent. Greg shrugged, deciding not to probe, but kept a light manner in his person and a cheerful tone in his voice.

"No problem, come on in, I thought we'd start by having a chat over a drink about what I have in mind. I've got Coke or Sprite; coffee if you prefer?"

"Coke's good," Jess replied with no emotion, following Greg into the room.

"Sit down, make yourself at home." Greg waved towards the two-person sofa and left to fetch the drinks; aware that the boy's eyes remained fixed on him, as if examining his every move.

He decided to remain cheerful and ignore Jess's reticence; opening a Coke for Jess and a Miller Genuine Draft for himself while recounting his day's doings in Larksville.

Greg said nothing about the attack on his tire and when he brought the drinks through he was pleased to see Jess looking more relaxed and with an emerging glow of life in his eyes.

"Thanks," the boy said with a thin smile as he took hold of the bottle of Coke and nodded towards the door.

"The air-con unit outside, is that the job you have for me tonight?"

Greg turned the desk chair around and sat down to face Jess.

"Oh that; that's our first deal." Greg welcomed the boy's curiosity as the first sign of his enthusiasm for their venture. "But before we talk about that, let's sit down with our drinks and get to know each other a little; then we can chat about what else we might do together."

Jess stiffened and looked up sharply. He moved himself further towards the front edge of the sofa and was half expecting Greg to ask him outright for favors there and then in return for his help. Greg noticed his unease and asked.

"What's up? You seem on edge about something tonight. Had a bust-up with somebody?"

Jess shook his head but looked down at the stained rug beneath his feet and murmured.

"It's nothing."

Greg sighed. "Come on. Out with it. What's wrong? If we're going to be partners we can't have secrets from each other."

This touched Jess on a raw spot. He jerked upright as if he'd received an electric shock, spilling his drink.

"Partners? We don't even know each other. You've been very kind. Why are you really doing all this for me? And why me, I don't understand? And what do you want back from me?"

Greg recognized a looming crisis. In dismay he bit his lip to keep his temper and stay calm. In one long gulp he drained his bottle of beer and tossed it into the waste bin. The jarring crash as glass struck metal echoed around the room. Greg stood up and faced Jess.

"I want nothing in return. I just want to help you to stay at school. Why do I want to do it? That's a difficult question. I don't really know why. I've never done anything like it before for anybody else, so it's a first for me too. But I can tell you this, I like you as a person and I'm kind of getting to like you more as we go along, but that don't mean I want anything from you in return."

Greg stood up to pace in front of the sofa and held up an arm with a finger pointing to the ceiling. "That's not entirely true. I do want something from you in return. I want to see you succeed and achieve your full potential. If you really want to take over from your dad and grow hay and melons for the rest of your life, that's okay, there's nothing wrong with it - it's your choice. But if you want more for yourself out of life, it means graduating from high school and I can help you do that."

Jess jumped to his feet to face Greg and blurted out, almost pleading. "But what do you want for yourself? Everybody wants something. Nobody does things for nothing. I'm not QUEER! … If that's what you want. I don't do that!" He flopped back onto the sofa. His shoulders sagged and he looked vacantly ahead; sitting still and silent.

Greg sighed in dismay, slumping back into his chair. He shook his head and spoke slowly.

"If you honestly believe I'm making up to you for sex reasons and it scares you, then there's the door. You're free to go, now and at any time. And, if you do have beliefs like that, then perhaps it's best you should go, now, and not come back and that'll be an end to it!"

Greg looked away from Jess and pointed at the door. The boy slowly rose to his feet, bewildered now, and more than a little anxious. For the second time in thirty minutes the means of settling his debt seemed in doubt. His jaw sagged and his brain reeled to find the right words. This wasn't happening right or how he'd expected their conversation to go. Greg should surely be professing things like- It's not at all like that... Jess stood motionless, looking at Greg sitting with his head to one side and his arm pointing to the door.

"I'm sorry."

Jess wasn't conscious of speaking until he heard his own voice apologizing. Slowly Greg turned to face him and Jess could see the upset in the man's face and wasn't sure if the light was reflecting from Greg's eyes or from unshed tears. They looked at each other. Both wanted to speak, but neither knew what to say and so remained silent until Greg stood, opened his arms and with a wry smile said simply.

"Come here."

Jess walked into Greg's arms and they closed around to hold him while his own arms returned the embrace. They held the hug for a few moments. Greg felt warm; family like feelings for Jess wash over him and that these same sentiments were reciprocated in the boy. Jess felt secure again. Greg's nose nuzzled into Jess's hair and smelled its fresh, hay-like odor as if the boy was his son or nephew.

Softly Greg said, "We don't know each other, that's true, but if this is going to work we have to trust each other until we do. I don't know what you've been through before and you don't know what I've done. But it doesn't matter. It's all in the past. Let's take things forwards one step at a time. If you have any questions, about anything at all, then fire way."

They broke away. Greg fixed them both another drink and they sat down to continue their talk. The visa anomaly troubled Jess like a persistent ache and he knew that this was his best chance to clarify the uncertainty surrounding Greg's intentions. He couldn't bring himself to ask a direct question, for not wanting to hear a direct, negative answer; and so he skirted around the issue.

"You said you'll set me up to put me through senior year and maybe even through college. Won't that mean you'll have to be here all that time?"

Jess's face flushed and he looked away in embarrassment as if he had asked an awkward, if not a killer question.

Greg pulled a long draught from the bottle of Miller, wiped his mouth with the back of his hand and replied without concern.

"Not if you apply yourself to what I'm going to teach you. If you accept what I tell you, and you do as I say; you'll be able to do it all for yourself without me having to be around."

"You are leaving then?"

Greg noticed the note of alarm in Jess's voice and its reflection in his body language and chuckled.

"Eventually, yes, I suppose I will. This isn't my home and the INS won't let me stay forever. My idea is to teach you enough so you can fend for yourself."

'Now, Now, Now,' ask him about the visa now. Jess's inner voice screamed in his head, but he shied away from the question, shaking his head in response to Greg's ideas for funding his schooling instead.

"That just can't be done. If it could, everybody'll be doing it. Wouldn't they?"

"That's the irony of it. Everybody can do it, but they think they can't and that's why they don't try. It makes it easier for those of us that do try. There's more to go round for us. I can see you're still not convinced."

All thoughts of the visa flew from Jess's head as he opened his mind to Greg's ideas.

"You're making it sound easy. But don't you need a grub stake and contacts and accountants and to be friends with important people?"

Greg dismissed the argument with a wave of his hand and butted in. "You need all of these things Jess and more, but how do you think you get them? You have to make a start, to try, and you have to be determined enough to see it through the bad times that will come along as sure as store bought eggs come from chickens in shells. You can still start small, and build up, that's as long as your will power is strong enough. Nobody said it's going to be easy, but remember this! The failures in business are not those movers who don't succeed first time; because if their idea is good, and their will is strong, they will try again and again until they do make it work. It's only those who don't try at all or give up after the first knock down and don't take another shot at it who are the real failures."

Jess found these words inspiring and Greg could see by the boy's alertness he was warming to the proposition. Jess clenched his fist, shaking it at the floor.

"But I'll need going on for thirty-two hundred to see me through senior year. I can't do all that business and be at school full time as well. Can I?"

Greg smiled at the note of wistfulness and doubt in Jess's argument. He went over to the desk, took a calculator from his briefcase and tossed it across to Jess.

"Put in what you want to make in a year - if it's thirty-two hundred, make it that. If you want more things, like clothes, entertainments, a car even - put those costs in too."

Jess stood holding the calculator with his brow furrowed by uncertainty.

"Go on," Greg chided, "put in thirty-two hundred for now and when you've done that divide it by three hundred and sixty-five, and that tells you how much you need to make each and every day to reach your target. Go on. Do it now!"

Jess carefully tapped the figures and commands into the keyboard then looked up, wide eyed in surprise and almost bellowed.

"That can't be right. It's less than nine bucks a day."

Greg grinned and took the calculator back from the boy.

"That's what you need to make. It's no more than you can get from cutting your neighbor's grass. Does it look more realistic now?"

Jess's face lit up and his eyes gleamed as the scales of disbelief fell away.

"And you think I can do that," he asked, "I mean make at least nine bucks a day and still go to school?"

Greg slapped his thigh and yelled.

"Wrong question! It should be do you, Jess White, think you can do it with my, Greg Mitchell's help?"

Jess mumbled, "With your help, yes I think I can."

"Not good enough," Greg roared, "Where's your resolution? What do I want to hear from you?"

Jess threw back his shoulders and said in a firm, confident voice. "Yes Greg, I can do it … with your help."

12

Greg paced slowly in front of the sofa where Jess sat watching and absorbing each of the man's words as he continued to explain his ideas for their enterprises.

"You got it! Good man, now listen, that's nine bucks every day including holidays and weekends. That's what you need to make after taking out any expenses. While you're training, I'll pay you four bucks an hour for two and a half hours a night - that will make you more than the nine bucks you need, - all you have to do is turn up every night and save your pay. There'll be even more if you work weekends. When you've learned the mechanics of trading, we'll do deals together and split the profits. That should earn you even more."

"That's great, but I do get schoolwork to do most nights."

Greg shrugged. "Come down after you've done it, better still do it here so you don't get distracted or waylaid and we can get started straight away, just as soon as you've done your prep."

"Prep?" Jess looked askance.

"It's what we called house work when I went to school." Greg replied with a throaty chuckle.

Jess trembled with excitement and Greg decided the time was right to introduce a note of caution. "But it's not printing money, don't think that for a second. Trades can sometimes go wrong. It's easier to lose money than make it if you don't know what you're doing or get your timing wrong. You always have to go in with your head against your heart when you do trades."

Jess nodded sagely. "Is that what the air-con unit outside is for - a trade?"

"Exactly. But we can talk more about that later. For now, let's have a general chat about business; just so you understand where I'm coming from and where you need to be going with this."

Jess sat attentively on the sofa with one leg drawn up underneath him while Greg continued pacing the room and delivered his lecture.

"Let me begin by asking you this question. What is business?"

Jess screwed up his face. "Making money I suppose."

"You could say that but what do you need to have or do to make money?"

Jess couldn't figure the answer for this question Greg might want to hear and shrugged it off. "A business I suppose."

Greg laughed. "So we've come full circle already and all around one word – business."

"What is it then?" Jess was put out by Greg's laughter until he explained.

"A business is an enterprise, that's any enterprise that buys or sells goods or services for a profit. That's its purpose, what it exists for. Okay so far?"

Jess nodded and looked on attentively as Greg continued to pace and speak.

"Good. To set up a business you need some money to start trading and to keep going, that's called capital. If you don't already have it you will have to borrow it. Next you need premises, machines and transport - what the economists call 'land'. Next on the list you need things to buy and sell - goods, services, raw materials, things like air-con units. Okay so far?"

"Uh-Huh."

"Great! Nobody can do everything at once, so next you'll need people with skills to do what you can't do and to support you: people like book keepers, carpenters, drivers, cleaners and lawyers. If you're a small business you mostly do all those things yourself, as much as you can."

Jess seemed mesmerized as Greg spoke, but at one point he raised his hand to ask a question, as if he was back in class at school.

"Do all enterprises do it like this - big and small?"

"That's right. It's basic economics." Greg clapped his hands; he was on his hobby-horse now and continued pacing to and fro in front of the sofa while he instructed his eager protégé.

"Whether you're General Motors or just a guy with enough cash to buy an old air-con unit and set out to sell it from a motel room – the principles are basically all the same. But ask yourself this Jess. If you got all those things together and hung out your business shingle, do you think your enterprise would be successful?"

"I suppose so? Why wouldn't it?" Jess wasn't sure of himself and Greg came right back.

"Then why do you think most business start-ups collapse in their first year? Think about it before you reply!"

Jess shook his head. Greg continued with his lecture.

"It's on account of they run out of money because they don't have four other important elements. Four abstract items you can't buy for love or money."

Greg counted out on his fingers. "First you need trust. You and your colleagues in the business, that's you and me, we have to trust each other - no secrets between us, and then, of equal importance; your customers have to trust you. You have to work really hard at getting customer trust; you'd better believe it. The business books all say it's five times easier to sell something to somebody if you've sold to them before than it is to get a new customer and I know that to be true from my own experiences. Most organizations spend time and big money chasing new customers instead of seeking fresh business from their existing clients."

Greg paused to allow this to sink in and thought he detected a slight discomfort as Jess wriggled on his seat. The boy made no comment and Greg continued.

"Secondly - you need knowledge not only about products, but about supply and demand. Where there's a demand for something, the person who can supply that need will get the business; providing the buyer trusts the seller."

"And the price is right." Jess interjected.

"Good point, but that's really about trust again in a way. You don't rip off your customer. You charge him or her a fair price leaving no money on the table, so he's satisfied and will come back to you again and again for his needs."

Jess's face had screwed up again and asked. "I don't get it. What do you mean by money on the table?"

Greg sat down on the sofa next to Jess, cradling his fingertips against his bottom lip.

"It's getting the price exactly right. Let me put it this way to you in an overly simplistic example. Suppose you know where you can get good cheeseburgers for a dollar. You meet a guy in the street who says he'd kill for a cheeseburger, but he doesn't know where he can get one.

You do, and you ask him how much is he prepared to pay - he says three bucks if you bring it to me here. You say okay and buy the burger for a dollar. You reckon a fair price for your time and outlay is two bucks, giving you a dollar profit, and you decide you'll charge him that. If you do you've left a dollar on the table. Providing you've taken the trouble to see he gets a good burger in as perfect condition as possible, he'll be satisfied paying the three bucks he offered you. And, because you've looked after him and given him a good buying experience, he'll trust you to do the same again and come back to you the next time he needs a burger."

Jess grinned and nodded vigorously. Greg pressed home the importance of this next point.

"Now do you get it? Businesses are not charities, a fair price and service that gives satisfaction will build business, and building business is the real objective of any enterprise looking for a future. That was the answer I was looking for. If you can build business for the longer term, making money will follow automatically on from that. There's no halfway house. You either make money by building business and succeed or you neglect to do so, run out of money and fail."

"Wow," Jess cradled his hands in his head. "There's so much to this - and is this what we're going to be doing?"

"You bet we are." Greg noticed an increasing air of excitement about the boy, which was encouraging. Jess's dour mood had vanished and he came back with another question.

"You said there were some other things, as well?"

"That's right. I did. Knowledge and information; knowing where you can get things from; who wants to buy these things; product information and right over there's where we can find a lot of it."

Greg pointed to the small pile of newspapers and leaflets on the floor. Jess half rose from the sofa to see better what Greg was pointing out.

"You mean all those flyers and things?"

"That's right, the advertisements, wanted ads, death notices, and new business openings; everything is information and no information is worthless. I picked that lot up in Larksville today. That's what you will be doing for your four bucks an hour to start with; studying them and finding us our opportunities."

Jess screwed up his face in disappointment. Greg ignored his reticence and continued with his lesson.

"Now just suppose we read in there somebody's asking for a window type air-con unit and you know where you can get one within the price he's offering to pay and it's a price that can give you a fair profit. You have found a demand. Since you already have a suitable air-con unit, you can provide the supply. All you need to turn it into a deal is a touch of customer service to tie it all up and you've likely got a trade that will put bucks into your back pocket."

Jess tensed with excitement as he now saw the real potential for solving his money worries in what Greg was planning for them to do together.

"I can see that. I understand!" He pointed to the door. "Outside, you've got an air-con unit, you've already bought one to trade, but who's it for?"

"I don't know, yet" Greg smiled at Jess's bemusement as the boy scratched his head. Greg waited patiently for him to explain his difficulty.

"That means you've just done something different than what you've just told me? You've bought a supply before you found a demand."

"It looks that way. Let me explain, it's all about gathering information and using all of it to advantage. I was walking about town this morning and I passed Mafferty's Emporium just off Main - it's what we call a second hand shop and pawnbroker in England. He's got an air-con unit sitting on the sidewalk outside his store and I watched a few people looking it over. He's got it priced at eighty-five dollars. It's older and in not such an apparent good condition as our one. I'm asking you now do you think Mafferty's are going to sell that unit?"

"Why for sure, people are always looking for air-cons when we get into the hot summer weather."

"Right…" Greg continued to explain. "That means I witnessed a general local demand and I also noticed today's weather's not yet hot enough to justify people spending the money he's asking for it. I used that argument to get the price of ours down to what I paid for it. I happen to know a new unit like that one will cost three hundred bucks. Ours is a better model and less beat up than the older one at Mafferty's. All we have to do is check it over to see it's in good working order, make sure it's clean and looks the best it can look; after that we will sell ours and make a profit on the deal."

Jess's brow furrowed with doubt.

"Do you know about air-con units and how they work?"

Greg bounced back with energetic confidence. "I don't have the slightest idea, but tomorrow I'll have an Internet connection in here and we can find all the information we need right there."

Jess still looked doubtful. He stroked his chin while he gave this some deep thought.

"But what about the price and how do we find a buyer - ads cost a grip o' cash."

"I'm not going to sell it. You are."

"Me?" Jess jumped off the sofa in surprise.

"Yes sir, you are. You are going to sell that to Mr. McKendrick so he can find the buyer for us. He'll do the selling while you are at school."

"But won't he want all the profit too?"

"Some, but not all of it he won't. We'll give him a choice. If he doesn't want to buy it outright we'll give him a margin of, say twenty dollars, providing he has it outside his premises and sells it in a week and fifteen dollars if he needs longer and sells it within a month. We need a quick turnover so we can use the cash to buy other things to sell on to make more profit. You have to average nine bucks a day, every day after expenses to make your target, don't forget?"

"Phew! Me? I've never done anything like that before. How'm I going to do that? Especially with Mr. McKendrick - he only just sort o' fired me."

Greg laughed and cupped an ear with his hand. "Remember what you said to me a few minutes ago? 'I can do it Greg', that's what you said. Keep telling yourself that. When you get over your nerves you'll find it not so daunting. I expect the opposite will be the case and you'll find it exciting - once it's all over."

Jess stood listening with a lop-sided smile on his face. He was still unconvinced. Greg chuckled, poking him lightly in the stomach with his finger.

"What happened to your confidence? Look at it this way. You're doing him a favor. You have a quality product to sell at a good price, one you know he will be able to sell on. What's he got to be worried about? Mafferty would snap your arm off, even though he's got one to sell already? You've got to believe in your product and you'll believe in yourself and for this first time, I'll be there with you all the way."

A broad grin swept over Jess's face and his eyes gleamed with eager anticipation.

"This is sounding like fun. More fun than learning in class."

"Not just fun Jess, but profitable fun. When you get the hang of these basics, we can talk about business planning and other things like that."

Jess thumped the sofa cushions with enthusiasm.

"What's next?" he asked.

"What's next is we fix that leg of yours. I'll fetch the medical supplies while you get yourself ready. Best take off your shoes, pants and shorts and get your self laid out face down on the bed - just wait while I put a towel over the bedding."

Greg watched the light and excitement drain out of the boy's face and nervous uncertainty cloud his features as Jess closed in on himself again.

Without making any comment, Greg spread a bath towel across the top cover on the bed. When he looked up he saw a child with big scared eyes, curled up in the corner of the sofa drawing his knees as far into his chest as his injury allowed. The bright, cheerful, intelligent Jess of moments ago was no longer there. In his place sat a small, frightened and contrary little boy.

Greg put his hands on his hips and hissed in exasperation.

"Do we have to go through this every time we meet? I told you I'd dress your leg that evening we came out of Doc Finch's office. If you're worried about me seeing your butt again, you can cover it with a cloth." Greg tossed a kitchen towel onto the sofa.

Jess's eyes seemed to grow even larger. He leaned forwards and pulled a cushion over his front, as if trying to hide behind it, his face had paled to an unhealthy gray color. There was no confidence in his voice as he asked.

"Greg where's your wife and family, and why aren't they here with you?"

Greg drew his breath sharply through his teeth His expression sagged as he nodded slowly.

"We're coming back to that old chestnut again are we? It's not only disappointing, but also downright hurtful that you still don't trust me or believe what I've told you. Consider this. I've made no move on you like that whatsoever, and anytime you think I'm doing anything you don't like personally, you can walk right out the door. I won't stop you. Now I want to dress that leg, so get your shoes, pants and shorts off; get yourself laid out on that bed and let's have no more of this childish nonsense."

Slowly and nervously Jess undressed. He kept his hand covering his boyhood as he lay face down on the bed wearing only his wife-beater; watching Greg all the time with pleading, 'don't hurt me' eyes.

Greg's eyes took in the white translucent skin of that young body and its rounded physique; the broadening shoulders narrowing to a trim waist and firm buttocks falling away to long, slender legs. It was a nice body, still not fully developed, hairless and with clear skin. Only the angry and violent colors of the bruises he had inflicted spoiled a figure that could serve as a model for any sculptor.

Greg would not be surprised to learn that men of particular tastes had propositioned Jess in the past. He was a good-looking kid with an attractive personality to go with a healthy body. Greg pulled himself away from admiring the boy to wring out and collect the first cold towel from the sink and said brusquely.

"Roll more onto your good side to let me get at the bruises."

"What're you doing?" Jess blurted out shyly, slowly rolling more onto his side and covering his crotch with both hands as his undercarriage became more exposed to view. Greg ignored the boy's sensitivity and laid the ice-cold towel over his injured leg.

Jess jumped up in shock, gasping as the towel covered his bruises. "What the…?"

Greg pushed down on Jess's shoulder. "Keep still and be quiet. It's a cold compress; it's good for contusions."

The room darkened as the sun dipped below the horizon; Greg switched on the bed lights giving the room a more homely atmosphere.

He pulled off the towel once it had warmed up and applied the second, colder towel from the sink. He carefully massaged the leg through the cloth, asking.

"Is that okay?"

Jess turned his face towards Greg and said with a broad smile. "It's kinda nice once you get used to it."

Greg dried the leg and gently smoothed ointment in and around the bruised area and Jess gradually relaxed under Greg's careful ministrations.

Greg continued to lightly massage the leg and threw out a light-hearted question by way of conversation.

"Tell me this, if we go to all this trouble to keep you in school next year, our time and effort won't be wasted will it? I mean you're not a dunce or anything, are you?"

Greg said it with a teasing ripple of laughter that Jess responded to, rolling further on his side to face Greg with mock indignation on his face.

"No I am not! I'll have you know I'm getting pretty good grades and in the top half of the class with a GPA of three point four and getting near on three point five."

"Well that's just great, but what about sports, do you play any sports."

"MMM," Jess murmured, "the big game at school is football, but they reckon I'm too small, so I play soccer and I've gotten to like the game. David Beckham's one cool guy, have you met him - he's English?" Greg chortled.

"I agree, he's one special guy and no, I've not met him yet. Are you any good, at soccer I mean?"

"Coach says I've got potential as a mid-fielder, but the game's still new in these parts and there's not many teams we can play."

Greg kept up the tease.

"You know what puzzles me. With you being so good at sports and schoolwork, how come the only real friend you've got is that latter day female prophet? My God she's one scary character."

Greg risked asking what might be a sensitive question, but laughed to convey the impression he was still speaking in a light-hearted vein. Jess rolled more to his side to look into and examine Greg's face for signs of tease.

"You mean Melissa, she can get carried away with her Bible studies at times, but she's a good sort and she helps me a lot. Her boyfriend's a College football hero."

Greg burst out laughing.

Jess looked bemused. "What's so funny?"

"Oh I was just wondering how they manage to get it together on a date. Her carrying all that religious baggage."

They both laughed and Greg began rubbing camphor cream gently into the bruised leg, first with lint and then with his fingertips. Greg enjoyed the sensation in his fingertips on the smooth silkiness of Jess's leg and the firm muscles underneath as they rippled in response to his attentions.

They talked small talk about the Community College, football, the town and local entertainments for another ten minutes. Greg learned that Jess liked to watch motor sport - especially Indy cars - and filed it away in the back of his mind as something they might go and watch together one weekend.

Greg urgently needed to find out about those three miscreants who had bumped into him on the street corner. He had convinced himself that they had just come out of the motel car park and were his prime suspects for putting acid on his tire. He judged that with Jess now in a more relaxed mood this was the moment to probe, but he needed to stay cool with his questioning.

He pulled out a large globule of cream from the jar and began rubbing it gently into Jess's leg.

"Did I hear you say everybody played sport this afternoon?" Greg asked the question in a casual manner.

"Not everybody," Jess replied, "But all of the junior high and senior school play sport Tuesday afternoons. I had to work the scoreboard 'cos I couldn't play on the wing for my team today - we lost, four two." Jess sounded bitter about the loss and Greg made sympathetic clucking noises.

"That's funny, 'cos I bumped into three of your lads, seniors I expect, as I came back here this afternoon."

He described Kyler and felt Jess's muscles stiffen under his fingertips as he spoke. He realized with grim satisfaction that Jess had recognized the boys he'd described

"Do you know who they might be?" Greg again asked the question as if in casual conversation.

"Why? Is there something wrong," Jess had turned around

suddenly, his lips quivering. Greg perceived that Jess was not only familiar with the identity of these persons, but they bothered him for some reason. His heartbeat increased, but Greg kept control of himself, forcing nonchalance into his voice.

"Nothing really, we just came around the corner at the same time from opposite directions and nearly bumped each other. I just thought it was strange for them to be out of school. That's all. I suppose they bunked off sports. Do you know who they were?"

Jess put his face into the pillow and muttered through the down. "Sounds like Kyler Reeves, he often bunks off sports."

Greg grimaced on hearing that name again; it was the same name Jess had mentioned and instantly regretted speaking last night at dinner. Greg continued massaging the boy's leg, but now spoke extra softly, so as not cause alarm.

"Who is Felix Gleitner?"

Jess jumped up as if he'd been electrocuted and swung his legs over the edge of the bed. Greg saw the boy's chest heave as he cried out.

"What did you say? Where did you hear that name? What's your problem? Why all the questions?" Jess became instantly distraught, his distress showing in the pallor of his face and the hurried, awkward way he began pulling on his clothes.

Greg remained calm and cleared away the medical debris to the bathroom, saying unemotionally. "No problem. It's just when you said that the boy's name was Kyler, I remembered where I'd heard it before. You mentioned his name and Felix Gleitner's yesterday when we were eating dinner. That's all. I just wondered who is this Felix character? He seems to bother you. What does he do?"

Jess was uncomfortable with this line of questioning and spoke through the side of his mouth without looking at Greg as he fastened the belt on his jeans.

"He's a really little guy that drives a big blue Buick and hangs around the College and the Truck Stop. He calls himself a facilitator. He can do and get things. I'd better go now. Thank you."

This reaction surprised and disappointed Greg.

"Do you have to go right now?" He asked. "I thought about sending out for some pizza. Don't you want some pizza?"

"No thanks, I'd better go. I just remembered I have things to do before tomorrow."

Jess could not leave soon enough and Greg decided it was best to let him go. "Baby steps, baby steps," he mumbled under his breath and then to Jess with an indifferent shrug.

"Okay, it's your loss. See you at the same time tomorrow then? We'll have the Internet connection running by then and be able to get to work on selling that air-con unit and sourcing some other deals."

"Okay Mr. Mitchell; thanks. You did say four bucks an hour right?" Jess moved to the door.

"Four bucks, that's right, and call me Greg. Hey! Don't you want me to drive you back to the school?"

"No thanks Mr. ... I mean Greg, see you tomorrow." Jess half ran out of the room as he left, slamming the door closed behind him.

Jess was plainly rattled by the mention of Kyler and Felix Gleitner. Greg stood looking at the closed door convinced now he knew who had doctored his tire with acid. What he didn't know was why? Those boys had most likely done his tire and they're close to this Felix facilitator. Not only that but Jess is running scared of them all; which also bothered Greg.

"I'd best check out this Mr. Gleitner."

13

Jess's reaction followed by his swift exit at the mention of Felix Gleitner's name astonished Greg and threw him off balance. The boy's panicky departure was as sudden as it was unexpected. Everything had been going along so well between them up to that point, but once again Greg witnessed a capricious transformation in the boy.

Greg stood staring open jawed at the closed door for several moments. A niggling doubt gnawing away at him that something was seriously amiss in Jess's background: possibly something sinister that he ought to discover before he got himself too deeply involved. Greg ran his mind over their conversations several times trying to identify what else might have caused him to run away. Each time he came up with the same answer. The single name - 'Gleitner.' He mumbled through closed lips. "This Gleitner character needs to be checked out and real soon!"

Jess's heart-rending question came next to mind 'Why Me? Why are you doing this for me?' It was a question for which Greg had no ready answer and he now asked it of himself "Why am I doing this?"

He looked around the room that purveyed such a cozy, almost intimate ambiance a few minutes before. In an instant it had transformed into cold, impersonal emptiness. Where there was warmth, joy and companionship only moments ago, Greg beheld only the shabby, worn tiredness of the room's appointments. For the first time he noticed the brown-rimmed hole in the sofa's yellow, plastic covering, burned by a long extinguished cigarette. The room became alien to him, causing him to shiver. Greg recognized it was Jess's presence alone that gave the place any positive character, which stretched to his reason for being here. But for what reason? It was a question for which he had no ready answer. Greg looked again at the closed door through which Jess had abruptly departed and it reminded him of another door that recently closed on him.

His mind strayed back to the day of his latest divorce settlement. He had looked on the iron bound, oak door of the courtroom that had borne witness to countless arguments and miseries, including his own misfortunes with gut-wrenching dismay. To Greg the courtroom door symbolized a barrier to his life and for him to either break down or overcome; and now the closed door of a motel room became another, standing between him and Jess.

Greg experienced a touch of faintness and sat down to cradle his forehead between his hands to work things out. He had run away from his problems then and it was tempting for him to do the same again. Once more he felt bitter gall rise in his throat as his mind traced memories of his second, failed marriage. It was his wife's small, provincial, family recruitment business he had joined and molded with his ideas and energy to bring it to national prominence. He had done that by preaching his particular business gospel to greedy executive ears.

Under his plan employers could avoid the legal obligations and heavy burden of costs associated with hiring permanent staff other than vitally important personnel, by taking on all employees on temporary contracts – temps!.

The strict employment laws, with the associated heavy costs and liabilities for employers enrolling permanent workers did not apply to temps or those working fewer hours than half a normal working week. This legal loophole caught most working mothers with school age children in its net and to their disadvantage.

Greg had built a system where major firms could outsource their recruitment to his company. Bailey's would fulfill the client's requirements from their own banks of registered workers or from other agencies with whom Bailey's had contracted to supply agency workers in those areas where the company had no local offices of their own.

The concept had been generally recognized as a masterstroke of modern business enterprise. The client received exactly the skills and labor they required, when and for as long as they needed them. They did not have to maintain an in-house staff payroll under the Bailey system. The client's central human resources department was only required to reconcile and pay a single, monthly invoice to Bailey's; who then paid the agencies, which paid the workers and completed all the other legal requirements associated with employment of temporary workers.

Bailey's owned only three of their own offices when he started expanding the company and so most of the temps came from other outsourced agencies. Bailey's had little to do but pass out the orders from the clients and reconcile the invoices submitted by the subordinate agencies; billing back to the client and keeping records.

The family applauded his ingenuity and industry, none more roundly than Ed Bailey, the bellicose Chairman of Bailey's who welcomed Greg into his home and family when Greg eventually won as his prize the hand of Victoria; Bailey's eldest daughter. Even although Greg married Victoria, he did not share the family's newest aspirations. Now that the family was more financially secure, their major quest became to seek social advancement.

This aim caused an unspoken rift. Greg saw this pursuit as an expensive diminution of their energies away from growing the business and derided these hankerings as trivial and foolhardy. As a consequence of his negative attitude the family regarded Greg as 'unsafe' and left him out of invitations they sent and received to various social functions for fear he would embarrass the family by openly speaking his mind against the inherent privileges of the aristocracy and thereby jeopardize the family's social ambitions.

In any event Greg did not fit the stereotypical mold of the slim, horse riding, chinless wonders that populated the fox hunting community. In only a short period of time the Bailey family began to regard Greg as less than their social equal. They drifted further away from him as they sought to become ever more accepted by the older, quasi-aristocratic families of the 'The County Set'.

The Bailey's believed, but never once mentioned to him, their fear that his abrupt, rough and ready manners, along with his disinterest in country pursuits would hold them back from full acceptance into the higher echelons of society.

Greg harbored only contempt for their ambitions in social advancement. The business would still be nothing more than a very minor local agency in a quaint southern market town in England without the application of his energies and personal ambition. It was his drive and enterprise that gave them the wealth to engage in their upper-crust pursuits.

Greg himself spent his every waking hour to advance the fortunes of the business. His overriding ambition was to make 'Baileys Managed Services' the biggest of its kind in the country. Ed Bailey was content to let him get on with it and never once had Greg betrayed that trust. While Edward Bailey supped stirrup cups at fox-hunt meets, and shouted *pull* enthusiastically at clay pigeon shoots, Greg would pound the streets from meeting to meeting at all hours of the day and night, growing the Bailey business concept until its shadow fell across the whole of the United Kingdom. The germ of international expansion was growing in Greg's mind as a next step when all came to an abrupt halt for him.

He was frequently away from home for several days at a time and often overnight. On these occasions his wife Victoria, would fill her time with horse riding and dancing in fashionable venues; accompanied increasingly by the impecunious third son of an equally impoverished Earl.

His lordship had recently put his ancestral home into the guardianship of the National Trust to avoid the high costs of its upkeep in exchange for private apartments for him and his family within the building and its grounds.

Greg despised these people whom he saw as indolent parasites belonging to a long past age; people who by accident of birth lived off the backs of others and enjoyed totally undeserved rank and privileges: an anachronism in the modern world. His firm belief was one good day's work would do them all a lot of good - probably by killing them off.

There was no chance of his wife's suitor ever inheriting his father's title, which would go eventually to his older brother, whilst he himself would remain The Honorable Mr. Palmer for all of his life.

Although there was no likelihood of Victoria ever becoming Lady Palmer should she eventually marry the Earl's youngest son, her parents nevertheless, secretly encouraged the discreet liaison of their daughter with her penniless, but well-bred lover. So while Greg toiled relentlessly to bring home the largesse that maintained the Bailey family in their luxurious lifestyle, his wife played away from home with this insignificant member of the junior aristocracy.

The situation couldn't last and came to a head the night he arrived home in a celebratory frame of mind after landing the last of eight major banking contracts.

Greg had rushed into the family home, where he lived with Victoria, carrying a huge bunch of red roses and a bottle of champagne. Victoria had met him in the hallway. She received him and the flowers stiffly, a wifely welcoming smile absent from her lips. She dropped the blooms disdainfully onto a side table without even pressing them to her nose to sample their exquisite scent. Victoria brushed her hands as if by touching the bouquet they had soiled them. Without any expression of emotion she had turned on him and as casually as if asking him to buy her a postage stamp the next time he visited the Post Office, informed him that they were to be divorced, because she wished to marry Henry Palmer.

Like a statue she stood in front of him, her face set as solid as chiseled white marble and equally as cold. He felt rather silly holding out a bottle of Bollinger in front of him, unsure that he had heard his wife correctly or that she was not indulging herself in some crude, silly game borne out of her boredom. She repeated her announcement and told him he would be sleeping in the guest room until the next day, when he should find himself alternative accommodation and abruptly turned on her heel. He remembered the sharp squeak it made on the marble flagstone of the hall as she strutted away from him, snapping shut the door behind her. The squeak was an insignificant noise, but to Greg it served as a telling note of protest.

Before he could recover from the shock of this encounter or assemble his thoughts into meaningful comprehension or a plan of action, Ed Bailey appeared alongside him in the hallway and caught hold of his elbow.

'Look at it this way old man' He had said with unctuous gravity. 'People make mistakes in life and people do change. It's just one of those unfortunate things. No use fighting it. It'll be hard at first, but there are no children and so that's a blessing - in the circumstances of course.'

Greg flopped into a chair. He sat listening to Bailey but not hearing his words. He watched the flowers he had bought become bare stalks as their petals fell from the bouquet onto the floor of the hallway following their rough treatment by Victoria. He gazed at them as they fell, like blood red tears, with the constant drone of Ed Bailey as accompaniment. There were no tears in Greg's eyes, but a burning anger building in his belly. He found his voice

'What about the business, what about ME and the business? And aren't you even going to ask me how it went today at the meeting with HSBC?'

Ed had patted his shoulder paternally and mumbled. 'Never mind about that now. This is family - far more important.'

Greg's thoughts came full cycle back to the present moment. He felt the cold sweat in the palms of his hands as he stared at the motel room door through which Jess had left and shook those past, hurtful memories from his head. He felt clammy and in need of a shower again. But his mind was not quite ready to let go of the past just yet. It returned briefly again to those painful remembrances while he tried to sort out his present motivations and find an answer to Jess's question of 'Why Me?'

He and Victoria had not enjoyed a passionate relationship; it had always only been a dutiful liaison. In many ways they lived their lives together more like 'kissing cousins' than man and wife.

For Greg, it followed naturally as the right thing to do to be married to Victoria, their marriage meant he was wedded into the business, becoming an integral part of the family hierarchy that controlled its affairs; for that was his life. It was the loss of the business he created from nothing that caused him the most resentment, much more than the loss of his wife. He realized he did not miss her company in the same way, as he seemed to be missing Jess's companionship. He covered his face with the palms of his hands and shouted through them.

"What the hell is happening to me?"

14

The idea did not arrive suddenly. It seeped slowly into Greg's consciousness like a dripping tap, but was so perfect a reason for his actions he seized and clung to it. At last he had found the elusive answer worrying Jess and himself.

Greg felt the blood pound in his ears as he said loudly, "I am doing this because I was shafted big time by the Bailey's and I know somebody or some people are trying to shaft Jess." Greg clenched his fist and shouted, "And I will not let happen to him what happened to me!"

Greg tingled with resolution. He now consoled himself with legitimate grounds for embarking on this endeavor, as much for his own satisfaction as it was for Jess's benefit. In a peculiar way he believed it would help rectify the wrong done to him by his ex-wife and her fickle family.

The buzzing of his cell phone interrupted his introspection and he rushed over to the table by the door to search for the instrument among the jumble of other items he'd dropped out of his pockets when he came into the room last night.

Greg picked up his phone hoping for a call from Jess; only to frown with disappointment when he read the confusing text from Bill Elbury.

X 4gt WnFshr B

Greg pondered this gibberish with dismay, muttering through his teeth. "Why the hell doesn't he use the phone?"

Greg was 'old school' and had not brought the modern text-abbreviated lexicon into his regular communications. He preferred to speak to somebody directly rather than sending out truncated, impersonal text messages. His initial annoyance dissipated in a wry smile a few seconds later when he solved the mystery of Bill's message. 'Don't forget Wayne Fisher, Bill.'

Greg was eager to take the next positive steps on his project and energetically pulled out his small, black address book from his briefcase to find Wayne's number and tap it into his keypad. He smiled sardonically when Wayne's familiar southern drawl answered his call.

"Wayne Fisher."

"Wayne it's Greg, Greg Mitchell."

They exchanged banter and pleasantries for several minutes before becoming serious while Greg outlined his plan, which entailed Greg asking for Wayne's help and advice in setting up a bio-diesel plant in Bamptonville.

Greg was completely open to Wayne, giving him a full account of his plans and intentions, holding nothing back. He mocked Wayne for his Dixieland accent, but fully respected the southerner as an astute and competent businessman; more than that, Wayne enjoyed Greg's respect. Greg heard a whistling in his earpiece as Wayne exhaled and asked.

"Let me get this right. You want me to help you set up a bio-diesel plant for you to give to a kid you bumped in your car yesterday so he can run it to put hisself through College?"

Expressed in that manner Greg's plan sounded ridiculous and more so after hearing Wayne's next question.

"Am I to understand you've not met this kid before you bumped him, so you don't know nothing at all about him, or his family or even if he wants to do this kinda work?"

Greg gulped, feeling a little silly as he replied. "Well Yeah! I suppose that's what it amounts to." Greg heard the whistling sound in his ear again, louder this time before Wayne replied.

"Holey Moley, what's happened to you man? Are you sick or somethin'? Where's that steel-hearted entrepreneur we all got to know and despise so much? You're soundin' almost human. You been smokin' somethin' you shouldn't?"

Greg laughed and shuffled his feet awkwardly, but some of his renowned hardness returned. "Okay, okay, enough of the inquisition. Can you help me or do I have to get heavy with you?"

Wayne chided with a discernible smile in his voice. "Dawg

Nabbit! That's more like the Greg Mitchell we all know and love t' hate. Listen. Do you really think this kid can work this thing on his own, or will you have to be there doin' it for him? It's a bundle o' work at first."

"I'll be there with him for a while, until it gets set up and running so he can take it on by himself."

"You mean you'll be happy to stick around there in cold, windy Nebraska for a year or more; 'cos that's what it'll take?"

It was a question that added to Greg's discomfort. He knew he had gone into this situation led by his heart, setting aside his golden rule to follow only his head. Wayne's businesslike questions were from the head forcing Greg to focus on his own 'head matters'.

"Yes! If that's how long it takes; Nebraska's not a bad place to be. It's mostly flat, but there are some nice parts to it with plenty of history around." Wayne's response was silence and Greg thought he'd lost the connection.

"Are you still there, Wayne?"

"Yeh, I'm here. Tell me this Greg, and I ask this question as a friend and business partner, just so's I can get a proper handle on this thing you're gonna be doin'. Deep down and personal, what is this kid to you?"

There it was again, the same question Jess had asked. The same query he had asked of himself. But Greg knew the answer now and he felt a glow inside when it rushed to the forefront of his mind, but he decided not to share it with Wayne not just yet.

"He's deserving."

"Deservin'? What's deservin'? Is that it?"

"That's it, can you help us?"

Wayne sounded peeved when he replied.

"Sure I can help you. It's business when all's said and done. We do more business selling plants and equipment than we do brewing bio-diesel these days. In fact that's only a small part of our business now. We're getting big on green energy production. I've been meaning to talk to you for some time about your position in the company."

"What position? I don't have one. I'm an investor, end of story."

"That's right, but you're an investor with too much hold on how we can grow. You might want to spread your wings with us and be a little more'n a silent investor. I don't want to rub salt into any raw wounds, but I read in the blogs about you an' Victoria splitting: so now you're not recruitin' mail men for Royal Mail anymore, we wondered about using you and your expertise in growin' our business?"

The idea instantly appealed to Greg, however, his business brain told him not to rush into anything and remained coy.

"I'm not sure. We'd need to talk. I'd need to hear your ideas and what you're offering, then do some research before I make a commitment."

"That's reasonable. But I can tell you're not against the idea and that's promising."

Wayne waited for a reply, but Greg knew that salesman's trick and kept quiet.

He heard Wayne sigh before he added. "Look, I have to go to Chicago soon. I can bring it forward to this week; get my business done there by Friday afternoon and come right on to see you where you are? I had the idea about coming to see you after I talked with your accountant, Bill Elbury, this afternoon and checked flight schedules. I could be in Lincoln by four in the afternoon. If you can pick me up at the airport, we can talk on the drive over and spend the weekend setting up this oil plant you've set your mind on building?"

Greg warmed immediately to this suggestion, not least of all because it meant he would have somebody here who was from his background and wholly for him over the weekend.

"Sounds good to me Wayne, what do I need to get done. Before you get here that is?"

"Get me a room where you're staying for Friday and Saturday night. Then get some premises we can look over for the plant - they'll need to have power and water supply with good drains. Can you still remember what we need to make gallon sized test batches of bio-diesel from clean oil?"

"I think so, I seem to remember buying crates of large soft drink bottles and emptying the soda down the drains."

"That's it, don't forget the thermometers and other gear; you pick-up the hardware and I'll send the chemicals and other stuff you need from here. Give me your address?"

"Hang on! What's the point of that Wayne? Don't get me wrong, I appreciate your offer, but...I mean making gallon batches out of clean oil? It's waste oil we want to convert?"

"Let's just say I need to see if you and your protégé have any aptitude and stayin' power fer the enterprise. I don't want to waste my time puttin' in a plant that won't be used after the first week. And, if you remember the process, you can oh so easily turn this stuff into jelly, then it's no good fer nothin' 'cept fer expensive dumpin'. Get the premises and meet me at Lincoln airport, Friday afternoon. Now give me that address an' expect an overnight package from UPS."

Greg rang off, rubbing his hands together gleefully. The project was coming to life. Greg knew of nobody with more expertise in this field than Wayne Fisher and he was coming here to set it all up. He could get all the stuff Wayne needed to make test batches of bio-diesel in Larksville tomorrow. But right now he needed a shower and then some food. He'd not eaten since his meal at Ma Tooley's and that seemed like yesterday.

After a quick shower and change, he picked up his wallet, car keys and phone from the table top, grabbed his jacket from the chair where he'd thrown it and made for the door. He stopped in his tracks as he opened the door, triggering a memory of the fear and surprise on Jess's face when he'd mentioned Felix Gleitner. Jess had said the man hung around the Truck Stop. Greg nodded sagely and spoke through pursed lips.

"They sell food at the Truck Stop. Maybe it's time I found out what this Felix character looks like close up?"

Greg spent several minutes checking around his car for signs of any fresh tampering before he climbed in and drove south towards the Truck Stop. A dark, lowering sky blew in from the southwest on a chill wind that threatened rain, adding another layer of gloominess to the atmosphere that perfectly matched Greg's present anti-Gleitner mood.

He scowled at the redundant diversion sign that had guided him into his present situation as he passed where it stood rusting, and leaning drunkenly to one side.

The Truck Stop was small compared to the big halts on the Interstate highway. This was just a minor fueling and refreshment station; used mostly by the local traders and those truckers who found themselves caught short in between the big halts. The Truck Stop also enjoyed a small, regular clientele of salesmen and truckers who preferred its quieter, more leisurely and less public facilities.

The Truck Stop's main vehicle park was to the left of the restaurant's single story building. It held no more than a dozen trucks and operated a single pump, diesel oil service point from the farthermost point near to the exit.

Greg drove into the entrance and swung to the right. He saw at once it was not a busy night with only three trucks parked side by side in the lot and two cars pulled up at the entrance to the restaurant.

The Truck Stop's boundaries were planted with hedges interspersed with clusters of bushy trees. It must have been Greg's subconscious concern for his safety after yesterday's events that stopped him parking in the open alongside the cars at the entrance to the restaurant. Instead he drove beyond them and reversed into the right hand corner of the lot. The added shade afforded by the clump of trees under which he parked added to the darkness of the night; further obscuring his presence.

Greg sat in the car for a few moments looking at the brightly lit windows of the restaurant to size up the scene. He enjoyed a clear view of the few diners munching mechanically over their meals and filled his waiting time pondering over Jess's sudden exit from the room tonight.

To the left, and attached to the main building, he noticed a rough, flat roofed structure. It appeared to be unfinished, a stark, unpainted, concrete block edifice without windows that gave the impression of an amateur attempt at building. Greg reckoned it to be a large storeroom, but learned soon afterwards it was a comfort station for overnight travelers.

Inside were basic bathroom facilities and a half-dozen cell like, windowless cabins, which for a few bucks, offered drivers slightly better overnight accommodation than the bunks at the rear of their cabs.

His observations were distracted by the squeal of braking wheels to his left as a large car rushed through the entrance into the lot. In the faint lume of the yellow entrance lights Greg caught a glimpse of white walled tires on an old, dark colored gas-guzzling sedan.

Greg identified it as a Buick and his pulse quickened. He sat and watched the car pull up facing the parked trucks and then reverse to the boundary wall to stop, still facing the parked trucks, but at a distance and on the other side of the entrance to Greg.

Greg was parked on slightly higher ground than the Buick allowing him to look down into the car. Its interior light came on briefly and Greg watched the driver's hands take something out of his wallet. From his vantage point, the driver's face was obscured. The interior light went out as soon as the driver had put away his wallet and sat there in darkness- waiting: as did Greg.

"That has to be this Felix character." Greg mumbled, tasting the acid animosity of his words prickling on his teeth. He wondered why the man had pulled up there so far away from the main building and made no move to get out?

His answer arrived moments later when Felix double flashed his headlights to be answered by a single replying flash from a Fourways truck facing the Buick parked on the opposite side of the lot. Greg was glad of the cover of night and the extra darkness of his tree shaded corner to shield him from their view. A man jumped down from the cab and strolled across to the Buick, getting in the car beside the driver.

"This Felix person is either over confident or getting careless."

Greg remarked. The interior lights came on in the car as the trucker entered. Felix did not bother to switch them off and Greg dropped lower into his own seat to better hide himself from view.

Greg witnessed a brief transaction in the seconds before the lights eventually went out in the Buick. Felix handed something to the trucker contained in the palms of their hands and too small and distant for Greg to identify. The trucker handed something from the palm of his other hand to Felix and then returned to his truck. Greg guessed it was money and he smiled wryly as he recognized the type of deal he had just witnessed.

"So Felix is into drugs." Greg spoke out loud, but softly, asking himself next. "Was Jess into drugs? It would explain his mood swings and why he was scared and didn't want to talk about Felix. Jess's words rang out from Greg's memory. 'Felix! He's a facilitator. He gets things for students.' "But Jess is broke. Drugs cost money. If he's into them, how does he pay for them?"

Increased activity at the Buick interrupted Greg's musings. He watched as another driver came out of a Greenfield truck parked in the middle of the line of three facing Gleitner's car.

A heavy, round man, with a long ponytail, languidly lolled over to the Buick. The lights came on in the car again, however, this trucker stayed outside the vehicle. Greg was able to see what happened as the Buick's door remained open and the interior lamps lighted. He watched closely as the two men conversed.

The trucker appeared animated, waving his arms around. Greg involuntarily strained to listen, a reflex action, as he was too far away to hear anything.

Felix waved the man down and talked into a cell phone. The moment he put down the phone the two men again talked earnestly. It looked to Greg as if they were arguing. The trucker threw his hands in the air in apparent resignation and began dropping things into the car. Greg craned his neck in an attempt to see what they were; his best guess was banknotes. With a disdainful wave backwards of his hand the trucker sauntered back to his cab, while Felix scrambled around inside the car to gather up his booty. The lights went off. Greg decided to wait to see what happened next, his hunger forgotten.

He didn't have long to wait before an elderly, soft-top Toyota swept into the lot and backed up to park alongside Felix. The driver got out and climbed into the Buick. Greg could see enough to recognize him as one of the kids in the group of three he had bumped into on the street corner before he drove to Larksville. The boy fitted a description Greg had given to Jess; who had reluctantly identified him as Kyler, the bully who worked for Felix. Greg now firmly believed this was the person that had put acid on his tire; but he had no provable evidence as yet. He made to get out of his car there and then and sort them both out, but listened to his inner voice telling him now was not the time and this was definitely not the place. Everything comes to he who waits.

Greg chewed his lip in frustration, sitting back in his seat to keep an eye on the Buick from the anonymity of the darkness inside his car. He couldn't see anything inside the Buick after the interior light went out, but did so moments later once it came on automatically as Kyler exited the car. Greg watched the boy stroll over to the Greenfield truck, climb into the cab and pull the door closed behind him.

Greg whistled softly. The picture became crystal clear to him; Felix was running a rent-boy operation from the Truck Stop. Now he understood the pressure Felix was putting on Jess. The boy didn't need to tell him any longer; it wasn't drugs at all; it was paid for sex that Felix planned for Jess.

The question that now troubled Greg was quite simply, had Jess already been forced to work in this way for Felix?

Greg's breath came in short gasps and he slowly wiped away the sweat from the palms of his hand on his knees as he pondered a point from his musings of last night. If Jess was already involved with Felix in this way - would Jess want or even need me to set up an operation to fund his schooling? More than that, would I still want to do it for his benefit? A chill passed through Greg as he considered these unpleasant possibilities.

The temperature seemed suddenly to have dropped by several

degrees. So many of the local people had advised him to move on, was it their way of telling him to stay out of this and not meddle where he was not wanted. Was that it? Was the acid attack on the tire only a warning? How many others were involved in these unwholesome rackets that Felix was apparently running so openly.

Greg entertained serious doubts about Sheriff Donovan since the man had met him on the way back from Larksville the afternoon his tire blew out and found that the man already knew about it. How could he have known unless he was party to what had happened? Surely a lawman, with his ear as close to the ground as Donovan's held his, would know for sure about Felix's dirty little scams at the Truck Stop; adding further to Greg's doubts about Donovan's integrity. Greg felt unclean, with the cold dampness of perspiration trickling down his spine.

"What about it Mitchell," he asked himself, "you don't belong here, get out while you can, this is much bigger than you, leave it alone, before you get hurt - or worse!"

Greg sat tapping his steering wheel with his fingers while his head fought a silent battle with his heart. It was an appealing idea of his to mentor Jess to help himself by schooling the boy in the ways and tactics of salesmanship. He was content when planning or doing things for Jess and even happier when the kid was around.

A question prompted by Wayne's and Elbury's perverse implications for his actions flashed across Greg's mind. 'Does this say something about me? Something I haven't woken up to yet? Am I expecting more out of this than just knocking down unfair barriers?'

Greg knew he was in a state of mental turmoil and he was undergoing a huge change in his life. He'd never bothered about other people before Jess came along. His long-standing practice was to take them for granted; even his wives. The sharp sting of unfair treatment after his divorce remained, but his general attitude to people was no longer as rigid as before.

He was always the one everybody else must follow. It was his ideas and agenda the others went by. The only thing that ever mattered to him was moving on to the next and bigger deal. He never considered the people working with and around him and a fanatical motivation absorbed him totally while he worked at Bailey's.

Latching onto Jess after 'bumping' into him was completely out of character for Greg Mitchell. In the beginning Greg opined he recognized a kindred spirit, a fellow victim of circumstance, another unfortunate suffering from the mauling and manipulations of other people enjoying the misplaced trust of their victims. In Jess he discovered somebody he could help thwart those that would put the boy down - battling against Jess's own nest of Bailey brand vermin.

Greg scratched his chin and listened again to his inner voice

You've changed since you met the boy, but it's looking to other people much more than a change in your attitude? Are you growing deeper, personal feelings for Jess?

Greg discovered he couldn't agree or dismiss that question with any degree of certainty or truth. His mind blanked and he couldn't make a positive decision one way or the other to settle the quandary. He convinced himself Jess was suffering the same unfairness as himself; that reason alone for his involvement seemed noble, normal and acceptable.

Greg could now be like a knight of old, sallying forth on a modern equivalent to a white charger to fight Jess's foes - because of Greg's arbitrary decision to make them his own enemies. The cerebral question returned to pester him for an answer.

But is that the only reason prompting your actions? Aren't folks like Elbury and others in town of the same mind; that there's more behind your doings than pure philanthropy? Are they right?

Greg didn't know and he didn't want to think about it. He was championing Jess, hoping to spare him the pressures Felix and the others might be putting on the boy without even knowing what they were or anything about the boy's background. Greg spoke out in a loud, clear voice.

"Is Jess already doing these things for Felix? If the answer is yes, like 'Jack' the next question in the box pops up. Does he truthfully want me meddling in his life - setting up something to fund his way through school for another year, or, has he got things boxed off for himself already and keeping it secret?"

Greg stopped to bring out his handkerchief to wipe his neck free of sweat continuing his deliberations.

'Perhaps it's not like that and all he wants is to go home and help his dad on the farm? Perhaps I'm wasting my time and making a damn fool of myself - again?'

It wasn't warm outside. The wind still blew cool from the southwest, but Greg had to take out his handkerchief again, this time to wipe the sweat from his brow: bringing another thought to the front of his mind to cause him even more concern and a quiver of alarm to his voice.

"What about that list of the town's 'Top Guns' the sheriff gave me, Can I trust them? Who are my friends in this place, who is here for me and on my side?" He shook his head. "I'm not sure. Maybe Bill Elbury, but only up to a point."

It was an uncomfortable revelation for him that Bill was possibly the only one he trusted around him at present. It would be wrong of him to trust Jess at this moment in time; at least not until he knew more about the boy and what mischief he might be involved in, and what the boy really wanted. 'Thank goodness Wayne Fisher's coming!'

A sharp pain stopped his self-analysis. Greg's hands were gripping the steering wheel so hard they cramped. He rubbed them vigorously to restore their circulation and sat back waiting for Kyler to come out of the Greenfield truck.

The time the boy entered the truck's cab Greg noted as twelve minutes past eight. He sat waiting in his car and when the youth dropped out of the cab to swagger back to the Buick, Greg looked again at his watch to note the time - eight thirty-four. Kyler's sojourn with the trucker was for a little more than twenty minutes. In the indistinct glow from the entrance lights Greg watched as Kyler stood beside the passenger door of the Buick. The youth wriggled his rear, as if smoothing out his belt and pants for increased comfort. The interior light came on as the boy climbed inside the car to begin an animated conversation with Felix, watched by Greg until the interior light went out. He saw no more until Kyler got out to stroll casually around to his own car and drive away.

Moments afterwards Felix got out and strutted across to the restaurant entrance. Greg appreciated what Jess meant when he said that Felix was a little guy when the man entered the pool of light at the top of the steps.

Even in the poor light Greg reckoned Gleitner could double for Danny de Vito in size. Felix paused before opening the door to go inside. It was then Greg noticed the man's pronounced, almost pointed, bald head growing out of an untidy shock of thick, stringy and unkempt hair hanging loose around his ears. The overhead light on his baldpate gave it a sheen that amused Greg.

He chuckled to himself at the incongruous sight, which relieved some of the tension building up inside him. He had at last seen the faces of those who would be his enemies. Now he needed to find out how many more there might be hiding in Felix's background. Greg needed to ascertain who they were and what were their weaknesses, just in case the right time arrived when he needed to take protective action. 'What did that old general say that time on TV? Attack is the best form of defence? Hmmm. There's a thought!'

Greg closed his eyes and several moments later spoke with fierce determination to the car's dashboard.

"You're staying Mitchell, just like you said you would; you're not running away no more. Not from this, from Jess or yourself; whatever happens - gets to happen!"

He got out of the car, stretched his limbs to free the tautness in his muscles and followed Felix into the restaurant. The waitress greeted him warmly. He looked around casually to note where

Felix sat at a small table for two in the far right corner. It was not lost on Greg that from where Gleitner sat he could surreptitiously observe the comings and goings into the park and restaurant. Greg kept as much of his back to Felix as he could while he requested a table on the left side of the building, well away from Felix, but in sight of the man. Greg wanted to watch his mark without being seen himself.

He shifted back his chair so he was mostly obscured by the counter and out of Felix's direct line of sight. By leaning backwards Greg could study the man at a comfortable distance from behind the counter.

Glimpse by glimpse, he took in the pock marked, flabby face, the uncombed mess of mousey colored hair around tiny ears and the large hooked nose between them. The man's rough tweed jacket was worn and shapeless.

The waitress interrupted Greg's observations by asking for his order. His appetite had returned in full measure and he ordered fried chicken, mashed potatoes and gravy with a side order of lima beans followed by Pecan Pie and coffee, with a Vodka, lime and lemonade cocktail on ice, to start.

Greg enjoyed a growing sensation of being more in control of matters; confident if push was to came to shove he could draft a workable plan to surgically remove Felix and his rotten crew from the scene: and that idea arrived with some good feelings attached to it.

15

At the same time as Greg was deciding whether or not to go to the Truck Stop, Jess ambled into his dormitory.

He expected to be ignored, shunned and shut out as usual by his roommates. There were only five in the dormitory when he arrived and Jess was agreeably surprised when they welcomed him warmly.

"Hi Jess, we're playing this Trivial Pursuit game. Do you fancy joining in?"

The invitation astonished Jess and made him wary, suspecting they were playing out some kind of prank that would ultimately be at his expense. This was the first time he could remember Ed Baines, a flaxen haired, pimply youth, inviting him to join in any game, or addressing him by any name other than 'sodbuster.' Jess decided to remain aloof, replying skeptically.

"Uh! No thanks. Another time. I got class work to do."

"Stuck on anything? Maybe I can help." Phil Proctor, a lanky youth who was dynamite on the wing of the school soccer team and equally as sharp at math, was another who had ignored him until now. Jess wondered what was going on and looked around for Kyler and his thugs, expecting to see them there, weaving their mischief; but they weren't in the room. Jess decided to find out what was behind this change in attitude towards him and took advantage of Proctor's offer.

"Actually, you can. It's that quadratic equation formula I'm stuck on."

"Let's do it", Phil called out, rising carefully to extricate himself from where he sat on a bed behind the makeshift table built out of chairs to hold the board game.

With Phil guiding him, Jess quickly got to understand the algebraic principles involved and finished the project. Phil remained cheerful and friendly right up until the moment Kyler appeared at just after eight o'clock and stood over them. Jess noticed the alarm coming into Phil's eyes and how his face fell as he looked up in anguish at Kyler; half rising to leave.

"Hi Kyler, I was just leaving." Phil's voice sounded apologetic, as if he shouldn't be there. Jess's spirits sank, but his resolve hardened. He now knew who was engineering his ostracism and why. He also realized that as long as Kyler and his cohorts thought he was going to work for Felix he would have no trouble with them. Fostering this belief would also guarantee his roommates remaining friendly towards him and with everyday life returning to normality; exactly as it should be. Jess quelled the spasm of anger rising inside him with a sharp cough and forced a smile.

"Oh Hi Kyler, we're just doing some math." Jess's voice feigned levity.

"So I see." Kyler addressed Phil. "You don't have to go."

Jess could see Phil was anxious to get away; his face paling to the color of chalk and decided to help him out.

"It's okay Phil; we're done here anyway. Do you want me for something Kyler?"

Phil slipped away from them, but before Kyler could say anything his cell phone rang. Jess heard Kyler utter *Yuh, Yuh* several times before he rang off, heading in haste for the door, muttering. "I gotta go."

The tension in the room vanished the moment Kyler departed with a resumption of the boys' more normal conversation and banter.

Jess wandered over to watch the group playing Trivial Pursuit until several other boys returned to the dormitory and more rowdy horseplay commenced.

Kyler returned later, red faced and highly excited, bringing tension back into the room with him; all banter ceased and the dormitory fell quiet. Everybody watched in silence as Kyler walked down to Jess's bed space and with an exaggerated flourish of his arm tossed two crumpled twenty-dollar bills onto his bed.

"Not bad for a few minutes o' real easy work is it sodbuster?" Kyler spoke through a lopsided leer. "You'd have to sell a lot o' bales o' hay to make that money. That's what you c'n be earnin' most days next semester." Kyler watched Jess closely as he waited for the boy's response.

Jess licked his lips nervously, shaking his head.

"I told you already. I don't do them things."

Kyler spun around. He pointed his finger aggressively at Jess and growled.

"Is that you sayin' to me you're not doin' the gig on Sunday?"

"I didn't say that! What I said was, I don't do what you did to get that moolah." Jess nodded to the two crumpled banknotes lying on his bed; scattered like discarded litter that had missed the bin when tossed away. "I haven't made up my mind yet about the photo shoot."

"Well make it up and fast." Kyler shouted. "You got 'til Friday sodbuster. Don't make me wait 'til then fer yer decision."

With that Kyler angrily snatched his money from the bed, deliberately ripping off the duvet in the process and stormed out of the dormitory. Several of Jess's roommates came into his space, one of them asked,

"What the heck was that all about?"

Jess pursed his lips and shook his head again.

"They're trying to make me do a nude photo shoot, for money."

"Lucky you!"

"What's wrong with that?"

"Nice work. I'd do it." Another boy exclaimed spontaneously. Jess smiled ruefully at him.

"Nothing I suppose. If you like doing that sort of thing."

Jess had trouble getting off to sleep that night. His brain reeled round and round in circles. He didn't know what to do for the best. He felt trapped between Felix and Greg.

He knew exactly what Felix wanted from him and, if Felix was right, Greg was after the same thing. Greg had mentioned he wouldn't stay for always, but had not said for how long he would stay. And, more importantly to Jess, he hadn't said that he couldn't stay after his visa expired.

Jess carefully rolled over to try lying on his injured side. The throbbing had gone, but set off an ache if he brushed the bruises against anything. A sharp pain ran through the length of his leg, forcing him to abandon the turn and roll back onto his good side. He heard loud breathing and snores from his slumbering classmates in the neighboring cubicles: but he lay wide-awake while his mind raced on.

Kyler was intent on keeping up the pressure on him. If he didn't do the shoot, things would be bad for him at school again - and might even be worse than before. The only sensible solution to the problem he could come up with was his earlier plan to quit school and go home for good this coming weekend.

He could go home, leaving all of them behind him in Bamptonville, and be done forever with them all and whatever their nefarious plans were for him. - Felix, Kyler and Greg included.

In truth, Jess welcomed Greg's ideas and promises to keep him in school until graduation. He'd like to do that, but what was Greg's hidden price for his help? Jess didn't know, besides, his father couldn't manage for much longer without his help on the farm.

Jess believed it was pipe dreaming to even suppose he could stay at school for another whole year, since he was bound to leave school to work on the farm some day. It made sense for him to simply walk away now and join his father a month earlier. He wouldn't have to worry about Felix, Kyler or Greg. That notion firmed in his brain as the right thing to do in these circumstances and with the decision made, felt more able to relax. Intense relief swept over him, bringing on drowsiness.

Jess was just dropping off to sleep when an alien remembrance intruded to jerk him back to instant wakefulness. He sat upright and gasping in bed. His subconscious mind reminded him that his troubles would not at all be over by running away. In exasperation, he punched the mattress with both fists.

"Damn it, I have to pay that schoolhouse bill before I can go home."

There was no way he could countenance leaving without settling the debt. The college would chase after him and force his family to pay. Jess couldn't let that happen. The emotional turmoil inside him made him feel sick at heart. His deliberations had gone full cycle only to bring him back to square one. It was as Kyler said. He was trapped; there was no other choice open to him; his doing the shoot on Sunday was inevitable.

Jess also knew in the kernel of his heart it would not end with the one photo shoot, no matter how ardently they promised him otherwise. Felix was bound to make even more demands on him and it would be harder to refuse next time having already worked for him.

Jess lay there contemplating the reality of the situation facing him. The idea of running away, cheating and being untrue to himself did not really appeal to him; it was a practical solution, but now that option was no longer open to him the temptation to run away also disappeared. He decided to remain true to himself. Jess forced himself to reconcile his situation with the only way he could think of settling his school bills before the end of the semester in a little more than a month's time.

He became calm as a flow of adrenalin clarified his thought processes. If there was no other choice except to prostitute himself to achieve the outcome he wished for, then in reality, the fact that he didn't want to do those things did not enter into the argument, it was inevitable and it could come down to a matter of choice for him between Felix and Greg.

With Felix he knew what would happen. He would be at Felix's behest and have to give himself frequently to unknown truckers, salesmen and people passing through the town? They would be mostly rough mannered, unattractive, dirty people.

The idea revolted him, but if there was a plus side, there would be no personal attachment to them. His involvement with them would only be during the minutes of the action they were paying Felix for him to provide. Perhaps afterwards he would be able to close them out of his mind and forget them immediately and would only have to endure the abuse suffered in the short time he spent with them; knowing he would likely never see them again.

Alternatively, Greg was an unknown quantity. Felix and others only surmised he was after sexual favors because of his extraordinary generosity. Greg had assured him this was not his intention. But! Supposing, as a worst-case scenario that it was, then Greg would be just one person to give himself to. On the down side, he would have to go with him time and time again at the man's whim and pleasure.

Jess pulled up his undershirt to wipe the cold sweat from his face before lying back on the pillow to work this through some more, searching for that elusive solution releasing him from bondage to either man.

After another hour's deliberations yielding no satisfactory solution Jess sighed as the reality of his situation forced him to reconcile himself to go either with Felix or Greg. The obvious choice was a no-brainer. It took seconds for Jess to decide to go with Greg. September's still months away when his visa expires and who knows, I could clear the debt long before then doing trades.

From what he knew of Greg already, Jess liked him as a person. Perhaps it won't seem like abuse if I have to go with him? His hand lightly stroked his injured leg and it brought back the memory and sensations from when Greg massaged the limb earlier. In a way, the touch of Greg's finger tips on his body and the man's careful ministrations had not been unpleasant.

If he asked Greg outright for the money to pay his bill it would immediately solve his financial problem. It might also prompt Greg to come clean should he have any veiled intentions and ask him outright for sexual favors in return, providing that was Greg's hidden purpose? Jess just didn't know.

The boy sighed, burying his face in the pillow, groaning into it in painful frustration. There was no clear answer to his musings; whenever one solution appeared another question arose to nullify it. Jess mulled this over endlessly until sheer exhaustion claimed him for sleep.

Greg sat eating his meal in the shadow of the Truck Stop diner, casting surreptitious glances across at Felix, who sat nursing a bottle of Schlitz at his table; making and receiving calls on his cell phone. Felix took no interest in what was going on around him in the restaurant and Greg became more conspicuous in his observations of this man he now perceived as his enemy number one.

The waitress was clearing Greg's table in readiness to bring out his pecan pie when he noticed a flurry of movement at Felix's table.

A short, wiry driver in a white coverall came in and sat opposite Felix; they immediately began talking earnestly with their heads closed together. Greg watched the driver's long, oily, black hair moving up and down as he emphasized various points of his conversation with emphatic nods. Greg was too far away to hear anything they said. The driver passed something to Felix who palmed the object as his lips split into a demonic grin. The driver rose abruptly. He pointed a challenging finger at Felix who waved him down with both hands. Greg lip-read Felix. 'Don't worry, I'll get on to it.'

The driver spun around and strode out of the restaurant. His coal black eyes swept over Greg who identified the man's swarthy complexion, beak-nose and mannerisms as Mexican. When Greg looked back at Felix he saw the man was busy on his cell phone. Shortly afterwards, Felix pocketed his phone and left the restaurant. Greg heard the roar of the Buick as it started up and moved swiftly out of the lot: just as the waitress arrived at the table with Greg's dessert.

"Enjoy," she said mechanically as she laid the dish in front of him. Greg ordered another cocktail. There was no hurry, he had to wait for Felix to come back and he could take his time over the remainder of the meal.

Twenty minutes later he decided Felix was not coming back after all. Disappointed, Greg called for his check, paid, lifted a toothpick from the pot on the table and walked out of the restaurant picking his teeth. He pulled up his collar against the damp rawness in the wind and hurried towards his car that he'd left parked in the corner of the lot, under the trees.

He walked into the darker shadows beneath the tree canopy behind his car when the Buick roared back into the parking lot screeching to a halt a dozen yards or more in front of the hostel extension.

Greg stood to watch as a woman emerged from the Buick on his side. Youngish. Lithe. Slightly built with long, black hair, falling below the waist. She looked around nervously and pulled a flimsy, black lace shawl closer across her throat. Greg saw her features indistinctly at this distance, but enough to recognize her as Hispanic or Mexican.

Greg stood perfectly still as he watched from the shadows. A door opened in the hostel block. A man in a white coverall stood in the doorway, his features obscured by the night. A white sleeve beckoned impatiently to the woman and she half ran across the lot from the car and into the building. The door closed behind them. Greg looked across to the Buick, which remained parked where it had stopped. He saw Felix's face in the flare of his match as he sat inside smoking, while he waited for something or somebody. Greg tossed the toothpick onto the ground and assumed Felix was waiting for the woman to come back out of the hostel.

"So you're into regular prostitution as well are you my friend?" Greg muttered with contempt, reflecting bitterly on the evening's discoveries as he climbed into his own car to drive back to the motel.

16

Sleep wouldn't come and Greg lay in bed with his hands folded behind his head, mulling over the day's events one more time. He retained mixed feelings about the day, some good and some less agreeable. Today's happenings taught him a lot more about Bamptonville and the differing natures of a number of its inhabitants?

Felix was against him for some reason of his own. Of that fact Greg was now certain. This small time pimp and drug pusher, who exploited juvenile bully-boys to get his own way, wanted him gone from here. It bothered Greg considerably that he didn't know the man's motive. Why did Felix want him out of the way to the extent of arranging an accident, and one that could so easily have ended with fatal consequences?

Greg had received no prior warning-off or threat he could think of, unless the advice given him in the sheriff's office counted as a warning? It must all be tied up with Jess and what Greg planned to do for the kid running counter to Felix's own plans for the boy. Even so, it was a bit extreme to sabotage a car. Greg sniggered with scorn as his mind drew pictures of Mafiosi and Al Capone with a pointed head driving a fifteen-year old Buick.

Following his observations at the Truck Stop last night a recurring doubt re-assailed Greg's mind. Has Jess already worked for Felix? Am I coming up against Gleitner's attempts to get the boy back into his - what did Jess call it- 'Felix's Remuda?' Greg wriggled himself into a more comfortable position on the hard mattress and pondered. Is that why Melissa was out to save Jess's soul? Because he'd already worked for Felix and she was pressing him to stop? It would explain her behavior and Jess's fear of Felix and Kyler.

Another question swiftly followed. If Jess was reasonably good at school and sport like he says, why has he only got one friend in Melissa? Could it be the others were keeping the boy at arm's length simply because he had got himself in too deeply with Felix at the Truck Stop? It all adds up well enough to be a plausible likelihood.

Greg rolled onto his other side to shake off such dark imaginings, but they remained in the forefront of his mind to press their points. Does Jess have a dark side that scares off the other boys: a side that he, Greg Mitchell, hasn't yet seen or experienced? Greg rolled back onto his other side again to listen to the counter argument from the opposite side of his brain.

What if he has done these things? Should it make any difference? He's of legal age for those things anyway and it's none of your business what or with whom he chooses to get involved with. He's still the Jess you bumped. Is he no longer worth helping if he does these things? What options does he have to fund his schooling in the short term now that his benefactor has died and can't support him any longer? That's all the more reason to help him so he won't have to continue going to the Truck Stop - that's assuming he's going there already - and you don't know that yet.

Greg sat up in bed and called out to the darkened room. "It makes no difference to me and it's in the past anyway. He doesn't have to work for Felix no more. I'm his benefactor now, if that's what he wants me to be! I just want him to come clean and be straight with me."

He punched the pillow into a better shape before laying his head back down, to dwell on his own reasons for doing this, raising another recurring doubt, - Why!

Greg viewed Felix and the others who would stop him as human versions of that iron studded, solid oak door in the English courtroom on the day of his divorce settlement. They shared a common purpose. They were all barriers.

He had taken far too much for granted in his earlier life, relying too heavily on other people, assuming they would perform exactly as he wished before discovering too late, and with no time to defend himself, before the Bailey axe cut into his neck. But it wasn't too late to do something for Jess and by doing so, help himself as well. In a strange way Greg believed helping Jess would make his life more balanced; so he was doing this not just for Jess, but also for both of them. They would each benefit from a satisfactory outcome. Jess would get the material benefit and Greg would enjoy the abstract success of beating the other guy and proving his own worth in the battle that he and Jess would win together. Winning was important to Greg. "Yes, winning was still everything!"

A familiar buzz wound up through his body strengthening the feeling of rightness his reasoning and commitment gave him. Yes! I will see this through! Greg now had a real purpose to stay.

The attack on his car made this quest personal and justified him continuing, even as another doubt cropped up to plague him.

'Was it only Felix who wanted him out of the way?' Greg knew he had to play things cool and watch out for himself, literally with every move and step he took - and he must resist any impulses to take any precipitous counter action. Contrary to his impulsive nature, he must stand back and wait. He had to wait to see what came out of the cracks in the walls around him in this extraordinary town.

Greg wondered again about the sheriff. Outwardly he was helpful and friendly. Yet the man knew all about him, he had extremely acute hearing, enabling him to listen to the other side of a telephone conversation. He also had sight of his communications from his Boston lawyers. The sheriff seemed altogether too interested in what he was doing and is perhaps too obliging. This close interest in his affairs bothered Greg. Has the sheriff set things up this way to stay in the background? Was his advice that strangers were not really welcome in Bamptonville and the suggestion for him to move on potential threats if he chose to ignore that advice? What could be Donovan's purpose if that did turn out to be true?

Greg had hoped to work with the sheriff and the town's people bringing them into his plans to make them all a part of what he hoped to achieve. In order for the plan to work, he must trust them all. Greg encapsulated the sheriff in a line from Shakespeare's Hamlet that sprang out from his memory; 'the lady doth protest too much, methinks.'

Greg smiled bleakly at the non sequitur, while questions continued to race through his head.

'Was the sheriff really a renegade? How did he know about the tire blowout if not? Is he a part of this move against me? Is the list of people he gave me as people to help me in fact a list of the principals against me? Are they all part of this new iron studded, oak door barrier I am coming up against in Bamptonville?'

Greg's mind raced on and he put his hands on his head to hold it still as his brain seemed to be lifting off inside his skull.

He gritted his teeth and muttered through them as he kicked his legs clear of the tangled mess of bed covers. "No I'll not run away from the barrier this time. I'll not let it close on me. Fortified doors expect to be knocked down; that's the only reason for them being fortified."

Greg relaxed. He felt comfortable again with his resolution, but was still ill-at-ease about the attack on his tire.

"Was it against me or was it against Jess?" The question regurgitated through Greg's brain for the thousandth time and his inner voice replied yet again. Time will tell.

This was a challenge, not a problem. Greg was familiar and content with tackling challenges. He'd not faced one with such violent personal overtones as this before, but in a way the hazards added to the thrill of the endeavor. It didn't overly bother him.

Greg woke refreshed, relaxed and early. He felt good about himself with the return of his characteristic buzz and energy. His reasons for doing what he planned to do here seemed as relevant first thing in the morning as they did when he thought them through the previous night. He was now a man on a mission to knock down barriers threatening to hold back Jess and himself.

He skipped across to the window, pulled open the curtain

and grimaced at the black, somber clouds rolling in from the southwest; hurling a verbal challenge at them; "not even you lot can spoil my day today!"

Greg switched on the TV and for a few seconds watched a panel of experts giving their opinions on whether Attorney General, Alberto Gonzales, should resign after firing eight attorneys through a flawed process.

Greg quickly switched to a country music station where Todd Fritsch sang a track from his latest album. The energy and bounce of the piece perfectly matched Greg's mood and he hummed along with the song as he went into the bathroom to shower. He opened the faucet fully and on hot for several minutes to fill the cubicle with steam, hiding its cracked tiles and the discolored grouting between them before he stepped underneath the powerful jet. He felt so good he began to sing.

It was after his shower, while smothering his face with shaving cream he recalled those darker accusations surrounding his relationship with Jess. He had no children, could his prime motivation be a latter day paternal compulsion or something else; something Elbury hinted at in his teasing? Greg rubbed the stubble of his chin and spoke to his image in the mirror. "Come on now, you've got growing feelings for the boy, but you know it's not in that way for God's sake. Sure, it was good to be close to him, but that's all part of this novelty, he's good company, you don't feel so alone with Jess, and that's all it is. You must have had too much vodka in those cocktails last night. Let's stick with knocking down barriers together and not grow anything else onto it."

He finished his ablutions, dressed, and with a skip in his step set out for Ma Tooley's across the street, nursing an appetite for a hearty breakfast.

The wind had backed round to the south. He pulled the collar of his jacket closer together against the freshness in the wind as he crossed the street, and screwed up his nose to the smell it carried. This was a newer, sicklier smell than The Noble Breath, a stink that reminded him of an old mattress he had once burned. He nodded at the redneck lounging against the wall beside the door of Ma Tooley's tiny diner. Greg's greeting was acknowledged by a twitch of the man's lips, raising the cigar end stuck between them ever so slightly in a reluctant nicotine tribute.

Greg went inside to find three diners eating breakfast and Ma Tooley lighting kerosene lamps. They cordially returned his greeting and he stood watching Ma lighting the four lanterns in some bewilderment.

Ma let out a whoop of laughter that rocked the bands of flesh around her ample frame. "I s'pose you wanna know why I'm doing all this. Right?"

Her question was like a cue for the lights to go out and she let out an even deeper hoot of laughter; wiping the tears from her eyes with her knuckles and said. "There's your answer, power outage. It'll be out for an hour. Happens everyday at this time and I is pree-pared."

Greg's jaw dropped and he grumbled. "I was hoping to get some breakfast."

"No problems," Ma Tooley's skirts swished outwards as she swirled around and headed back to her kitchenette. "Them lamps fer heat an' light, but I is cookin' on gas, man."

She burst out laughing and everybody, including Greg joined in her paroxysm of mirth. Greg ordered his meal, excusing himself as he pushed past the diners to reach the vacant table next to the single tiny window; taking care not to spill anything from the mug of coffee Ma thrust into his hand.

Greg learned later that the restaurant had been Ma's front room before she opened it as a diner after Pa Tooley passed away four years ago. The room held only four small, homemade rough pine tables, each with a plastic chair to seat a single diner.

"Now tell me how's your day goin' so far," she asked as she passed over his plate of eggs, bacon strips, sausage patties, hash browns and whole wheat toast with another steaming mug of freshly brewed coffee? Greg grasped his meal from her in both hands with relish.

"That smells a whole lot better than the street outside Ma."

The other diners grumbled their agreement and Ma's ample bosoms jerked up and down as she laughed yet again.

"We call's that one the Not-So-Noble Breath. Do you want jelly with that toast?"

"No thanks, why Not-So-Noble Breath?"

One of the diners wiped his mouth on a paper napkin prior to providing the explanation.

"When the wind's from the north we get the Noble Breath from Ross Noble's sheds an' the other chicken farms up there. When it's from the south-east we get the smell from Frank Fawley's plant at the back of Whitewater."

Greg's face showed his confusion. "But why Not-So-Noble Breath?"

Another, younger diner chortled, tapped the table with his index fingers and clarified the reason for the name.

"The big man around these parts is Ross Noble. The man who would like to be the big man is Frank Fawley. He runs Fawley Grain and Feed and prefers being called 'Mitt' Fawley, after one of his political heroes. Fawley put in a chicken processing plant on his lot a year or two back. When he burns off the feathers and all, we get the stink in here and call it the Not-So-Noble Breath, 'cos it's a big stink, but, like him, not quite big enough."

Greg shook his head in disbelief. "That's incredible. Are you saying you have two grown men in this town who should know better, vying with each other for local supremacy?"

"Not really." The first diner replied. "Mitt Fawley would like havin' his own way, but Ross Noble gets his own way."

It was another name and insight into local politics for Greg to take on board.

"Thanks for that, I'll bear it in mind," he said, turning his attention to his breakfast. Ma watched him eat, and when Greg forked the last mouthful of food from his plate into his mouth and drained his coffee mug, she called out,

"More coffee," holding up the coffee pot?

"Later perhaps, I have to rush off. That truck pulled up outside the motel is for me. How much do I owe you Ma?"

She waved him away, "Close out with me later, you'd best get goin' these deliv'ry men don't wait none."

The technician had the satellite system installed and running on Greg's laptop in less than twenty minutes. After showing Greg around the peculiarities of the set-up he was done and gone.

Greg busied himself exploring the Internet and making a shopping list of the equipment he would need to buy in Larksville to make up the test batches of bio-diesel. He still had to write this down by hand in a paper notebook and the first item on his list was 'Printer/scanner and computer supplies.' He stuffed that in his pocket, tidied himself up and decided to leave for the Town Hall to introduce himself to the mayor.

Greg examined his car carefully for signs of any tampering before driving out into Greener and Main heading south for three blocks before taking the right turn down towards the Town Hall.

Greg smiled grimly as he passed Deputy Bronsky on station in his car parked on Main, just opposite Charmain and mused. Can it really be only three days since I ran into Jess? It seemed much longer.

Half a block farther along he noticed a tall, ramrod straight man with gray hair swept severely back on his head and wearing storekeeper's whites, placing goods on the sidewalk outside his store. Greg looked up and read the sign over the shop-'McKendrick's Stores'. Greg looked at his watch. He was in plenty of time and swung across Main to park outside the store.

The storekeeper regarded him quizzically as he climbed out of the car and approached the store.

"Mr. McKendrick?" Greg asked with a friendly smile, holding out his hand.

"Ay, that'll be me." McKendrick replied, taking the proffered hand in a light grip while his suspicious, steel gray, eyes fastened on Greg.

"Good Morning, I'm Greg Mitchell." Greg was not fazed by McKendrick's lack of warmth. He had met that reserve scores of times before on first sales meetings and launched directly into his spiel.

"I'm staying here for a while to help young Jess White set himself up for next year at school. It was me who knocked him down by accident last Monday and it cost him a job with you. I kind of feel duty bound to set him up with another."

This wasn't coming out as well as Greg hoped, he saw McKendrick's bushy eyebrows rise and his eyes harden.

"I've given the job to somebody else Mr. Mitchell. I don't have another job to give the laddie."

Greg chuckled nervously, but kept his cool. "I'm sorry Mr. McKendrick. I'm not making myself clear. I'm not here to ask you to give him a job. I'm here to make an appointment for him to make you a proposition. I'm creating a job for him. One that will let him take care of himself and give him enough income to finish high school and graduate."

The storekeeper's eyebrows rose higher on his forehead. "And just how do you plan to do that?"

"By trading, Mr. McKendrick. It's what I do. I'm a businessman when I'm not on vacation. I reckon I owe the boy that much, since it was my fault he lost the job with you."

The storekeeper's brow creased into deep furrows. He blew out heavily through quivering lips to show his impatience and said.

"He would not be making enough money on my job to see him through next year at high school. What makes you think you can do it in a few days in a place like Bamptonville? It's not London, if that's where you're from? I'll thank you not to waste your time or mine Mr. Mitchell and not to build up the boy's hopes either; his family has already suffered badly by the loss of his supporter. You do know about the sad death of Colonel Stewart - a fine man, so he was?"

"Yes sir, Jess told me about the colonel and what he was doing for him before he died."

"Not just for Jess, but for the whole family. Art White is a hard working, God fearing man trying to do better for one of his sons than he could for himself."

"I didn't know that Mr. McKendrick. I haven't met Mr. White."

"What!" The storekeeper gasped in surprise; his voice turned hard and sharp. "You mean to stand there and tell me you're filling his boy's head with big ideas and you don't even have the father's permission? Didn't you think his parents might have something to say about it and even have plans of their own for their boy? Thank you, but no, you take your plans elsewhere Mr. Mitchell. I'm busy now, getting ready to open." The storekeeper made a dismissive gesture with his hands.

Greg shuffled his feet uncomfortably and knew his face had flushed red by the heat it generated.

"That is remiss of me Mr. McKendrick and it is something I need to put right, but at the right time. You don't have to listen to me. I am the new boy in town, but this is about business, not me or the White family."

Greg looked beyond the man and into his store. "From what I see around me you can ill afford to turn it away. At this moment in time Jess needs help his family cannot give him and what I'm trying to do is build some confidence in him so he can learn to take care of himself. All I ask is for you to let me bring him here and listen to his pitch. I can teach him to trade so he'll be able to fend for himself. We're not selling snake oil. It's a genuine deal he'll offer you and you can make yourself some easy money, with no risk to you or your own business."

McKendrick crossed his arms over his chest, his chin jutted forwards belligerently.

"You owe him nothing except to move on and leave him to get on with his school work."

A hot surge of temper rose in Greg that burst out in a stream of indignation.

"That's all I ever get in this town. This backward looking town that has no future. I just want you to listen to Jess. That's all I'm asking. Give him a fair hearing when I bring him here to put a real business proposition to you."

McKendrick looked uncertain and his eyes flickered from side to side. "What business proposition can he possibly make? He's a student in junior high school?"

Greg pushed his jaw closer to McKendrick's face.

"Jess will make his first trade under my guidance. He's got a good offer to put to you. All I ask is you give him a fair hearing, and when he stands in front of you, don't see and listen to a young boy talking, instead listen to a young businessman with a good proposition that could make you both some money. Is that too much to ask of you? If so we'll go to Mafferty's with this. He'll not shut it out without examining it first?"

The mention of McKendrick's main competitor in town, galvanized the storekeeper's thoughts.

"Mafferty's? Mafferty's," he repeated, "what business deal do you have that could possibly interest Mafferty?" Greg sighed.

"Not now. I'm not telling you about it now because it's Jess's deal. Let us make an appointment so he can to tell you about it."

Greg gave the shopkeeper no time to think of a negative reply. "When can we come to see you tonight Mr. McKendrick, shall we say five-thirty or would a later time suit you better?"

McKendrick was outside of his comfort zone and stammered without thinking. "Five-thirty make it Five-thirty if you must; but no promises mind!"

"Thank you Mr. McKendrick, until this evening then." Greg turned on his heel, got into his car and drove away, exhaling deeply to relieve his tension.

He glanced in his rear view mirror and saw McKendrick standing with his hands on his hips, gazing after him. That had been a hard call and did not go as well as he had hoped. McKendrick had raised another legitimate problem

What about Jess's parents? I really ought to see what his father has to say about all this. However, his inner voice told him it would be better to see his folks after Jess had completed a couple of successful deals and not before, when it was still only a dream, with no substance to prove it can work. They could then talk about their plans from a position of strength and show both Jess and his father that this plan can work.

"Yup! That's the best way to go. Approach his dad after the boy's had some success to prove he can do it." Greg glanced at the dashboard clock. "It's time to meet the mayor."

17

Greg pulled up on the parking lot outside the Town Hall, brushed himself down and fueled by his new resolve, plus the energy from his breakfast, ran up the steps into the Town Hall entrance foyer.

The foyer gave into a long corridor resembling a church with high, vaulted ceilings, flagstone floor and long, oblong windows with arched tops at the far end; cathedral windows without the stained glass.

Greg shuddered. He was not sure if it was from the cooler temperature inside the building, or the dim, funereal atmosphere of this mausoleum of a place. There was nobody around and Greg walked slowly along the corridor towards an arrowed sign pointing to a doorway with a sign reading RECEPTION.

His footfall on the flagstones echoed from the walls as he walked. Greg stood outside the heavy wooden door, a lump in his throat and his fist poised to knock. He swallowed and then rapped boldly three times on the door putting his ear to its panel to listen for a 'come in' from the other side. Instead the door swung open making him jump back in surprise.

An elegant, petite lady, a few years older than Greg, with large, horn-rimmed spectacles and wearing a close fitting, black business dress showing her well kept figure to advantage stood looking curiously at him. She held her head on one side with a mischievous half-smile playing across the fullness of her mouth.

"Ohh!" Greg muttered in surprise and her smile became a pleasant chuckle as she said.

"Hello I am Miss Broeckner, the mayor's secretary. Can I take it you are Mr. Mitchell?" She held out her hand and her eyes sparkled, teasing him.

"Umm, yes, that's right," Greg, stammered, taken unawares and discomfited, his fingers went to fiddle with the tie he was not wearing.

He shook her hand, agreeably surprised by its firm softness as she gave out anther friendly chuckle. Greg felt relaxed and rather silly at losing his composure upon meeting the attractive Miss Broeckner.

"Bill Courtley said you'd be along and the mayor's expecting you Mr. Mitchell. I'll take you right along." He followed her closely to the far end of the corridor. The clip-clop of her high heels echoed around the cavern of a passageway drowning out the noise of his footsteps. Greg's eyes gravitated to the gentle sway of Miss Broeckner's hips and the ripple of her buttocks under the tightened fabric of her dress as she walked towards the long windows at the end of the corridor. She stopped and knocked on the last door on the right, putting an ear to its panels.

Greg heard the throaty 'Come' from the other side as he stood a half step behind the secretary, looking at her throat with its tiny gold chain and crucifix. She opened the door and with another coquettish smile, stood aside.

"You can go inside now Mr. Mitchell. Can I bring you some coffee?"

"Uhh No thanks, I've just had breakfast." Greg was still taken aback by this alluring woman and she knew it. She flicked her eyelids at him as she stepped back and said. "I see."

Greg walked open mouthed into the large room; its walls decked with flags, bookshelves, pictures and Native American souvenirs.

Harvey Denton sat behind an oversized oak desk in the far corner of the room, brightly lit from the natural light streaming in through the double French windows forming the outside wall of his office. Harvey was vigorously packing a large, curved Meerschaum pipe from a tin of 'Half and Half' tobacco. The dulled, blackened bowl along with the chewed mouthpiece spoke of long usage.

"Mr. Mitchell, come in, come in" The mayor waved him in with his free hand and flashed a broad smile of welcome.

Greg stood and pointed at the closed door behind him.

"Good Morning Mr. Mayor! Pardon me for saying so - but that is one appealing lady."

Denton laughed as he stood up and came around to the front of the desk, his pipe in one hand and the other outstretched in greeting to Greg.

"Miss Broeckner, she sure is, and a very efficient secretary too," he said as they shook hands, "but don't you be getting any ideas, ain't no man yet been able to get near her and many have tried, believe you me."

Here was another riddle, Greg fancied the secretary would be good company over dinner, but he was not in the mayor's parlor today to solve any puzzle surrounding Miss Broeckner. The mayor placed an arm across Greg's shoulder and led him towards the French windows.

"I've been hearing some good things about you Mr. Mitchell and I'd like to hear some more about those ideas of yours people are talking about. It's brightening up outside and I thought we'd sit out on the terrace. Do you smoke Mr. Mitchell?"

"No sir, it's not one of my vices."

The mayor looked peculiarly at him as he opened the doors. It seemed he was about to follow up with another question, but changed his mind, clamped his pipe between his lips and shepherded Greg outside onto a pleasant stone flagged terrace, shielded from the wind by tall, flowering shrubs. Greg recognized the long, drooping fronds of forsythia covered in close clusters of yellow flowers. His nose caught the heady scent of jasmine. Greg stopped himself in time from remarking on the pleasant change of smell from the more prevalent odors of Noble and Not-So-Noble Breaths.

Harvey Denton ushered Greg across the terrace to a white, wrought iron table and matching chairs under a candy striped canvas canopy.

"Sit down Mr. Mitchell, you don't mind if I smoke?" The mayor lit his pipe without waiting for an answer. Greg pulled out a chair to sit opposite Denton to wait for the mayor to reappear from behind a cloud of white smoke. The mayor waved it away with his hand once his pipe was drawing to his satisfaction.

"Did Miss Broeckner offer you refreshments Mr. Mitchell?"

"She did, thank you, but I've not long since eaten breakfast. I must say it's a real nice place you have here Mr. Mayor."

"That's true, but sadly it's too big for us now. This used to be a regional administration building with a company of US Cavalry billeted here in the bad old days before Nebraska became a state and bigger towns grew up elsewhere, leaving Bamptonville in a bit of a backwater; where we've been paddling along ever since." The mayor finished speaking with a guffaw of laughter, pleased with his watery analogies

Greg nodded his appreciation. "You can sense the history here."

Denton struck another match, holding it to his pipe, sucking noisily before answering.

"That's then and this is now, have you met Ross Noble yet?"

"Not yet sir, I'm meeting with him next Monday."

"Good! Good! Now I'm hearing all sorts of things about you Mr. Mitchell, mostly good I must say."

Greg bristled slightly. "You mean you are hearing some things that are not good about me sir?" Greg's tone conveyed his indignation and the mayor brushed it away with a flourish of his hand.

"Not bad things, maybe a bit of uncertainty's more the thing. That's all. Folks hereabouts take a while to get used to strangers. The word on the street says you knocked down young Jess White and are putting him to rights with his medical bills, even got yourself some ideas to help him stay on at school?"

"Yes sir, I knocked him down by accident and it stopped him getting a job at McKendrick's Stores. His benefactor died recently and it's my understanding he needed that income to help support himself at school."

"Yes, yes," the mayor shook his head, "bad business Hiram Stewart going dying sudden like that. Nobody knew he was unwell you understand?"

"Yes sir."

"So you're planning on filling the gap?" The pipe came out of the mayor's mouth and his eyes widened as they scrutinized Greg and waited for his reply.

"That's right sir. It seems I was last in a line of bad luck that boy encountered and he was at his wits end to find a way to carry on. I am presently at a loose end and can help, so I thought - Why Not?"

The mayoral eyes remain fixed on him, but without immediately replying to Greg's explanation, raising an uncomfortable doubt that the mayor did not believe his story.

"Do you doubt me sir?"

"No, no, not at all it's just that you'll have to stay here a long time, just to see things through. Don't take offense now, but I believe in plain talking and some folks are saying you might have other intentions after getting to know the boy better. It's just what some folks are saying mind, and I'd like to get your take on that rumor?"

Greg gritted his teeth and slapped his thigh in irritation.

"Let me put you straight on that sir. Whoever's saying that is spreading lies, malicious lies. I have no designs whatsoever on Jess White other than to help him cut through the barriers that are stopping him completing his education. In a way it will knock down barriers put up against me. I don't expect you to understand that, but I believe any barrier to a person's advancement is a barrier to society itself."

"Wow, that's in too deep for me, so tell me how you're gonna do this."

Greg spent the next ten minutes explaining his ideas for setting up a bio-diesel plant, recovering the waste cooking oil, converting it to diesel and selling it on to consumers.

The mayor forgot about his pipe and leaned forwards towards Greg to be sure he caught every word. When Greg had finished he lit his pipe again and asked with a tremor of excitement in his voice.

"Are you sure this is safe and it'll work?"

"Absolutely sir, all the chemicals and poisons used in the process are already everyday household items. The fuel produced is as good as any diesel you can buy at any gas station."

"Then how come everybody's not doing it?"

"In most other places they are and have been doing so for years. In some countries the major oil producers are mixing ten percent of bio-diesel with normal refined diesel oil. Nobody on record has been injured by it and no serious accident has ever taken place where people have exercised sensible precautions handling the chemical agents. We're talking drain cleaner and stove oil here."

The mayor looked confused and Greg spent the next five minutes explaining the process and finished by saying.

"I invested in a company doing this in Florida a couple of years ago. It's now a leader in the field. Wayne Fisher, the company's president is coming to spend this weekend with me. I could bring him around to see you if you are interested in hearing what he has to say on this."

The mayor was clearly interested, but waved away Greg's offer to meet with Fisher.

"That won't be necessary. Tell me what does it cost to convert this oil to diesel fuel. Fuel costs for my school buses as well as getting rid of the waste cooking oil are a humongous headache to me and I don't mind admitting it. Now tell me this. Could I use this in my school buses? Can they be converted to use this bio-fuel? How much would the conversion cost me before they can use it?"

Greg allowed himself a half-smile and experienced the distinctive buzz of triumph passing through his body whenever he successfully closed a sale in his past life as a salesman. He kept his cool and the excitement out of his voice when he replied.

"If your buses are old, their rubber fuel hoses will need composition replacements. That is all. They will need no other conversion and will run on this fuel as well as they do on regular diesel oil, or a mixture of the two. In very low temperatures, like in deep winter, it might be better to mix the bio-diesel with regular fuel to ensure it doesn't crystallize. That can happen with bio-fuels made from tallow and animal fats, but waste cooking oil should be okay all year round."

"Yes, yes. But what does it cost?" The mayor leaned right across the table, plainly captivated. Greg pursed his lips as if in thought to keep him waiting.

"Well sir, that's the sixty-four dollar question and it depends on a number of things."

"What things?" The mayor's impatience to know was encouraging for Greg.

"Well sir, we'll need secure premises with drains, power and water"

"We got 'em right here; the old stables out back ain't being used, would they do?"

Greg looked out over the courtyard at the back of the Town Hall where the four, yellow school buses were parked ready to go out and behind them a neat row of solid stone built stables flanking the roadside.

"They would be perfect, but when could we move in; and what rent would you charge?"

"Never mind the rent and you can move in as soon as you like, what other costs are there."

"There's the cost of equipment."

"Yes, yes, but once you've got it, it's paid for, what I want to know is how much does it cost to turn a gallon of waste oil into diesel fuel?"

Harvey Denton's keen interest showed in the way he twitched and shifted around on his chair. Greg kept him waiting for an answer to feed the mayor's growing impatience.

"Then there's the cost of labor and the collections. I don't know what that will come to, but it will govern how much waste oil we need to collect on a weekly basis."

"But won't you be doing that yourself? Collecting and converting and all that?"

"Not for always sir; but in the beginning I will. I intend setting up this business so Jess White can run it; and he can't do that full time and be studying at school, he'll need help. I can't be here for ever - otherwise folks will think I have improper designs on young Jess and what's likely keeping me here anyway." Greg couldn't resist making the snipe and gave the mayor a crooked smile. Denton's face flushed red with embarrassment.

"Point well taken Mr. Mitchell, but you still haven't told me how much the process costs?"

"At present commercial prices, and I checked them on the Internet only this morning. We can buy methanol at two to three dollars a gallon and caustic soda at five-hundred a ton."

The mayor looked perplexed. "That doesn't mean too much to me Mr. Mitchell."

"Bear with me sir. The amount of methanol we use is the same every time: for every four gallons of filtered waste oil we need to add one gallon of methanol to give us a little less than five gallons of bio-diesel."

The mayor started tapping his fingertips and his lips quivered as he counted.

"I make that between forty and sixty cents a gallon. Jumpin' jackrabbits, why ain't we been doin' this already? Why ain't nobody told me about this before?"

The mayor had risen to his feet. His pipe dropped onto the table and his face flushed a deeper shade of red.

"Do you know what happens here right now Mr. Mitchell. We have to pay a contractor to come in from Alliance to remove it and he'll only come in when there's five hundred gallons minimum to take away. Folk have tried feeding it to chickens and hogs, but there's too much of it over a year and it builds up. A lot goes into landfill to feed rats and if what you tell me is right, and I've no reason to believe otherwise, what you're planning can be the answer to two of my biggest problems. If it works, it's a winner - a vote winner."

Greg smothered his elation as the mayor sat down sheepishly having said too much, which Greg was quick to pick up on.

"I take it you're up for re-election soon sir?"

"That's right, later this year." The mayor continued to look embarrassed and began stabbing the bowl of his pipe with a penknife. Greg moved the discussion forward by asking.

"May I ask how much you pay the contractor and how often you call him in?"

"No problem. It's five hundred dollars a time, dollar a gallon. It varies with the time of year, but he comes about three or four times a year."

Greg pursed his lips and Denton, sensing his dismay, leaned across to grasp Greg's forearm, "but there may be more. I suspect the caterers are pouring a lot down the drains to get out of paying the contractor's fee."

"Even so sir, we'll need more oil than that to make this work. I've been doing some calculations and we'll need to collect about a hundred and eighty gallons of waste oil minimum each and every week; that should give us a hundred and sixty gallons of good oil to sell out as fuel at two dollars a gallon after processing."

The mayor looked agape. "But I thought you said the chemical cost two - three bucks a gallon?"

"That's not all the costs, there's another chemical we need as a catalyst, sodium hydroxide, caustic soda, drain cleaner by other names, it costs five hundred bucks a ton."

"And you'll need to use a lot of that stuff in the process, will you?"

Greg was on firm ground now.

"The amount of caustic we need depends on the quality of the waste oil we collect. I suspect it's been boiled up a few times before it gets thrown out?"

"You can bet your life on it," the mayor said with a chuckle.

"That means there'll be a lot of water and cooking debris in it. We have to do what they call a titration test. It's not difficult, but it is important and this will tell us how much caustic we must add to each batch of oil. Normally you put three grams per liter for good, clean oil to catalyze the process. In plain language that comes out at about six pounds on one-eighty gallons."

The mayor whooped, slamming the table with his fist.

"But that's peanuts at five hundred bucks a ton?"

"Yessir, but I reckon we'll need double that for the rough oil we'll be collecting."

"Even so," the mayor protested, "it shouldn't bring the cost up to two bucks a gallon."

It was an accusation and Greg uncrossed his legs slowly to take time to reply.

"It's labor costs that puts up the price. I believe there are unemployed folk in the town that would like to work. I'm hearing about a bunch down at Whitewater. We'll have to pay them to do the collecting and for helping Jess. Then again, it's not a foolproof system. There's likely to be losses, especially when we first start out. If we get the measurements wrong the whole batch of oil turns into a worthless jelly we'll have to pay someone to get rid of. To make a decent profit to put young Jess through school, we'll need to charge two dollars a gallon. That's still a good price with regular diesel presently at two-eighty and rising. It's a twenty-eight percent saving, plus you won't need to pay for collection charges because you'll get the waste oil collected for free every week, instead of every three months like you do now and nothing going to landfill or down the drains."

"Yes, yes," the mayor studied his fingers as they fiddled with his pipe on the table. "It's not so good as I was hoping, but it's still good enough. My school buses each make a round trip of fifty miles twice a day, five days a week. The buses average out at eight to ten miles a gallon. We could use all you produce for the school run. I'd want the best price you can give me."

"Yessir, we'll see what we can do."

"Tell me Mr. Mitchell, are there any downsides to this, such as dangers, wastes or anything you've not mentioned."

"No sir, with normal precautions it's safe. The only waste is the residue after processing and that is glycerin, which is a useful degreaser and we can hand it out as goodwill to those who might want to use it."

"Or sell it to bring down the price of the finished fuel."

"We could do that too sir, but then there would be other costs, packaging and more labor charges mostly, making it non-viable as a sideline."

The mayor grunted and stood up.

"Would you like to see the stable block?"

"Yessir, I would."

The mayor led Greg down into the courtyard and along to the farthest stable door nearest to the road entrance and opened it up.

Inside Greg saw tether positions for eight horses on a solid, cobblestone floor under a sound, tiled roof and lighted by small fanlight windows. He found the water supply in the farthest corner near the door and opened it to run.

After a few moments of gurgling noises, brown water spurted out of the faucet. Greg ran it into the drains until the water ran clear. He was also pleased to see that the drains functioned to carry away the water. The stable was perfect for their needs. The mayor switched on the lights, but nothing happened.

"I'll get our contracted electrician on to this. When would you want to start?"

"This weekend if that's possible Mr. Mayor?"

"Call me Harvey when we're off parade, you'll want to lock it up so I'll get Miss Broeckner to send you round the key. Or would you prefer to come and collect it from her office," he asked with a wry grin?

Greg forced an innocent expression onto his face, "Why Harvey, whatever are you suggesting? Of course I'd rather collect it from her - I mean from her office."

Denton roared with laughter and slapped Greg's back. "I thought you would say that, but I'm telling you, you're wasting your time there with that one."

The mayor walked Greg to the entrance and called in on Miss Broeckner's office to say cheerio. She said her good bye from beneath lowered and fluttering eyelashes. Both men knew she was playing with them.

Greg stood with the mayor on the Town Hall steps to shake

hands and make their farewells. Before they parted Denton asked.

"It looks like you'll be staying around Bamptonville for a while. Does that mean you'll be staying on at the motel?" There was mischief in his eyes as he cast a backward glance that suggested, 'if you have designs on Miss Broeckner, you'll have to do better than a motel.'

Greg chuckled. "It's only temporary accommodation. I might buy locally if something suitable comes on the market."

The mayor walked down two steps with Greg and then gripped his elbow with his face set serious. "Don't get me wrong here Greg, but this town is eighty-eight percent ethnic white. Their families have been here a long time, for most there was nothing here when they arrived. The twelve percent of ethnic other people mostly live out at Whitewater, the suburb you mentioned. They're the ones mostly out of work and living on social benefits. I just wanted to say we have had some closures recently at the Fawley Food and Grain plant and we have a few good folks looking for work who don't live in Whitewater. What I'm saying is this; you won't need to go out to Whitewater to get your labor. You catch my drift now?"

The meeting had gone well up to this point, but the mayor's meaning came across crystal clear. Greg noted the pained urgency in the mayor's question and in his body language. It sounded like a threat and it marred the geniality of what passed before between them. A dirty taste came into Greg's mouth as he shook hands with Denton for the last time that day.

"I hear you Harvey. Yessir, I hear you."

"That's good; we got an understanding. You can move into the stable whenever you want, rent free, collect the key tomorrow. Good bye for now."

The mayor turned and walked back into the building without waiting for any reply. Greg watched the door close behind Denton and spat the foul taste in his mouth onto the steps as he walked down them and speaking through nearly closed lips.

"It seems we might have a bit of a race issue here and he's just told me to steer clear of it. Well I might or I might not! I just don't know yet. I'd better find out some more about what makes this town get through its days."

The good that came out of the meeting overrode the badness at the end and fed the spring in Greg's stride as he walked to his car to drive to Larksville. He switched on the radio giving out that Todd Fritsch number that he heard first thing this morning. Greg recalled enough of it to hum along with the tune.

18

With the memory of the blow out and his near escape from serious injury fresh in his mind, Greg drove cautiously until he passed the last of the rows of chicken sheds to the north of the town and then pressed his foot to the boards to open up the engine. The drive was nowhere near as effortless or smooth as the BMW and he noticed the strained roar of the smaller car's engine when pressed for speed along the level carriageway that runs as straight as a Roman road all the way into Larksville.

Greg shuddered involuntarily as he passed the point where his tire had failed. He glanced to the side of the road and blanched at his lucky escape from harm when he saw the road was raised a full five feet above the deep ditch draining the flat countryside through which it passed. The route cut through fields of sorghum, grain and grazing pastures interspersed with tree plantations. He only noticed the wind had backed to the east when the car suddenly sheered sharply to the left as a gust of strong wind funneling through a gap between two tree plantations hit the side of the vehicle.

Greg shouted in surprise, fighting the wayward motion with deft touches of the wheel to regain control of the car and return to his musings. He still felt good about his plans, in spite of the warning about employing ethnic minorities and the attack on the car yesterday. After mulling over the incident innumerable times since it happened, he was now sure in his mind that it had been an attack on him personally. The question that vexed him still was, 'Why'?

The Hertz clerk confirmed his fears when they met on the forecourt after driving into the station.

"Regional office wants to keep your car for detailed examination Mr. Mitchell." The clerk's face pale and deadpan; he spoke in a dour tone, giving Greg the impression the man was hiding something from him.

"What's the problem?" Greg spoke nonchalantly as he got out of the car and shook hands with the man. The clerk looked uneasy and shifted the subject.

"What do you think of the little Geo, it's not in the luxury class but it's got a game little motor?" He forced a smile, but his eyes remained shifty and wouldn't meet Greg's gaze; slapping the roof of the little car as he spoke. Greg abruptly brought him back to the subject in hand.

"You were telling me that your regional office wants to examine the BMW. Why is that?"

The clerk shuffled his feet uneasily and then let go what was worrying him in a deluge of words. "It's like this Mr. Mitchell. The company mechanics that looked it over think the damage was done by acid, and they got an idea it might be more'n an accident. I'm not supposed to tell you this, but you asked me and I guess you have a right to know, 'specially if someone has you in their sights for somethin'."

Greg felt a cold hand clutch his heart, but remained calm. "What happens now then?"

"Well, they can send you out another BMW, but they'll need to get a Five Series in from the East for you. You can keep on with the Geo if you prefer? I've got a Contour coming in later that might be more suitable"

Greg raised his hand to interrupt. "I was talking about the tire. What happens now?"

The clerk gulped and his face reddened. "Well sir, they've passed it over to the police for forensic tests. Depending on what comes back from them, it could become a police matter. You might have to make a statement."

"That's not a problem. There's not much I can tell them. I'd only been in town for a day or so when it happened and I've met nobody I could say I upset enough to want to do that to me. But why haven't they got me a replacement car? You said yesterday it would be here today?"

Greg watched his question cause extreme discomfort to the clerk whose face colored a deeper shade of crimson while the man's throat gurgled nervously. Greg stared at him, silently waiting for a reply.

"To be plain honest with you sir, the company's worried somebody might have a vendetta against you. They don't want to lose another expensive car if they try again. That's the regional franchisee's opinion I want you to know and not the Hertz Company itself saying that."

"That's why we all have insurance isn't it?" Greg asked the question with false bravado.

"Yessir, It is, but please note these are not my words, the regional manager said they might get lucky next time and it'd be plumb bad fer publicity havin' you crash and maybe die in one of our cars. Bizness and competition being hard as it is these days."

Greg didn't know why he laughed at this, it wasn't funny at all, and inexplicably he became light headed.

"What you're really telling me is they'd prefer me to hand over the keys to this car and go away?"

"Yessir, I can't deny it in these circumstances; until the person that did this is discovered they think it would be in their best interests for you to do as you just said." The clerk looked distraught and shrank away.

Greg stood in silent reflection for a few seconds before presenting the keys to the Geo and said as if it was of no concern to him, "There you are then Mr… ?"

"My name's Yocum sir, Alfried Yocum. My family owns this garage."

"Thank you Mr. Yocum, thank you for your honesty and forthrightness. Can I take it you don't work for the rental company? That it's not your main business here?"

"No sir, we're a family business of automobile and farm machinery engineers. We are only a local sub office of a regional franchisee for Hertz."

"I was thinking on the way over here today that a rental car's not suitable for what I have in mind. I need to buy a small truck or pickup: diesel engine, reliable and not too costly. Can you help me?"

If Mr. Yocum's face had been winter, Greg's question turned it instantly to spring.

"I just might have the very thing for you, it came in only yesterday. She's a Ford F-350 pick up; 1996 with one hundred an' eighty-seven thousand miles showing on her clock. She's been worked hard, but there's a whole lot of good work left in her."

"Would you show me Mr Yocum?"

"Sure, call me Al, everybody round here does!"

They spent the next twenty minutes looking over the truck with its faded, chipped, white paintwork and grime encrusted interior, reeking of old oil and nicotine.

"We can get all that cleaned up for you." Yocum's words were spoken as an apology.

Greg mumbled an acknowledgement and asked. "Does anything need replacing?"

Yocum caught his enthusiasm and replied warmly. "I'll get her through the bay for servicing and inspection. She'll need new rubber on the wheels real soon, but it all seems good at the price."

"What is the price?"

"Fifty-seven hundred as she stands."

"I know nothing about these trucks or their prices, but that sounds reasonable from what I've seen of prices on others like it on forecourts I've passed."

"It's a bank repo. The owner couldn't keep up the payments. We only have to get that for it. It's a steal at the price."

Greg screwed up his nose as he said. "That's the way of this world today, one man's misfortune is another's good fortune and only the banks win - every time."

Yocum nodded his agreement.

"Can I do a deal on this without it coming off your commission?"

"I guess we can try. I'll have to talk to the bank about it; it's their shout."

"If you have that talk with the bank, then service it like you said and put on new rubber I'll give you five grand for it today. You do take Amex don't you?"

Yocum grimaced. "They charge too much commission. We only take it if we have to and I'd have to talk to the bank about that as well."

"You do that Mr. Yocum and give me a call at Bill Elbury's office when you're done. If the bank goes for it they'll have to pay the credit card charges, plus I'll not need a rental car from you. If they don't, then I will - unless you can find me another truck like that F-350 over there."

Greg declined Al Yocum's offer of a ride to Bill Elbury's office, preferring to walk through the town to find his way around and gather some inspirations for future trades for Jess.

The clouds had parted to allow shafts of sunlight to pass through their gaps and brighten the dullness of the day. People were coming out into the streets, their presence creating a busier more pleasant atmosphere. Notebook and pencil in his hands, Greg looked in shop windows as he passed noting the goods for sale and their prices. He found two interesting shops selling used goods and stood looking in the window of 'Daniel's Cave' for so long that Daniel came out to invite him inside.

"Another time thank you, Daniel," he had replied affably. Greg was encouraged by what he had seen and strode briskly to Bill Elbury's office, stopping only to buy a local newspaper.

The office door was open. Greg wondered if it ever closed? Inside, the room seemed more crowded than before with larger piles of papers strewn about the furniture and floor space.

Elbury was deep in thought when Greg arrived; pacing the two or three steps to and fro behind his desk and dictating to an auburn-haired woman in her thirties with shapely legs sitting on a chair in a corner of the room surrounded by more piles of papers she had obviously moved from the chair. Greg stood back out of sight until he heard Elbury say 'Yours etcetera' and then followed his single knock on the door into the room.

"All you have to do now is find the computer and printer under all this junk and you can get that letter out Miss." Greg joked to the woman through a huge grin, she returned it with a surprised gape.

"Greg, come on in," Elbury followed his expansive greeting by adding, "meet Jennifer."

"Pleased to meet you Jennifer, I'm Greg Mitchell," Greg held out his hand. Jennifer smiled to show the tiniest and most even teeth Greg had seen in a person. He stared at them, fascinated, as he shook her hand. Her voice focused his mind back to the moment.

"Hello Mr. Mitchell. I am pleased to meet you too. I've heard quite a bit about you already."

Bill butted in from behind the desk before Greg was able to reply. "And all of it bad. Jennifer helps with the office work."

Elbury quipped, following up with a loud guffaw and stood smiling with his hands on his hips. He was in shirtsleeves with the cuffs rolled above his wrists and wearing no tie. Greg ignored him, glancing around the office with disdain and spoke to Jennifer.

"However can you manage to do any work in a place like this?"

She put her hand to her mouth and giggled. "It's the system and you get used to it. I have my own office down the hall where I use most of my elbow grease."

Bill laughed again and waved his arms around in front of him to take in the room.

"It's all in here somewhere." Then spoke to Jennifer. "We'll send out for a working lunch. Do you want to join us, Jen?"

"No thanks Bill, I've some shopping to do. I'll get your letters ready for signature later this afternoon."

She turned to Greg with a pleasant smile. "Can I get you anything from town while I'm out Mr. Mitchell?" She asked with a slight flutter of her eyelids. Bill laughed from behind the desk to add to her embarrassment. Greg ignored him again and fished out his list.

"Actually I've quite a list of things I need to buy. It's quite a lot and maybe too much to ask." Jennifer took the list and studied it solemnly while Greg thought she doesn't wear glasses, then wondered why he thought that. She folded his list and held on to it.

"I can get this for you. It will not be a problem." Greg fished out two, one hundred dollar bills from his wallet.

"Thank you very much Jennifer, I'll be much obliged. Do you think two 'Franklins' will cover it?"

She covered her mouth again to stifle her laughter as she took the notes and tittered from behind her hand. Greg saw her shoulders shaking with mirth.

"What's wrong?" he asked.

She took away her hand and laughed openly. "Wherever did you learn that expression Mr. Mitchell? I've only heard that in gangster movies."

Greg felt his face heat up, showing his embarrassment. "I think John Travolta said it in Pulp Fiction."

"Never mind," she said with a smile, "I understand what you meant and yes, it should cover your purchases. I'll be off and see you both later." She fluttered her eyes again at Greg as she left and Bill acknowledged her departure with a limp wave of his wrist.

"She likes you!" Bill said after she had gone, pulling up the waistband of his pants.

Greg waved a hand casually in front of his face and joked. "It happens all the time. It must be the English accent."

Bill dumped a pile of bulging paper folders from his desk onto the floor and picked up another. He removed a file from half way down the pile, dropped it on his desk and dumped the remainder back on the floor. He pointed at the chair where Jennifer had sat and ordered, "Sit!"

Bill Elbury was back on the job. Greg had learned to read upside down from his years of facing clients and prospects from across their desks. He saw the folder was labeled 'G. MITCHELL' in red capital letters and was already an inch thick.

Our boy has been doing some work, he thought as he followed instructions and sat in the chair still warm from Jennifer's presence. He made himself comfortable by crossing his legs to wait for Elbury to open the proceedings.

Bill Elbury sat at his desk and flicked open a file. "I've been doing some work," he announced in a flat monotone.

"I was just thinking that," Greg chortled, "judging by the thickness of that folder…." Bill raised a finger for silence and continued.

"Have there been any more incidents?" Greg shook his head.

"No, I think the tire attack was probably a one off, but I'm keeping my eyes and ears open. The sheriff knew about it when I met him yesterday, and that's a bit of a concern."

"What do you mean, concern? It's his business to know these things."

Greg sighed, noting Elbury's rush to defend the sheriff and recrossed his legs slowly to gain more thinking time, taking care to formulate his reply.

"The sheriff came out of town to meet me on the way back yesterday. He knew all about the incident as you call it, and I wondered how that was possible, that's all."

Bill shrugged it off. "One of those things. I wouldn't worry about it. Flik Donovan's paid to know what's going on. It wasn't a secret here in Larksville. One of his callers from here would likely have mentioned it."

Elbury's answer was plausible, but Greg remained unconvinced and pressed his lips together to keep his darker thoughts to himself. The accountant laid the palms of his hands flat on the table and leaned forward before speaking in low, confidential tones.

"I've been talking to a contact at Hertz. They've taken your Beemer to Omaha for a detailed examination and sent the burst tire to police forensics for tests. They want to determine whether or not this was a deliberate acid attack. Forensics has come back and confirmed that it was, so watch out for yourself. It seems someone doesn't want either you or BMW's around these parts. I reckon you should come into Larksville; if not for your own good, for the benefit of Hertz's hire car."

Greg sat bolt upright in the chair and shook his head. "Nah, I'm staying where I am."

"Why for goodness sake? Do you like courting danger? Set yourself up here where you won't need to look over your shoulder or wonder what's waiting for you round the next corner."

Greg slapped his thigh in exasperation.

"Not my style, Bill. Not anymore. I'm done with running away. I'm pretty certain the cretin behind all this nonsense is a creep called Felix Gleitner."

"Gleitner?" Elbury sat back in surprise, gaping with incredulity, "Gleitner? He's a small time low life that runs crooked labor crews for equally crooked chicken farmers. How can you possibly have got in his way to upset him this bad? Besides, it's not his style to do a thing like that."

"He doesn't have to. He's got hoodlums to do his dirty work for him. I believe Gleitner runs a vice ring out of the Truck Stop using high school kids for hookers. I bumped into three of his string coming round the corner from where I'd parked my car before I drove over here yesterday. I thought they looked shifty at the time and now I reckon they did the tire job for him."

"But that don't prove anything unless you saw 'em do it! And a vice ring! With high school kids! Out of the Truck Stop! What you just said has to be this season's number one fairy story. The sheriff would never let him or anybody else get away with anything like that in Bamptonville, 'specially with school kids. Donovan's ears are much too close to the ground. He'd run Gleitner into jail so fast his feet wouldn't have time to make tracks in the dirt."

Greg sighed again. "Maybe so but It's no fairy story, I can't prove it - not yet, but it is happening. If the sheriff doesn't know, then his informers are either not working or they're compromised. Of course, if he is aware it's going on and has done nothing about it; doesn't that implicate him too? That would better explain how he knew to come and meet me on the road back to Bamptonville yesterday."

Elbury's fist slammed the desk. "That's enough. Talk like that can cause a whole heap of trouble. You've no proof of any of this and Flik Donovan is a much respected, church going citizen and a damned good lawman. Implicating him in any way doesn't explain why Gleitner or anybody else is coming after you?"

Greg now leaned forwards and stressed his next words.

"What is said in this room stays in these four walls remember?" Elbury nodded and Greg continued, uneasy that Elbury might not accept his beliefs. "...I just know what I know, and I know what I've told you is true and I also believe Gleitner is trying to groom Jess for his depraved business purposes."

They sat silently looking at each other. It was an impasse only broken by the abrupt ring of the telephone.

"It's for you," Elbury said, passing the instrument to Greg.

"Mitchell here," Greg forced as much lightness into his voice as he could muster.

"Hi Mr. Mitchell, Al Yocum here. Bad news I'm afraid. The bank won't shift on the price, not one wooden nickel. More'n that, they said they won't accept Amex at any price either. It has to be cash. What do you want to do sir? The Contour's come back early and can be ready for you if you want to stay with a rental car. I don't have another truck to offer you just yet."

"That's okay Al, pity about the bank not moving on my offer. I'll still take the truck. If I drum up the cash to take the F-350 could it be ready for me by late afternoon today?"

"Why yes Mr. Mitchell sir. No problem at all, I can have it all done in a couple of hours excepting for the new tires. I don't have that size in stock right now. I'm expecting a delivery in the next couple o' days."

"That's a deal Mr. Yocum. What will be the all-up price, including new rubber all round?"

"That'll be fifty-seven hundred still."

"But won't those costs come out of your commission Mr. Yocum?"

"It do, but I reckon on getting you fer a customer to balance it out over time."

Greg chuckled. "That goes without saying Al. I'll need to be leaving here by four o'clock this afternoon."

"No problem Mr. Mitchell. She'll be ready for yer."

"Just a second Mr. Yocum." Bill Elbury was tugging Greg's sleeve.

"What's going on?" Bill mouthed without speaking.

"I'm buying a truck from the bank through Al Yocum. I'll need five-thousand seven-hundred cash by half-three this afternoon."

"No problem. Is that the Mid State Farmer's Bank?"

Greg relayed the question to Yocum and the mechanic's answer to Bill.

"That's right!"

"I'll call the bank," Elbury said with a firm nod of his head.

Greg confirmed the deal and rang off with Yocum. Elbury called the bank and guaranteed the cash against Greg's cheque to obtain release of the vehicle. He rubbed his hands together and grinned when he hung up.

"You've decided to stay for the longer term then, since you're buying a vehicle. Sounds like a good price."

"Bank repo."

"There's a few of them around these days and a lot more coming soon. Al Yocum's a good man, you can trust him to give you a straight deal."

"I found that out already. Are you always so damned pessimistic?"

Elbury sighed deeply. "It's not pessimism it's reality. I don't want a recession anymore than you do. That raises another question. If you're planning to start businesses here you'd better get yourself onto a proper visa. I've had a word with your lawyer, Dean Halburton in Boston. We talked on the phone about this. He'll contact you about getting a green card."

"Hang on a minute," Greg half rose out of his chair, "I'm

starting a small business or charity to help one US citizen finish his education. I've no intention of becoming a US citizen myself as part of the process."

"You'll not become a US citizen, you'll be getting a green card. Sure, it's a step on the road to citizenship, but what it will do is let you do what you want to do here according to the law of the United States and not the law according to Greg Mitchell."

"What's wrong with the visa I've got already?"

"It says you have to leave the USA before September third and it's not the visa for what you want to do in the longer term."

"Shit!" Greg rapped his knuckles on the desk in frustration. Elbury flicked open his file and read a paragraph.

"I've been doing some more checking and it says here you worked twenty-five hours every day, weekends and holidays included, to build Bailey Recruitment and you did so successfully in only five years by putting your heart and soul into it."

Greg seethed inside hearing these words; the hurt and the memories they evoked were still fresh in his mind and painful for him to contemplate.

"So what? What's that got to do with anything we'll be doing here?"

"If you put everything into building that business, how come you have cash lying idle for two years in Wayne Fisher's company?" Elbury held up a spreadsheet from the folder.

Greg wriggled on the chair and looked down at his feet in embarrassment. He liked to think of himself as super-efficient, but reluctantly admitted his negligence in following up on these particular matters.

"This is personal, I don't want to go there," he said with a dismissive wave of his hand.

Elbury was not put off by this and came straight back at Greg.

"This is just between us two and it's important Greg. Unless you've filed an IRS tax return here or declared that money to your UK tax authority, you could go to jail. I'm not trying to be superior or awkward. I'm just trying to do my job as your accountant and financial adviser. It's what you're gonna be paying me for and I need you around long enough to sign my cheques."

Greg regarded Elbury in open jawed astonishment. "You're putting me on? Jail?" Greg laughed it off, but Elbury wasn't laughing.

"Yes jail Greg, and there are no jokes in what I said. The IRS is merciless about tax evasion. What we have to do, and we have to do it fast, is get those Fishers profits turned round from evasion, which it looks like at present, to avoidance: which means legally paying no tax on it." Elbury's deadpan facial expression matched the severity of his words.

Greg shook his head.

"I don't understand." Greg's voice rose with irritation. "I've been doing business in the States for years on this visa and now you're telling me I need a different stamp on a piece of paper. Is that just here, in Nebraska, where everything seems to be put in the way of anybody who wishes to get forward, or the whole of the USA?"

Elbury kept his cool. "It's the law. The federal law," he emphasized, "and it applies across the whole USA, not just in backward Nebraska. I'll explain it to you after you tell me how and why this money's in Fisher's company in the first place. I also need to know exactly how long it's been there and where you got it from?"

Greg sat silently regarding his shoelaces for several moments before he looked up and asked for water. Elbury left the room and returned with a plastic beaker of iced water. Greg swallowed the contents in one draft, took a deep breath and commenced talking in a slow drone.

"Bailey's was a small market town recruitment firm in Southern England. It was going nowhere when I joined and the owners were living beyond their means chasing superior social status."

Elbury interrupted. "You told me some of this yesterday, but explain that social status thing."

"They wanted to be like aristocracy. The real aristocracy would ordinarily have little to do with them: among themselves they despise the newly rich people with aspirations beyond their social station. The real aristocrats all have massive, crumbling houses and castles to maintain and are now without the financial means or income to do so. They have this thing called inheritance tax in the UK - death duty by another name. Each time the owner dies the estate has to pay a percentage of its value to the State. In order to keep themselves going and maintain their position in Society - with a capital 'S' - the landed gentry have to hob-nob, even marry into the wealthier middle classes; who sometimes get titles along with the wedding ring, like 'Lord' or 'Lady'. In return the real aristocrats get funds from their new in-laws to support their upper class lifestyle and pay for building repairs."

"It's a class thing then?" Bill's mouth twisted as if it had tasted something foul.

"Very much so."

"Why Society with a capital 'S'."

Greg stood up to explain. "Because there are still two societies running one above the other in England. There's the usual one, meaning everybody under the government of the state, and there's the superior one, headed by the sovereign and her nobles. Centuries ago that used to be the establishment before democracy changed everything, however, the old blue-blooded families still cling to their ancient belief they were born to rule. They don't give much of a damn about what other people think. They dislike this nouveau-riche class most of whom act and think like the Bailey's; and believe they're now good enough to be raised to the aristocracy because of their wealth. These wannabes act superior and look down their noses at lesser mortals. The ordinary people in the street call them 'snobs'."

Bill Elbury laughed and shook his head "No wonder there was a tea party in Boston all them years ago. Go on, I'm enjoying this." Greg coughed into his hand and sat down before continuing.

"I got myself into recruitment because it was a source of good money for not doing very much or having to set up more than an office with a phone, a desk and a photocopier to be in business. Then along came the Internet and the Super Highway to give it all a new dimension. Before Tim Berners-Lee gave us the public Internet the common belief was that in order to be both big and national a company needed a head office in London; paying the higher salaries, rents and expenses that entailed. I could see the benefits of using this modern technology to set up a national organization covering the whole country from anywhere; including a small market town in Southern England."

Bill frowned and snapped out his next question, pointing a finger at Greg.

"Why didn't you go to one of the big boys in the market, surely they were already doing something like this? They would already have the necessary credibility in the marketplace to go nation wide from a place in the middle of nowhere?"

"That's true, they were trying to put something together, but surprisingly, they were not that well organized and were slow to pick up on national managed services contracts. They were still hide-bound by the past, clinging to their old ways and practices. They weren't able to shed their skin to emerge leaner and fitter for the modern Internet age. For that reason they wouldn't take in executives with that knowledge from outside to let them streamline their organizations for them. Their existing managers took the view anybody coming into the firm with any rank from the outside was a personal threat to them rather than an asset to the business."

Bill had rested his elbows on the desk, supporting his head on his hands as if bewildered; he lifted his head to ask and wave his hands at Greg, encouraging him to continue.

"I see where you're coming from. It would be easier to start fresh with an outfit that had no baggage. But that would mean you've got no presence in the markets; and that means no credibility. How'd you get over that obstacle?"

"Slowly and painfully at first, working every day at full speed. I started by putting together a Supplier and Client contract using a friend who was an employment lawyer. Then we put together… together…"

Greg's voice broke away in small, choking coughs.

"Are you okay?" Elbury stood up, leaning towards Greg in concern, supporting his weight on his hands.

Greg massaged his throat vigorously between his thumb and finger, forcing an embarrassed smile and croaked. "I'll be okay in a second."

"I'll get you some water."

Elbury picked up the empty beaker on the desk in front of Greg as he left the room.

19

"Here y'are," Elbury said simply when he returned seconds later. Greg gratefully accepted the refilled beaker in both hands. The accountant stood to one side with his hands on hips watching over Greg as he took several sips of water, returning to his seat behind the desk when Greg said,

"That's better. Now where was I?"

"You and a friend were putting contracts together." Elbury stabbed a pen in Greg's direction as he spoke.

"Ahh yes," Greg held onto the beaker of water as he continued with his story. "Next we put together another contract to sign other High Street agencies to supply workers to our client through the Bailey system I set up. The idea was Bailey's would have the exclusive right to supply temporary workers to the client who would benefit by having only one supplier to deal with: uniform terms and conditions throughout the UK, one point of contact and only one invoice to settle each month. Bailey's would manage the recruitment, delivery and payment process sourcing the temps from other suppliers."

Greg paused to put the beaker onto the desk and give Elbury an opportunity to ask questions. The accountant said nothing, sitting rigid and attentive, waiting for the rest of the story. Greg obliged.

"Once we got our first client and proved the system was reliable and more cost effective on our lower overheads, profitability followed automatically. We weren't burdened by the costs of running our own offices and staff in every town where we were now doing business. We used the existing local agencies, many of which were already supplying the clients directly before we took the business away from them by signing the client to our exclusive contract. If they still wanted to supply the client with the temps on their books they could only do it through us, and on our terms and rates."

"Did they go for it or try supplying through the back door?"

Greg smiled thinly, appreciating Elbury's question as the product of an astute mind.

"Some tried that way and some delivery managers preferred doing it the old way. We watched the back door and closed them down when it happened, making the business flow through our channels."

"How come? If you had nobody locally working directly for you, how'd you find out it was going on through the back door. You wouldn't have had any orders to check back on if the local supplier went direct?"

Greg threw back his head to laugh easily.

"What's so funny?" Elbury's face screwed up in confusion.

" You'll never believe this when I tell you."

"Try me."

"The agencies who supplied through the back door told us. They came onto us complaining they hadn't been paid. We built into our contract a system whereby the client could only pay for all agency personnel it employed through us, but we could only bill the client for staff supplied through us. I built that in as a safeguard against such black market or back door operations. There was no way other agencies supplying outside of our contract could get paid."

Elbury whistled in admiration. "Good thinking Greg. Nice piece of work, but that don't get you over your lack of credibility in the marketplace."

"At first we used only those regular suppliers the employers already trusted until we built up a track record for reliability. That's where we got over any credibility obstacle. They had to work for us or not supply the client at all, and the arrangement worked well; except the suppliers didn't make us much as before. They worked for lower margins and it's from those reductions, coupled with our increased technical efficiency, that delivered the reduced hourly costs of temps to the client."

Elbury waved his hand above his head and said, "It's a common enough business model. I know how it works, what I don't understand is this. With you putting everything you have into this business - even going so far as marrying the daughter so you were wedded to the family and the business; how come there's cash over here in Fisher's company that don't belong to the Bailey's? To be perfectly blunt Greg, I need to know if it's honest money you came by and you weren't creaming off Bailey's or laundering monies from other sources?"

"No, Bill, it's nothing at all like that. The money is mine; it's honestly come by and traceable from Bailey's to me. They were commissions I received when I landed big contracts. I built a small address commission into the main contracts for myself when I wrote them. I thought I was being clever. When I got the first one I did consider giving it back, but it was a legitimate business charge and decided instead to let it mount up and maybe give it back later, as presents; like a new horse for Victoria. I set up a small company in UK. It's still going and receiving commissions from the contracts I signed with clients that Bailey's haven't lost or renegotiated since I left."

"So why didn't you give it back as gifts like you intended?"

"I was still making my way with the family when I started signing off the big national contracts. The family didn't think I was as good as them, even although I was producing the cash to fund their social graces. Victoria and I weren't married yet, but getting closer and it would seem like treachery if I drew attention to it by giving it back. They would think I was not fully committed to Bailey's and feathering my own nest at their expense."

"Weren't you?"

"No, of course not! These are legitimate brokerage commissions. They would have nothing at all without me. Then as things went on I was getting ever more absorbed into the family. I was expected to act, think and behave in a certain manner. I was told to play tennis instead of watching Premier League soccer. I needed something to keep me being me. I was scared of being absorbed into the Bailey family mold and losing my identity; especially when Victoria's family decided we were to be married"

Elbury exploded. "What! Are you telling me you're marriage was arranged by her family? Are you saying these things happen in England today? It's preposterous."

"But true nevertheless."

"But I thought you said they didn't like you at their parties and things."

Greg laughed and slapped his knee. "Our wedding was one of commercial convenience, it was not so I could be consort for Victoria at their social functions. There were enough 'Hooray-Henrys' from the right side of the social bed to accompany her to those. It was because of business. I had to attend quite a few business functions. These are the black tie dinners and wives' long dress events arranged by companies we were doing business with or whose business we were courting. I needed a wife on my arm to go with me. There was none better for the purpose than the owner's daughter; particularly one whose picture was seen most months sat astride a horse, or holding a champagne flute in the County and Society magazines."

Elbury sat still, as if he was in shock before whispering, "Good God man, why ever did you put up with it?"

"Simple. I was a man on a mission to get to the top. My own mug shot was all over the business glossies. TV often interviewed me to make a comment on business trends. I was somebody in the forum and going places. I wasn't there yet, and still needed to make Bailey's the biggest, the richest and the best in the field to get there. I was working on changing the name to Bailey and Mitchell later this year; soon as I finished renewing the Royal Mail contract I was in the process of renegotiating. The job wasn't finished yet. I told you. I was a man on a mission with that single thought in my head."

Elbury's jaw sagged. "Your marriage was loveless, is that what you're saying? What about children?"

Greg laughed, a short and heartless sound.

"Children? Bailey's was my baby. Besides, there was no chance of that. Victoria would not wish to chance spoiling her figure with childbirth. On our wedding night she changed into a slinky silk off the shoulder piece, she looked ravishing and had supped just enough champagne to be loose. She wagged a finger at me and rubbed her other hand slowly over her body, pushing the fabric against her curves and hollows. She had a body to die for and she stood there and said to my face, 'Let's start as we mean to go on. By which I mean, don't get ideas about having children, I value my figure too much'."

"WHAT?" Elbury erupted. "And you let her get away with that as well?"

Greg nodded as he laughed. "For the good of my business ambitions I did. I don't know why I'm telling you all this, it's personal and I only met you yesterday, but it's good therapy for me to talk about it."

Elbury didn't reply, but picked up another piece of paper from his folder and rubbed his thumb and forefinger over his forehead before he looked up and shook the paper.

"While we are talking like this, it says here you were married before you wed Victoria?"

Greg laughed derisively, "That's right, dear Elsie, she had her own ideas about marriage. I was for Tuesday and Sunday nights and paying the bills. Every other day or night was for some other woman's husband."

"You've not been very lucky with women have you?"

"I don't know, I've never been in love with one, but I don't think I'm queer if that's what you're leading up to asking?"

"Not queer! You told me that the other day, how about bi-sexual?"

Greg didn't answer at first as his thoughts briefly queried the feelings he experienced as he massaged Jess's leg.

"I don't think that's me, but I have no abhorrence to the practice as long as it's for the right reasons."

"And what are the right reasons?"

"Love and not lust."

Elbury sucked his lip for a few moments while he took that on board and then spoke crisply.

"I'm here to help you in business. Your personal life is your own affair, but it helps me to help you knowing what you've told me. Thank you for being so candid and free with your backstory Greg. It can't have been easy for you talking like that to a stranger, and I respect you for it."

"Thank you Bill. I feel rather silly right now."

"Don't! You still haven't told me how this money came to be in Fisher's company?"

Greg shifted again to make himself more comfortable on the hard chair.

"Victoria and I were married for just over two years. It was about three months before our wedding. Victoria and her brother were invited by the Simpson's to accompany them on their yacht, cruising the Adriatic Sea."

"Adriatic Sea?" Bill looked perplexed and Greg explained.

"It's a Gulf really, part of the Mediterranean between Italy and what used to be Yugoslavia. This happened in the August of that year. The firm was mostly closed for annual holidays and working on a skeleton staff. I took a month off work and with nothing to do and nobody to do it with came to the States. I like the States and had done some international business there for Bailey's; and some other firms before I joined Bailey's. I've always enjoyed doing business here; I like the open style where people take you at your word and you just have to be honest and do the business and not having to be recommended by a third party beforehand. I came into New York Kennedy, hired a car and drove down the US1 taking in and looking around the old Civil War sites. By the time I got to Georgia, I was bored."

Elbury interrupted again, "How long did it take you to get to Georgia?"

"Five days."

"You couldn't have learned much about the Civil War by then?"

Greg waved away Bill's objection.

"Enough. If you've seen one battlefield you've seen most.

In my opinion victorious generals of any army applauded for winning campaigns are only successful because the opposing generals actually lost the battles for them."

Elbury snorted. "Touché. So what happened after Georgia?"

"I picked up with an old seafaring pal in Florida who had opened a profitable sideline importing all sorts of sports and manufactured goods from Russia. Things were going well for him and there was enough cash on his wife's side of the family to fund his ventures. He was telling me how difficult it was for start-ups to get funding from the banks. He told me about a young guy with a great idea for converting waste cooking oil into diesel fuel who couldn't get bank funding because he had no provable business background and no realizable assets to support a loan."

Elbury nodded "Fisher told me some of this on the phone. He said that you said it was crazy that nobody was doing this commercially and maybe only California had more waste cooking oil than Florida."

Greg grinned. "That's right, but after we met and talked, the kid ticked all my boxes. He showed me over his plant. It was in his dad's garage. The plant was up and working. It was producing quality fuel and I could see he knew what he was doing. I stayed with him over the next week. We worked together to make a couple of batches of oil from start to finish. The diesel price was topping two bucks on the forecourts and here he was making fuel just as good for fifty cents. I was sold, not only on the idea, but also on him. He said he needed fifty thousand bucks. We sat down together. I crunched the numbers and reckoned fifty grand wasn't enough and he'd need half that much again."

Bill intervened. "He said he laughed in your face because he couldn't get a dime out of the bank, much less seventy five grand."

"That's right he did. Then he asked me outright, 'where will I get that sort of money?' I said, 'From me.' When he saw I was serious he jumped up and down hugging me."

Bill chuckled. "He told me he ran inside to his folks yelling 'I got the money, I got the money'."

Greg nodded. "He did and it gave me a chance to examine my own reasons. I was hoping this would be something for me outside the family. I didn't expect things to go so badly with me at Bailey's, but I needed something to cling to that was my own - like I already told you, this would be my identity outside of the family. I'm really glad I did it now after what happened. Anyway, I'd worked with Dean Halburton before on contracts. I talked to him on the phone and we worked out a program and a contract. I invested twenty-five grand for twenty percent of the business and loaned him the other fifty grand on a performance related variable interest rate and as far as I know he's prospered ever since."

Bill rubbed his chin, "And some. He's coming to see you about that contract on Friday."

"No Bill, he's coming to see me, and help me set up a bio-diesel plant in Bamptonville."

Elbury exhaled deeply and stood up to pace behind his desk and talk as he walked.

"Wayne Fisher is grateful to you for his start. He wouldn't be where he is now without your help. But he's also a businessman who needs to move his business forward. It seems your past help is now a hindrance to his future."

"What's that you're saying? How can that be?" This news startled Greg.

Elbury raised his hand again for attention.

"Let me explain it like this Greg. You have so many tie-down clauses in your contract he can't move without offending one of them. Your loan and its accompanying terms are now an encumbrance to him. He considered selling the firm to start out all over again, just to get rid of you, but Dean Halburton told him he couldn't even do that without your permission." Elbury looked sideways at Greg before adding. "Apparently you were always too busy to give this your attention or respond to his enquiries. Meanwhile this money accumulated in his accounts and it's a false entry, since it belongs to you and he cannot do anything with it, except let it stagnate until you remember it's there."

Greg stood and shook his head. "It wasn't at all like that. I didn't deliberately ignore him. I had to keep this secret from the family. These deals grew and became something of a monster. I was negligent. I admit it, but I wasn't uncaring. I'm here now to visit them all."

"Them all? You mean there are more Wayne Fishers' out there somewhere?"

Elbury pointed to the window as he spoke. Greg nodded dumbly at its curtain while it fluttered in the light breeze.

"That's right."

Elbury clasped his forehead.

"Holy Shit! How many?"

"Four or five."

"Four or five! Four or five?" Elbury paced to and from behind his desk for a few moments to think and came to a decision.

"One step at a time. Let's deal with Fishers' for now. His business has moved on. He does more plant sales and installations now than he does converting waste oil. He's heavy into green energy - gas from manure, electricity from wind, solar and heat pumps. He's coming to help you set up, but also to give you an ultimatum."

"Ultimatum? What ultimatum?"

"You either join him, because he can use your money, contacts and expertise or you get out altogether."

"Do you mean buy me out? He can actually afford to do that now?"

Elbury chuckled. "It's ironic Greg. The very bank that wouldn't lend him a dime to start with is crawling over him morning, noon and nighttime with offers of loans at preferential rates. He's a triple 'A' customer in their books now."

Greg was temporarily lost for words and couldn't believe the young entrepreneur's good fortune.

"I thought he liked me?"

Elbury grimaced at the self-pity, but it was all Greg could think of saying at that moment, however, he soon recovered his balance and composure.

"I never intended to hold him back at any time. I knew I couldn't be here to watch over things myself. Those clauses are there to protect my interest. If he wants me out we can come to terms. It shouldn't be difficult. How much is his company worth now?"

Elbury casually shuffled the papers in his folder. He picked one out and read from it nonchalantly. "At the last audit, and that would be last December, it was valued at four million. That's a paper valuation of course and things have improved some since then."

Greg was flabbergasted and slowly rose to his feet.

"Did you say four million? Is that dollars?" His voice croaked and his brain reeled under the enormity of this news. Greg had no idea Wayne Fisher had done so well, which proved again how negligent he had been in keeping in touch with his investments.

"That's right, four million dollars. Your share is worth eight hundred grand and your loan, let me see, where is it... Ahh, here it is, your loan value is currently one hundred and fifty thousand dollars."

Greg collapsed into the chair. He now knew the sensation of winning a lottery prize. Elbury sat and waited for him to come to terms with the good news.

"How come?" Greg muttered.

"How come? I guess Wayne Fisher is a good businessman. The markets like him and what he's doing. Just like you did when you loaned him the money. What I can't understand is how you didn't keep track of it or even know about it."

It was Greg's time to wipe his brow. "Honest to goodness Bill, I was too busy, it was a sideline so was out of my sight."

Elbury pointed a finger at Greg to emphasize his next words.

"Now you can see why we have to get you straitened out with the IRS - they'll be anxious to get either the tax they'll say you owe on these assets or have your hide tanning to a striped sunburn behind bars inside a federal jailhouse. They don't much care which in these cases. You'll have a lot to talk about with Wayne. You're currently as free as a bird and looking for a new place to roost, could be an easy solution there. He's got some really big ideas and he would much prefer to have you on his board of directors for your abilities and assets. It's not sentiment; he's going national and needs someone to direct the operation, just like it seems you did before at Bailey's. He can tell you all about his plans when he gets here. Now I'm hungry and I'm going out for some Subways. What can I get you in your sandwich?"

Greg's head was fit to bursting with this news and he only half heard Bill. "Anything at all, whatever you are having." Greg was in shock.

Elbury chuckled again and tossed a pen and a pad on the desk.

"While I'm gone you write down every other investment or asset you own or have owned or part owned in the US of A and put down any losses you've had as well. I'll want addresses - contacts and everything you can think of to do with them. I'll be about twenty minutes; be done for when I get back."

He left. Greg sat down at Elbury's desk and began writing on the pad.

20

Good to his word Bill returned twenty minutes later, laden with packages and a bulging Subway bag.

"I met Jennifer downstairs, she's got most of what you wanted and she's now off again to look for some mail scales, whatever they are. You finished writing?" He spoke in staccato gasps, panting and breathless from his exertions.

He placed the Subway bag carefully on the desk and dropped the other packages on top of the piles of papers and books on the floor. Bill picked up Greg's notepad and read from it out loud.

"R.A. Austin - 'Phoenix Az, Guns and computers'. That's a strange mix?" Bill raised his eyebrows to ask for clarification.

"He's a Vietnam vet who got into computers and is good with them - equally as good as with guns. The bank said he was too bad a risk to give a business loan."

"No, no, no," Bill exhorted, "it's not like that. There's all sorts of help available for vets; mortgages, loans, education, everything."

"I think he used all that up making guns his main business and computers the sideline. There's too much cutthroat competition in the arms trade in the USA, and it seems to me it works out best for anybody in that business if the place of worship they attend meets on Saturdays. I gave him a loan on condition computers become the core of his business and guns the sideline. I reckon it's worked out well enough for him. He's not hiding from me as I've been getting a Christmas card from him every year."

Bill grunted. "I'll be checking him out." He read out the others on the list.

"What on earth went through your head when you put this portfolio together? There's no theme or balance to your investments. They're all bottom of the heap, risky ventures."

Elbury slapped the pad emphatically. "You've got money in a

fishing boat in the Keys, a boatyard in Louisiana, a beauty salon in Houston and a deep pit grill and bar complex in Kentucky. They're also all in the South and a long way from Larksville."

Greg shrugged as he teased. "They seemed like good ideas at the time and as for the South; the weather's generally better down there."

"Tell 'em that in the hurricane and tornado seasons," Bill commented and then clapped his hands. "Okey-dokey let's eat and get to work."

He rummaged in the Subway bag and passed over a wrapped sandwich with crackers, Coke and napkins. "Hope you like meatballs?"

"Meatballs? In a sandwich?" Greg held the package away from him in horror.

"Why sure, I eat 'em all the time. Delicious. You just don't need to be going anywhere except the laundry after you're done eating, that's all."

They laughed, and got down to work as they ate. After two hours of intensive application they rose to stretch their arms and legs. Elbury closed the paper folder and said.

"That looks like a plan. I'll work with Dean Halburton in Boston on the legals. He can make a start on your application for a green card. Meanwhile we'll use your secret little company in the UK as the parent for your current operations. We'll need to open a bank account for it - what's its name?"

Greg flushed with embarrassment and mumbled under his breath, "It's registered as Ghost Enterprises Ltd."

"Jeeesus! It gets worse!" Bill wrote down the name, his hand shaking with equal embarrassment. "I'll get that set up. You want it at Bill Courtley's bank?"

"Yeah, let's keep it all local to Bamptonville as much as we can."

"Got it; which will, meanwhile, keep you legal with the INS and the IRS since you're working here for a foreign company. It'll take a month or so to get your status sorted out to something more suitable. I'll make a start getting your money out of these investments. You must've done well for bonuses at Bailey's and these - what did you call them - address commissions? I think we call them overrides this side of the Gulf Stream."

Greg grinned. "I didn't do too badly. If you're interested, I made a few smaller investments in UK and France and I own a sixty-fourth part of a theater-club in Amsterdam as well."

"Don't tell me anymore," Bill threw up his hands in mock horror, "but leave me the contacts for Ghost Enterprises Ltd. I take it you'll be starting these trades with your young man quite soon."

"We start tonight. I'm going to teach him how to sell a used air-con unit. And for the record, he's just a young man, not my young man."

"Anything you say Greg, anything you say," Bill spoke with a twisted smile, exaggerated to tease Greg's sensitivity on how he preferred others to perceive his relationship with Jess. They were interrupted by the arrival of Jennifer, laden with more packages.

"What's that about a young man? What'd I miss?"

Bill smirked. "Nothing at all Jen, Greg was just saying he's got to get back to his young man."

Greg balled his fist and made out to threaten Bill, but the disappointment flooding across Jennifer's face arrested his move.

"Oh no," she said, with an unmistakable note of sadness in her voice, "not you as well Greg; you're not another one of those gay folk are you?"

Greg's cheeks burned with embarrassment. "No I'm not Jennifer. It's just Bill having his little joke. And thank you very much for doing all this shopping."

"Oh that's fine," Jennifer's face found its smile, "there are a couple of bigger things downstairs, and there's change." She said it like a child reporting an award of good grades at school. Greg took the cash from her, putting it away in his pocket with a grateful smile.

"Thanks again Jennifer, that's a great help to me. I'd like to repay your kindness, can I entice you to accept an invitation to lunch?"

Her eyelids fluttered and her lips quivered.

"Lunch?" she asked feigning chagrin, "Dinner could be nicer?"

"Well yes, I mean no, I mean I don't know, you see I meet a young fellow every night when he comes out of school - oh hell this is coming out all wrong. I'm helping him pay his way through high school. He does things for me"

Jennifer's face paled in horror. Greg remembered the advice of a British politician who made a mess of the UK economy in the 1970's. 'When you're in a hole, stop digging.' Greg stopped talking and the only sound in the room was the deep belly laughter of Bill Elbury. Jennifer turned on her heel and left without saying another word.

"Now look what you've done with your damn fool jokes." Greg blamed Bill who hugged his midriff in a bout of uncontrollable laughter.

"You can laugh," Greg shook a finger at Bill as he spoke, "but you can put on your next shopping list the biggest bunch of flowers you can find for Jennifer and put in a note from me; 'It's really not like it sounds and may I please have the pleasure of your company at dinner sometime next week?"

It was just after four when they loaded Greg's packages into Bill's estate car to drive over to Al Yocum's garage.

The F-350 stood bright and almost shiny reflecting the afternoon sun as it stood on the forecourt waiting for its new owner.

"It doesn't look so sad now." Greg said with a note of proprietorial pride.

"She's all ready for you Mr. Mitchell," Al Yocum came out wiping his hands on a rag before shaking hands. "She'll need new disks for the hand brake, but it won't matter as she's an automatic. Just leave her in 'Park'. I couldn't see anything else seriously wrong, just fair wear and tear, that's all. I got some new tires sent over from Henshaw's Garage at Plaisance. They had 'em in stock, so they're all fitted."

Greg had a lump in his throat as he thanked the garage owner for his time and trouble. Bill watched while they completed the paperwork in the office and Greg wrote his first check on Courtley's bank for fifty-seven hundred, handing it over to Al Yocum who passed him the vehicle's keys.

"Nice doing business with you Mr. Mitchell," Yocum spoke with sincerity as he wrote out the bill of sale.

Elbury took it. "I'll take that and put my place as Mr. Mitchell's address for the change of owner notifications. Give me a call Al, if you need anything else."

Yocum helped shift Greg's purchases from the car to the truck. Greg swung into the driver's seat and felt good with his hands closed over the big steering wheel.

"That's it then, thanks everybody I'll be in touch."

"Not quite Mr. Mitchell." Yocum's soft tones stopped them all in their tracks.

"What else is there to do Al?" Greg said.

"You'll need insurance to drive."

"Shit. I forgot about insurance."

Yocum grinned. "I can help you there. I'm an agent for Fire, Auto and General. I can fix you up with a month's emergency insurance to get you on the road. It's not cheap, but I can do it for about seventy bucks. That'll give you time to get your driving experience evidence over here from England or where you've come from and we can get it a good bit cheaper for the longer term."

Fifteen minutes later Greg had his foot pressed to the boards with the powerful roar of the seven-liter engine sounding like music in his ears; he was heading for Bamptonville and running late for Jess. It had been quite a day already, and in many ways, it was just the beginning.

Al Yocum and his team had made a good job of servicing the F-350, it ran and smelled as sweet as a mountain stream on its new tires. They not only serviced the vehicle mechanically, but also cleaned it up inside and out. The throaty roar of the engine seemed to echo the truck's pleasure at its new lease on life. It was as if it felt good about itself again; like a horse after a careful grooming.

Greg switched on the radio to a country music station and together with the swish of the tires accompanied Dolly Parton as she sang 'Jolene'. The truck was happy and with the sun lowering in the sky, casting longer shadows from the west, Greg also felt more content and at ease.

It had been a full and memorable day starting out with meeting the mayor in the morning and finishing up so far with Bill Elbury shocking him with the revelation he was almost a dollar millionaire in the afternoon.

Greg felt a twinge of pique that Wayne Fisher believed their contract was holding him back.

Greg recalled the day they signed. He had forced his own way on the deal on the grounds that he was taking the bigger risk by putting his money into an unproven venture.

Wayne was thereafter meant to stay beholden in gratitude to him forever, to jump when Greg said jump. After all said and done he, Greg Mitchell, was the big man; everybody else took secondary place. That was the way Greg worked then. He couldn't remember now why it was so important to get this particular deal completed in such a hurry, but he had forced the pace on the final negotiations, refusing to take any 'No's' or 'Maybe's'.

Greg recalled dressing the part of a youthful business tycoon for the sign-off meeting, wearing a tailored summer suit with silk shirt, matching tie and Italian shoes. For a second he relived the thrill of the kill, enjoying the memory of how he had twisted the last dime of benefit for himself out of the Fisher deal and screwed the operation down tight; exercising a level of control his minimal investment in loans and shares did not truthfully warrant - especially now the business was flourishing.

Greg had invested seventy-five grand into the business with another five grand spent on legal fees. Conversely, Wayne had put everything he possessed into the project, including himself. In two short years he rewarded Greg's trust by increasing the value of his investment ten fold.

Greg had given no consideration to Wayne personally, or for that matter to any other people with whom he conducted business. He didn't do that. For Greg, the deal alone was what mattered. His concern for any other parties involved in his deals was merely whether or not he considered them capable of delivering their part of the bargain. It was small wonder Wayne wanted him out of their contract; it had to be stifling him. Comparing himself with the man he was then to what he had become startled Greg into recognizing he was altogether a different person now, with non-identical views and harboring dissimilar priorities.

"What a bloody pompous, self-indulgent prick you were back then Mitchell."

Greg castigated himself under his breath and cringed with embarrassment at the memory of the person he saw as himself just two short years ago. Jess floated next through his musings and Greg wondered if the catalyst for changing his views on life generally resulted because of meeting up with Jess.

He definitely saw things differently now after his divorce. He had no inclination to make deals for their own sake or do business for the sole benefit of people who did not deserve the rewards that stemmed from his successful endeavors.

The buzz wasn't with him any longer for negotiations making money for the purpose only of making more money. Instead, he was growing more towards prosecuting transactions that knocked down barriers holding people like Jess back in life; folks that deserved better fortune than fate or circumstance was handing out to them. He savored the genuine pleasure he found he could bring to others now - like the big-eyed, grateful smiles Jess gave him. "Of course I'll change the contract with Wayne and let him fly free from my cage."

The thought of a top job waiting for him at Fisher's provided additional excitement. It was a big job and one he was confident was within his capability. Living in Florida could be great; perhaps

Jess might go down there with him? The boy could finish his education in the Sunshine State? It was an appealing, but silly idea borne out of the exuberance of the moment, with the roar of the engine, swish of the tires and Dolly Parton's song ringing in his ears.

These daydreams and flights of fancy were dismissed with a vigorous shake of the head as Greg slowed the truck on approaching the lines of chicken sheds on the northern outskirts of Bamptonville. Ahead of him he saw a line of slower moving traffic and needed to concentrate on driving.

The vehicle in front of him was a dirty blue Buick and it had to be Gleitner's car. Anger flared instantly inside Greg. His first childish impulse was to ram the Buick and drive over its twisted, deformed steel, holding inside the trapped and broken remains of Felix Gleitner.

Greg derived a brief moment of satisfying self-pity in the pipe dream, but dissipated his emotion by gripping the wheel tightly and settled in twenty yards behind the Buick. More than ever he was convinced Gleitner was the man behind the attack on the BMW. He couldn't prove it yet, and he wondered who else might be involved in Felix's dirty tricks chain?

He knew Kyler and his gang were in this Felix 'remuda', but what about the sheriff? Could he really be in it with them, a man of his standing? Could Donovan be taking bribes to ignore the going's on at the Truck Stop? If so, he wouldn't be the first or even the last lawman to fall prey to temptation. Greg continued to convince himself that the sheriff was not as lily-white as Elbury and others painted him. His inner voice spoke to straiten his thinking. 'The sheriff didn't put acid on your tire; you'd best concentrate your thinking to expose those that did.'

Having failed last time, will they try to get at him again, and if so how would they come for him next time? The questions made Greg uncomfortable and took away much of the gloss from his day.

For perhaps two seconds he thought about buying a gun, but he was a foreigner here and would have to buy it and hold it unlawfully. I can't walk around town with an illegal firearm hidden under my coat. Greg dismissed the notion, but decided to buy a pepper spray to keep about his person instead. If somebody did move to attack him, it could be a useful deterrent.

Greg eased off the accelerator as he entered the town limits and followed the slow moving stream of traffic heading south until he turned off at Greener and drove into his space outside one-ninety-six. He was delighted to see Jess already waiting for him. The boy was sat on the bench outside his room wiping a J-cloth over the air-con unit.

It had not been one of Jess's best days at school. Melissa endlessly spread her malicious gossip about him and Greg; tittle-tattle based on her own assumptions after he went off the campus with Kyler yesterday.

Jess mentally kicked himself for telling her they were taking him to the motel; it was stupid of him. Her twisted mind instantly put two with two to make five and went around telling the whole school throughout the day that Greg was sent by the Devil to corrupt Jess and was using Kyler and Felix to help him. And, it was already too late for Jess, because she was sure that English devil's disciple had carried out his evil desires with the boy last night.

Kyler and his crew helped exacerbate this particularly juicy rumor, even though they knew it to be untrue, since it suited Felix's purposes to split Jess from Greg.

The story raised some whoops and hollers among the students. Jess had come in for heavy ribbing from some of his peers throughout the day, but mostly the others couldn't care less what he and Greg were doing, as long as it didn't affect them.

The teasing continued throughout the day once the class saw how sensitive Jess was to their jibes. They were able to get a rise out of him whenever they brought it up. Melissa maintained her diatribe without let up whenever she had an audience. Jess missed his lunch to avoid seeing her in the cafeteria and his stomach growled to remind him it needed food.

The best moments of the day for the boy were during class lectures when he allowed his mind drift off to recall Greg's teachings about business and his ideas for them making deals together.

Jess did some work on his sales pitch. Several times he wrote down what he had to say to Mr. McKendrick later that night. He didn't find it an easy task. The words would not come readily and he ripped up several failed attempts before he found what he thought were the right things to say. He began feverishly writing them down in his workbook, unaware that the teacher had stopped his lecture on North American history.

Mr. Sloan had quietly walked across the room to stand poised over Jess like a vulture while the boy continued writing, oblivious of the teacher's presence. Meanwhile, the class grinned and waited with relish for the finale when the teacher pounced on Jess.

Jess came to with a jerk when the teacher pulled his workbook away with the challenge.

"Of course you know all about Farragut's attack on Mobile don't you Jesse White; and so you can just sit there day-dreaming through the class?"

Before Jess could apologize, Ethan Cartwright bawled out from the far side of the classroom

"He'll be dreamin' about last night with his new boyfriend sir."

Uproar in the class followed this catcall. It went on for some time. The teacher did not understand the joke, but left Jess in order to stop the pandemonium and settle the class down.

Fortunately for Jess the bell rang for the afternoon break and he ran out of the room and into the schoolhouse, mounting the stairs to the top landing above his dormitory.

This was the roof space where the janitor kept tools and equipment behind a stout door, double locked with a chain and padlocks. There was a small open landing at the top of the stairs with a tall dormer window overlooking the yard and a wide windowsill, making a convenient seat.

Strictly speaking it was off limits to students, but Jess had lately got into the habit of hiding himself there whenever he needed privacy or wished to avoid meeting up with anybody in particular.

Apart from Melissa and her constant rants, Jess also wanted to avoid seeing Kyler today. He knew the older boy would pester him relentlessly for his decision about the Sunday photo shoot the moment they met up. Jess wasn't ready to make that decision and preferred playing for time.

This had been a long day for Jess, one he was glad was drawing to its end. He became jumpy, feeling constantly on edge and with his mind playing tricks; Kyler or Melissa appeared to him among student groups, even when they were not there.

Avoiding Kyler or Melissa when school was over for the day became his first priority. In order to make a quick get away Jess excused himself ten minutes before the end of the last hour under the pretext of visiting the restroom. Jess's ears burned as he left the classroom with Ethan Cartwright's next outburst ringing in them. "He's really off to a hot date with his new English boyfriend!"

Jess ignored the taunt and ran out of the class, stopping only at the locker room to put away his satchel of books before he jogged all the way to the Melody Inn to wait for Greg. He sat on the bench outside one-ninety-six feeling miserable, with a dry throat he could not ease by repeated swallowing while his stomach growled for want of sustenance. More than once, before Greg arrived, he wondered if he was doing the right thing.

The uproar caused by the class bursting out with laughter at Cartwright's jibe as Jess left early angered the teacher.

Mr. Marks took them for geography in the last hour and was a no-nonsense, strict disciplinarian. He held back Ethan Cartwright and two others once the bell rang for the end of the session, questioning them under threat of report.

What he heard, he didn't want to believe, but couldn't ignore. He dismissed the trio with a warning and walked briskly to the principal's office, tapped on the door and walked in once he heard the invitation to 'Enter!'

Dr. Armstrong sat in his armchair reading a college prospectus and looked up in surprise at Marks's creased brow and anxious attitude as he walked briskly into the room.

"Mr. Marks, whatever has happened? You look most distressed. How can I be of assistance to you?"

Marks fidgeted uncomfortably for several moments before replying.

"It might be nothing Dr. Armstrong, but I have reason to believe that Jesse White in the junior high school is being corrupted into an homosexual affair by a British visitor to the town."

Armstrong gaped at Marks in astonishment. The prospectus in his hand fell to the floor beside his chair.

"Heaven help us!" He exclaimed in horror. "Are you absolutely certain? This is extremely serious. You had best sit down and tell me all about this, but best first close the door for privacy."

21

Greg took Jess's early arrival as a sign of enthusiasm for their projects following the previous evening's lecture session, adding to his delight in seeing the boy waiting for him outside the motel room.

Jess's listless movements as he brushed the air-con unit with the cloth; his general languid attitude and lack of a smile rapidly dampened this belief. Greg felt a spasm of annoyance swell inside him as he watched Jess through the rear view mirror after parking the truck. The boy sat on the bench without acknowledging Greg's arrival or offering a wave in greeting. He looked miserable, making only an apathetic attempt to clean the air-con unit.

This is not how it should be. After all, I am doing this for you. Greg expected the boy to rush over to him full of joy and gratitude. Impatience mixed with disappointment and self-pity urged Greg to yell in exasperation, what the hell's the matter with you now? Fortunately he stifled that impulse by biting on his lower lip, subduing his sense of affront at Jess's apparent, casual indifference towards him.

Greg had no knowledge concerning the passage of Jess's day or of the boy's remaining underlying fears - fueled by Felix's glib and plausible arguments that gnawed away constantly in the youth's subconscious. In spite of constant protestations from Greg to the contrary, doubts about the man lingered at the forefront of Jess's mind. 'Was Greg truly for real?'

Greg calmed down rapidly, putting Jess's mood down to pre-first sale nervousness. He forced a smile to hide his own feelings, waving casually as he called out.

"Good to see you here so early, Jess. We're in plenty of time for our appointment with Mr. McKendrick. You can help me unload this lot from the truck."

Jess sauntered over, hands in his pockets; shoulders hunched forwards and head hung low. Greg ignored the negative body language, climbed into the back of the truck and passed down packages for the boy to stack on the verandah.

"What are they," Jess asked, showing the first glimmer of interest?

Greg answered with a chuckle. "They're the beginning of our bio-diesel operation."

While they unloaded the packages Greg talked about making test batches of bio-diesel from clean oil this weekend to familiarize themselves with the process and gain confidence in carrying it out before they tackled dirty oil.

"These, young man," Greg expostulated, standing proudly on the back of the truck, adopting a Napoleonic posture with his fingers tucked inside his shirt. "These, my boy, are the valuable pieces of equipment to help us do it. Here we have plastic bottles, dustbins, funnels and scales among these treasures."

Jess laughed out loud at Greg's silly pose and claims of value in everyday, cheap household items. He entered more into the spirit of the enterprise, putting his melancholy behind him. Jess rapidly returned to his normal, cheerful and enthusiastic self. Greg rendered silent thanks for restraining his impatient impulse of a few moments ago to strike out verbally.

They carried the packages inside the cabin and Greg brought Jess up to date with the positive aspects of his visit to the mayor and the offer of a free loan of one of the old stables for their refinery. "Best of all Jess, he's going to buy all the oil we can make for his school buses."

That called for a 'happy high five' a lot of yelling and bouncing on the balls of their feet for a few seconds after which Greg spoke of his trip to Larksville and buying the truck.

Jess was astounded. "You mean you handed in the hire car and bought that truck, just for us to use in this waste oil business?"

"I certainly did. How much waste oil do you think you can load into the trunk of a BMW?" Greg chuckled through a broad grin. He refrained from mentioning he was almost a dollar millionaire.

These revelations served to ease Jess's doubts of what Felix claimed to be Greg's prime purpose with him. He lightened up even more and asked with a reddening glow in his cheeks and a glimmer of excitement in his eyes.

"Are we really going to do this Greg? Can we really do this thing?"

Greg opened his arms. "Look around you Jess. Look at the things we unloaded just now. Isn't it all happening in front of you? Can't you see it yet? Of course we can do it and Wayne Fisher will be up from Florida tomorrow night to set up the plant and show us how best to work it. The time for this sort of business is now. There's a lot of money to be made. Wayne has done it already and you'd better believe we can do it too."

Jess was speechless and put his hand on Greg's shoulder, while his eyes said, I can't thank you enough. That was more than enough for Greg, he coughed, finding himself choking with emotion and changed the subject.

"First things first; you had better concentrate on selling our used, but good air-con unit." Greg shepherded the boy across to the small bedside table by the new Internet connection.

"We've got satellite broadband in here now," Greg announced with a proud smile, opening his laptop in Google Search.

"Wow, that's fast." Jess was impressed.

"This is a satellite connection; not as fast as broadband ought to be, but it's good enough for what we need." Greg's mind was already working on the job in hand. "We'd best get to work on your pitch Jess, and for that you'll need some up to date facts and figures about what it is you're selling."

They sat side-by-side, perusing the screen of Greg's laptop, pulling off details of models, performance and prices. Jess noted salient facts in the pocket notebook Greg pushed towards him and read them through several times to memorize for use afterwards.

With ten minutes to go before the time of the appointment with McKendrick, Greg shut down the connection and put his arm across the boy's shoulders to say softly and confidentially.

"Just be yourself. Take control of the interview. Always remember, you have other options open to you - other potential customers. Do not for one moment think he is doing you a favor. It is you who are doing him a favor. Remember that, should he get heavy with you."

Jess paled and looked nervous. His left eyelid twitched slightly. Greg shook the boy's shoulder to give him encouragement. "You'll be okay. I just know it. So don't worry. You'll get a feel of how it's going once you start into your pitch and then you'll know how best to play it from then on. Okay?"

Greg paused, waiting until Jess nodded shyly and Greg continued. "Good. If you see he is interested, but not yet fully convinced, a good play will be to act as if you're taking it away from him. You say something like, I have to have your answer on this now Mr. McKendrick, I've got Mr. Mafferty waiting. That should move him of the fence, one way or the other."

Jess looked up sharply to ask. "How will I know when to say that?"

Greg shrugged. "The idea will come to you at the time. It's one of the things about closing a sale; you have to ask for it. You'll just know the right moment to ask for the sale. Trust me! You'll know."

Jess's dubious assent was almost drowned by an intense grumble from the boy's stomach. Greg laughed. He suspected the boy had missed his meals and brought over a Snicker bar from the refrigerator, tossing it to Jess.

"You'd best chew on that on the way over to McKendrick's."

"Thanks Greg," Jess seized the bar ripped off the wrapping, stuffing it into his mouth with relish. Greg noted the boy still looked pale, but he saw also a brighter gleam of excitement in his eyes. Greg put both hands on Jess's shoulders and said with a thin smile, "You can do this Jess. I know inside of me you can do this. Just be sure of what you want at the outset. It's easy to get distracted, but if you know what you want and hold out for it, you'll not get sidetracked into a lesser deal."

Jess's head snapped up in alarm.

"What do we want?" he spluttered through an open mouth half filled with chocolate and peanuts.

Greg felt a fatherly glow pass through him and squeezed Jess's shoulders again.

"What you want is for him either, to buy it outright for seventy dollars, or to sell it on commission for ninety. His take will be twenty bucks if he sells it in a week, reducing down to fifteen at the end of seven days. It's up to him and how he goes about selling the unit and how much he'll make. Remember, there's no outlay or financial risk for him to take - only profit."

"Won't he want to see it?" Jess asked grasping Greg's elbow, "aren't we taking it round to show him?"

"Not tonight. He can see it another time if he's interested. Take a photograph with your cell phone, that'll be enough to show him for tonight."

Jess's head dropped again. "What's up," Greg asked, "don't you know how to take a photograph?"

Jess looked up sheepishly from under a lowered brow. "Yes, but I don't have a phone."

Greg concealed his surprise, fumbled in his pocket for his own cell phone and passed it over.

"No problems. Take this." Greg teased, "Umm! You do know how it works?"

"For sure I do," Jess replied, snatching the phone to examine it. Greg chuckled as light replaced dullness on Jess's countenance. The boy took pictures of the unit from several angles and distances. He would have taken more, but Greg intervened.

"We'd better get going. Mr. McKendrick doesn't do late. Remember? All done?"

"All done." Jess replied with a toothy grin, slipping the cell phone into his own pocket. Greg gripped the boy's arm to hold him back as Jess moved away.

"Just one more thing on top of everything else." Greg held up a finger to emphasize his next words.

"Don't push a bad position. Remember, there's always another day and another customer. If you think it's going badly and you can't pull it back to your way; call it off and get out of there. Don't be scared of doing that. I won't criticize you. Use your own judgment. Don't wait for him to send you away. Just relax, be yourself, take control and you'll be fine. Let's go. It's show time!"

Greg gave the boy's arm another squeeze as they set off for their rendezvous with storekeeper Elias McKendrick.

The light evening breeze had come around to the North, bringing with it a slight taint in the air of the noxious Noble Breath as they walked briskly out of the motel and across Main towards McKendrick's Stores. Greg held a handkerchief over his nose while Jess ribbed him good naturedly for being girlish.

The storekeeper was waiting for them on the boardwalk outside his store. He stood rigidly with his arms folded belligerently across his chest, as if ready to do battle. He had already cleared away for the night the goods he placed for sale outside the store during opening hours. Judging his manner from a distance, it did not bode well for their sales meeting.

The duo heard the distant chime of the Town Hall clock strike the half-hour as they approached the shop. They walked side by side, but Jess began to hold back as they came nearer to McKendrick. Greg placed the flat of his hand in the small of the boy's back and pushed him forwards, whispering, "You'll be fine. Go get him Tiger."

Jess threw his shoulders backwards and walked directly up to the unsmiling storekeeper.

"Good evening Mr. McKendrick." Jess greeted the man cheerfully as he climbed the step from the road onto the boardwalk with his hand outstretched to his man and meeting him eye to eye.

McKendrick remained standing upright and distant, like a picture of a stern, old Indian Chief without the feathers in his hat. The storekeeper's hand moved, not to shake Jess's proffered hand, but to look at his wristwatch. The corners of his mouth curled downwards as he muttered.

"You just made it on time. I wouldn't have waited for you."

Jess lowered his hand. Greg was relieved to notice that McKendrick's refusal to shake the boy's hand did not create any adverse effects on Jess, who moved into his introduction with a determined confidence.

"Right on time Mr. McKendrick. I know how much you value time and being on time for appointments. It's a valuable lesson I learned from you." Jess maintained a winsome smile as he spoke that threw the storekeeper off his mental balance as much as it bemused Greg.

The storekeeper became less rigid as Jess maintained a respectful attitude with a polite, professional smile to confirm he was conducting a serious presentation.

McKendrick tapped one foot uneasily on the timber boardwalk and grumbled "Eh! Okay! What's this all about then?"

Greg glanced from the storekeeper to Jess, willing the boy on and saw no signs of nerves or lack of confidence.

Jess was into his second wind and launched into his pitch.

"Mr. McKendrick. I have a proposition for you. Can we discuss it inside sir?"

"What's wrong with out here?" The storekeeper argued grumpily.

Jess was not thrown. He looked around into the street with self-assurance gushing from every pore of his body. "Because it's in the street sir. I know you don't discuss your private business on the street and neither do I. Can we go inside please?"

There was no doubting the determined insistence written across Jess's face as he faced down the prickly storekeeper.

McKendrick was completely unnerved by Jess's unexpected mastery and conceded gruffly, "If you insist." He strode inside the store, closing the door with an excess of effort once Jess and Greg followed him inside.

"You little beauty!" Greg muttered under his breath, forcing himself to stay in the background; silent, but inwardly rejoicing.

The boy was proving himself to be a natural salesman. Jess had just taken control of the meeting.

Inside, the dimly lit store was piled high with bales, boxes and bundles of every description. A riot of odors pervaded the space: soap, sawdust, ripe fruit, camphor and a whole range of concentrated domestic aromas.

"Now then! Tell me what's all this about?" McKendrick turned to face them, folding his arms across his chest. The storekeeper addressed Greg, but it was Jess who replied.

"You've known me since I was born sir and my family even longer. You've been good to us in bad times. It's for that reason I want to give you the first option on this opportunity."

The storekeeper's eyes flickered from Jess to Greg and back again. He uncrossed his arms, showing the first signs of becoming receptive.

"Are you saying this isn't about me not giving you the job? This is not some prank to get back at me?"

"No sir! Nothing like that at all. This is a genuine business meeting." Jess spoke with such convincing earnestness that McKendrick visibly relaxed. He managed to force a semblance of a smile once his doubt was resolved, listening intently as Jess outlined the deal and studied the pictures the boy had taken on the screen of the cell phone with a close interest.

The storekeeper asked questions to which Jess gave answers that earned him satisfactory grunts in return. Greg was content to leave all the talking to Jess, adding only a silent nod of verification when McKendrick looked his way for a confirmation. Ten minutes later and McKendrick was sold, but with one reservation.

"The problem I find with these things is not just the cost of the unit, it's the extra charges for an electrician, if you can get one this side of a blue Monday and maybe a carpenter too. It all gets too expensive if you don't want to cram it into an existing window and make your home look like something out of Whitewater."

Greg had already learned Whitewater was the rough end of town, where mostly the ethnics and long term unemployed lived. The customer service element of building business mentioned in his lecture to Jess last night came through and he butted in to ask.

"If we could get a labor only price for fitting, plus a reasonable start date to offer with the unit, would that make it a better proposition for you Mr. McKendrick?"

"It sure would," the storekeeper replied clasping his hands together in a display of newly found enthusiasm, "but I don't know where you'll get 'em under two-hundred bucks a job or before the end of summer? That I just don't know."

"Neither do we just now Mr. McKendrick, it's another problem, but electricians are out there somewhere and I guess it's up to us to find 'em." Greg then noticed that Jess's cheek's had reddened and the boy was bobbing up and down on the balls of his feet like a small boy in desperate need for a pee. Both men looked at him with their eyebrows raised for want of explanation. Jess gave in to his heart and blurted out.

"I think I know someone who can do it well and cheaply too. Can I check him out and come back later?"

"Not tonight you can't, I'm going home now," the storekeeper's arms folded across his chest and delivered his statement with a glare that said he would brook no argument. Greg seethed inside. Jess had just lost control of the meeting, but he relaxed in pleased surprise a moment later when he witnessed his protégé regain the upper hand. Jess continued undeterred.

"I was thinking about later tomorrow morning Mr. McKendrick. I can't be sure I'll find the man I'm looking for at home tonight."

McKendrick looked skeptically at the boy across the rims of his spectacles.

"Won't you be at school tomorrow?"

Jess sighed. He had forgotten all about the need to go to school, but with swift thinking recovered with an acceptable retort.

"That's right sir, but I could send my assistant, Mr. Mitchell here."

"Cheeky beggar," Greg heard himself say in outrage and then burst out laughing. His mirth was infectious and all three laughed heartily.

McKendrick wiped his eyes on the bottom of his apron and said. "You sure can Jess. You, or your assistant." That gave rise to another bout of laughter after which the three said their good byes.

As they were leaving Jess turned back to face the storekeeper, his face set and solemn.

"Before we go sir, I'd like to be clear on one thing. Can I take it that if we come back with somebody who can fit the unit for about a hundred dollars for labor and can do it sooner than a blue Monday you'll take the unit?"

"Providing he's properly qualified you certainly can young man. I'll be taking the commission option and let me clarify, the unit retails at ninety bucks and you get seventy, is that right?"

Jess grinned and shook his head. "Only if you sell it within seven days sir, otherwise our take goes up to seventy-five"

The old man laughed and looked proudly at the boy.

"You have yourself a deal young Jess and here's my hand on it."

The handshake went into overtime and Greg tugged at Jess's arm to get him outside in case he came off subject and started talking generally to McKendrick.

Both gave vent to their emotions in the street. Greg whooped, "You did it, you did it. You just closed your first deal. I knew you would. You're a natural born salesman. Did I or did I not tell you that?"

Jess jumped up and down in a high state of excited energy. He threw his arms around Greg to give his man a fierce hug borne out of sheer elation.

"I did it, just like you said Greg, I love it, I love it, I love it, I love it. I love McKendrick, I love you, I love everybody." They were soon inside the motel and off the street and out of sight.

Melissa sat by herself in a window seat in Harry's Place across the street from McKendrick's Stores, an opened, but as yet untouched bottle of Coke in front of her. She had watched

Greg and Jess go into the store and waited for them to come out, expecting Jess to join her and share the drink as usual. Her mouth twisted as she gasped in horror when she saw them go straight back into the motel together. She had observed with dismay the joy they shared in their togetherness, not understanding why they should be so happy with each other tonight.

She cringed when she saw Jess's ecstatic display of affection for Greg. Her eyes narrowed, her face paled as her lips formed into a thin, dark line and her fingernails pressed into the palms of her hand until they cut the skin and drew blood.

"He's with the Devil. The Devil's taking him. He's having him now. I must save him from the devil's disciple. I must save Jess's soul." She muttered this over and over with increasing volume until she finally rushed out of the diner yelling, "I must save his soul."

Her voice carried over the sound of the jukebox. People stopped to look inquiringly at her, but she was gone and they went back to their conversations. The full, abandoned bottle of Coke bubbled itself into lifelessness on the table: the only evidence of her presence.

22

Greg smiled, watching Jess as the boy skipped along the motel verandah towards the motel room in a high state of euphoria following the meeting with McKendrick. "I did it, I did it," the teen called out repeatedly as he danced and pirouetted over the decking.

Greg followed behind in a more sedate, but no less euphoric state of jubilation. After his rather lack-luster meeting with McKendrick earlier on in the day, he could not believe the evening rendezvous had gone so well.

The success of the meeting was entirely due to Jess. The boy was a natural salesman and handled the encounter brilliantly, as if he was already experienced in the art. Greg was astounded by Jess's confident performance. He mentioned all the right things at precisely the right moments to build trust with the skeptical storekeeper and a successful outcome would be his reward - providing they found an electrician qualified and capable of installing the unit for under a hundred dollars.

Jess bounced up and down on the spot in his hyped up state while Greg unlocked the door to let the two of them inside the room. He was pushed to one side as Jess rushed past to work off his exhilaration with jumps and twists in front of the sofa, chanting, "I did it, I did it."

Greg smiled and a new warmth rose inside him as he stood for a moment to watch the boy and savor his joy.

Jess noticed Greg observing him and stopped cavorting around the room and walked across to the man; eyes shining and his mouth agape in wonder.

"I did it Greg, I did it," he spoke in almost a whisper, as if doubting his success. Greg smiled proudly.

"You certainly did, where on earth did you find the right things to say at exactly the right moments? That's what I can't work out."

Jess did not reply, instead he threw his arms around Greg, jumping up and down on the spot and yelling like a dervish, "I did it. I did it." His rapture became infectious and Greg fell under its spell and joined the ecstatic celebration. Together they hugged, jumped and screamed for several seconds, like fans applauding a home run in the Yankee stadium; and then Greg's professionalism kicked in and brought them both back down to base level.

He broke away from the huddle, took out his handkerchief, wiped his face and said, "It was a really great start for you Jess, but it's not over yet. The deal's not done until the cash is in the bank. We have to find an electrician, and fast. Who's this guy you said you know who can do the job? Without him we're sunk."

Jess came down from his high by blowing air noisily from his puffed cheeks. He inhaled through his nose, held his breath for a short while, then with a large grin through a puff of exhalation said.

"His name's Mr. Ali. He lives in Whitewater. I did some child minding for him and his wife a couple of times when they had to go to pre-school meetings or something."

Jess felt rather than saw Greg's dubious look and was quick to add. "And I've been there a few times since, delivering boxes from the food bank."

"Food Bank!" Greg exploded like an artillery shell, raising his eyebrows to the top of his forehead. "This is getting worse by the second. Deliveries? With the money electricians make these days they should be contributing to food banks, not making withdrawals."

Greg was shocked. He was more than a little disappointed since he now doubted Jess's judgment overall; and not only in finding the man they needed for this job.

The boy came right back at him in a determined counter attack; punching Greg lightly on the arm.

"That's just it. Mr. Ali can't get work. And it's not for the want of him looking for it. Nobody around here'll give him a job. He's fully qualified and experienced. He rewired the condo where he lives for the landlord all by himself. It's still working okay. No one got fried yet."

"No, No, No, I'm not having any of that," Greg strutted across the room, dismissing Jess's explanations with short shakes of his hand in front of his face. "How come he can't get work? There's always work for a good tradesman. If he's done bad work, or if he's rough, unreliable, rude or badly behaved, or if he over charges he'll get a bad reputation. It'll be no good us expecting McKendrick to take him if that's the case."

Greg began to worry. He continued pacing, nibbling his knuckle while he deliberated to find another solution.

"Who else can we get," Greg asked brusquely? He had already given up on Ali.

Jess looked on Greg's self-inflicted distress with pained amusement.

"That's just not necessary! I told you already, Ali's not done any electrical work around here to get a bad reputation."

Greg stopped pacing to stare at Jess, slowly absorbing what the boy had said, then made a snap decision to trust the teen's faith in this electrician.

"Right-ho, We'd best check him out. Let's Go."

Greg picked up both sets of keys from the table, tossing the truck keys across to Jess. "You know the way, so you drive."

Greg opened the door and stood to one side for Jess to pass through so he could lock up the room.

Jess caught the keys deftly, but remained rooted to the spot, holding the keys in his open hand.

"Come on," an edge of impatience sounded in the tone of Greg's voice. "It'll be dark in an hour or so. We don't have all night. Get in the truck and drive."

"I can't..." Jess whimpered like a child. He stood on the spot, a silly expression on his face, half shame and half disappointment. "I can't drive."

"Oh! I see," Greg contained his surprise. He held out his hand for the keys and Jess tossed them back, looking humiliated. Greg caught the keys and with them came an idea to ease the boy's obvious embarrassment. He pulled the lobe of his ear and asked as a by the way.

"Do you want to learn to drive? Everybody does these days."

"Sure I do Greg, but driving schools cost a grip of cash and I don't have no one in the family to teach me or even a car to practice in if I did."

Greg grinned knowingly at him.

"Well you do now. We need you driving the truck to collect waste oil once we're set up. Do you have a provisional license or whatever they call them over here?"

Jess's face lit up like a streetlight. "You mean an LPD, a learner's permit? No I don't."

Greg chuckled. "Remind me we have to get you one tomorrow. I just thought driving lessons are something else we could do together. Come on get in the truck."

Jess directed Greg to drive out on to Main and turn left down Charmain towards Whitewater. Greg nodded dispassionately as he passed Deputy Bronsky sat in his car, on what appeared to be his permanent station at the junction with Charmain.

Greg noticed out of the corner of his eye the sidelong glances Jess gave him from time to time. No longer were they the furtive, suspicious looks of doubt and mistrust. They were now happier, more contented peeks that held a promise of trust blossoming between them. A pleasing surge of pride swelled up inside Greg as Jess directed him in the manner a son would a father along an unknown route.

"Take the next right," Jess called.

Greg swung the truck hard right into another narrow street and grunted, "These roads look strangely familiar."

Jess laughed, slapping his knees, "they should do. This would be the way you came in from the Interstate the first day you got here."

"Well I never did," Greg snorted. The atmosphere between them was light and carefree with a total absence of tension. The process of bonding was underway and while they were in this mood Greg judged he could risk asking Jess a question bothering him since he last broached it over dinner the first night they met.

At that time Jess declined to give an answer, but in his present, more relaxed mood, it would be a good opportunity to ask again and clear up any doubt concerning whether or not Jess was involved in shady activities with Felix.

Greg glanced across at Jess and saw the boy was fully at ease, nodding his head and tapping his fingers on his thigh in time with the music from the radio. Greg swallowed deeply before asking,

"Jess, tell me, just how exactly did you plan to cover your costs at school for the rest of this year if I hadn't come along when I did?" He finished his question with a chuckle aiming to convey the impression he was simply making a casual, conversational enquiry.

Wrong question.

Wrong moment.

From the corner of his eye Greg saw Jess sink back into himself. The happy-go-lucky, outward looking Jess vanished. The frightened, threatened, silent youth of yesterday reappeared in his stead.

Greg knew he'd blundered by asking the question too soon in their fragile relationship for Jess to answer completely: but by the boy's agitated response, Greg now knew there was something surrounding this subject Jess wished to hide.

Greg sighed and decided not to push the question or his luck. He looked ahead, nonchalantly whistling the melody of 'The Last Dollar' playing on the radio in the hope of restoring the casual, carefree ambiance pervading the cab before he asked that poisonous question.

A few moments later, Greg pretended to look into his wing mirror on Jess's side and was relieved to see the boy straightening himself up and apparently relaxing. He was even more pleased when Jess spoke, breaking the silence, but not by what he said.

"We should've turned left there."

Greg laughed it away, screeched to a halt, backed up, made the turn and continued whistling.

Greg noticed with distaste that the town was becoming unpleasantly more dilapidated and untidy the further they progressed southeast from Charmain into the Whitewater section proper.

The streets were strewn with litter; food wrappers blew in the breeze like tumbleweeds. Greg saw overflowing refuse bins with rubbish piled in front yards, some with even more rubbish piled loose alongside or spread across sidewalks onto the streets.

The people they passed regarded them with vacant, hostile looks, while their mangy, underfed domestic animals ignored them completely; crossing the road in front of their vehicle with imperious disdain.

The general atmosphere outside the truck became thick and threatening. Greg felt his flesh crawling under his shirt. They drove past an old, rusting Corvette; jacked up on bricks, with no wheels. Greg sighed deeply, this time with despair.

"This is depressing," he moaned, "are you sure we can find a good man for our job in a place like this?"

Jess had good powers of recovery. He gave Greg a thin smile with a determined nod of his head, showing no signs of his recent upset as he replied confidently, "I'm sure, I'm sure."

Jess sat back smiling, offering no further explanation. Greg chuckled and drove on. "I'll take your word for it, but if you're wrong, I'll have to beat you." Greg spoke with mock severity.

Jess took it in good part. He flinched in feigned terror, holding up his arms and wailed. "Not the belt, not the belt; please not the belt with the brass buckle."

They both roared with laughter. The real Jess was back and he picked up the conversation again.

"Not everybody who lives in Whitewater is bad, you know." He paused to think, Greg waited for him to continue. "And them that are, it's mostly not their fault. They got no other choice."

Jess's sincerity illumined his statement like a spotlight, stifling

Greg's intended argument. He drove on in silence to the far south-eastern corner of Whitewater; which Greg discovered was also the south-easternmost extremity of the Bamptonville urban district.

Jess directed him to pull up in front of a wood framed condominium. The building looked different to the depressing environment they had driven through and Greg couldn't determine exactly why at first.

It was still shabby and tired, reflecting poverty like the rest of Whitewater, but then he realized this building was cared for, in small ways, unlike the neighboring dwellings. There was no loose rubbish or litter scattered around this condo. The front yard boundary with the road was marked with small, hedging bushes; neatly clipped into round shapes. The space between the boundary and the condo was packed earth, but looked as though it had been recently swept.

A group of five young children were playing in a group with glass marbles and stones. Greg saw that their clothes were old and faded, bearing signs of frequent repair, however, with the exception of the dust of the day, they were washed and pressed. The children were also clean and tidy, with their hair combed or brushed. This condo and these kids were cared for.

Greg sat in the truck for half a minute to take in the scene. The condo, with its black painted woodwork marked with streaks of gray, white and brown where used boards replaced rotted or broken cladding timbers and were as yet unpainted to match the others. This small block of modest homes was an island of hope in an otherwise sea of despair.

The air even smelled fresher, the atmosphere more homely. Greg breathed deeply and with the air he inhaled came a glimmer of understanding. The people who lived in this building were not giving in to the life of losers that the local society had decreed for them. They were not like the other inhabitants of Whitewater who had scowled at them as they passed on their way here; these were people who seemed to accept their given lot, but at the same time not giving up hope that life will get better.

Unlike their neighbors, these condo dwellers were maintaining standards and holding out for a better deal. These people could use help and because they had not given up hope of trying to better themselves, deserved help. Greg now believed he understood this before he had even met them; just by the way they maintained their homes and children.

Greg sniffled as he looked across to Jess, who sat in the truck watching him curiously, with his door half open, ready to get out.

"You're right Jess. I do think we might find our man here after all." Before Jess could answer, Greg dropped out of the truck and stood looking at the condo and the huge, wooden building towering over it to the rear and to its right. It seemed to come up to the right hand end of the condo itself. Jess had come to stand beside him. Greg pointed to the building and asked, "What the hell is that?"

Jess chuckled. "That's Fawley Grain and Feed mills, the home of the Not-So-Noble-Breath."

Jess laughed, but Greg kept a straight face. He could find no humor in Jess's words. He looked behind him to see that the road they had arrived on swept sharply to the right at ninety degrees to run along a tall, wire security fence. Greg screwed up his nose in disgust. 'Those fences belong around penitentiaries, not around communities.' The enclosure separated the road from a range of industrial buildings beyond and stretching out to the I-80 to the south.

This condo is the very last residence in Whitewater; light industry takes over all the way out to the I-80. Greg was finding his bearings. He pointed west along the road, where it curved away to the right in front of the condo.

"Where does it go from here?" He asked Jess.

"Out to the Truck Stop. It's the road you came into town on, but you turned off at Cleaver before you got to here."

"You mean we could've come from town that way and avoided all the unpainted houses with boarded up windows and mean people outside with their even meaner cats crossing the road?"

Jess didn't know if Greg was joking or serious and half-laughed as he quipped.

"But you would've missed the sights of Whitewater."

Greg quickly thought about that. Jess was right. He needed to understand what he was up against here. He could appreciate now why the mayor wished him to employ people who lived elsewhere other than Whitewater. Perhaps there were no racial motivations in the mayor's advice after all. Greg hitched his pants involuntarily while he looked at the shabby tidiness of the condo and its happy, cared for kids playing in its dirt and sucked air through his teeth. He had made another decision. The people who lived in this condo had impressed him for trying to maintain a good standard of life when all around them had given in to the system that held them down. Hope was alive here and if these people wanted his help to get on, they could have it, in spite of the mayor's advice to the contrary.

23

The group of kids stopped playing their game to sit on the ground and regard Greg and Jess with big, wondering eyes. A little black boy, about six-years old, broke from the group, rushing towards them with open arms, calling out Jess's name, "Jess, Jess."

He ran into Jess who gathered him up high above his head with practiced ease, twirling around and acknowledging the youngster's call. "Hi Jasper, you doing good?"

Greg saw Jess's face light up like a beacon as he revolved with the youngster and reckoned he must have younger siblings at home on the farm.

The front door in the middle of the condo opened to distract him and a powerfully built Afro-American with a three-day stubble on his face filled the doorway. He pushed back the fly screen with unnecessary force and regarded the goings-on suspiciously, his expression severe and bearing no sign of welcome.

Jess put Jasper down on the ground. The juvenile eagerly grabbed Jess by the hand in his excitement, pulling him towards the group of kids sat in a circle in the dirt.

"You gonna play farmyards with us Jess?" Jasper pleaded, turning to the other kids to announce, "Jess is here. He's gonna play with us."

Greg stood back to enjoy the happy scene, aware that the man in the doorway was studying him from a distance. Greg assumed this was Jasper's father. The man came out of the doorway and with loose-limbed ease floated towards them. Much of the hostility left his face when he recognized Jess, although his suspicions regarding the stranger remained palpable.

Jasper shook Jess's arm. "Come on Jess, you can look after the cows in the field over there."

Jasper pointed to a patch of dirt ringed with stones to make a toy farm field; inside were six red glass marbles they were using for cows. The scene took Greg directly back to his own early school days when kids let their imagination run and made their own toys and fun out of anything they could get hold of.

He felt at home here and smiled at the tall man who now stood in front of him, holding his head to one side and his thumbs stuck pugnaciously under the bright, red suspenders holding up his threadbare, faded jeans and digging into the shoulders of his wife-beater.

The man spoke sharply to Jasper. "Not now Jasper, leave Jess be, go off play by yourselves."

"Ahh Pa!"

"Go on now, do as I say, or you wanna feel the flat o' my hand across yer rump?"

Jasper sauntered off in sullen disappointment to rejoin his little gang.

The man now spoke to Jess, but his eyes never left Greg's face.

"What brings you out this way Jess, not trouble I hope?" The man smiled mechanically to finish his question on a non-threatening note, revealing his strong, white teeth. Greg judged Jasper's dad to be about six-four and two-hundred and forty pounds with no visible fat about his body. The man's eyes now flashed between Jess and Greg asking the unspoken question, 'tell me who is the dude, Jess?'

Jess stepped forward to shake hands and make the introduction.

"Hi Mr. Ali, good to see you again. This is Mr. Mitchell. He's from England, come here to do business in Bamptonville. I'll be working for him."

Ali's brow creased, his nostrils flared belligerently and he spoke directly to Greg. "What sort of business? Why Bamptonville?" He spoke with a raised voice as he leaned threateningly towards Greg, his chin jutted forward and teeth clenched.

Greg was not fazed by the man's reaction. He had seen this response all too many times before back in UK when he had worked on government projects aimed at getting the long term unemployed back into work. He judged it to be a universal defensive attitude against rejection in those whom work had spurned for a long time. Greg understood how Ali was feeling and stepped forward with his hand outstretched and a winning smile on his face. He knew he had to build trust.

He studied Ali swiftly, noting his clothes were old, but clean and the man smelled of soap. He wore torn deck shoes, but without socks.

"Trading! Trading in mostly household and everyday goods Mr. Ali, how do you do? I'm pleased to meet you." Greg kept his hand extended towards Ali. The man regarded it dubiously and appeared to be out of his comfort zone. Slowly and reluctantly he took hold of the proffered hand. Greg felt the man's worn, calloused skin against his palm; the result of hard manual work, and also sensed the enormous reserves of physical strength in the body to which it belonged.

Ali's lips quivered as if struggling to find words. Greg filled the silence with a light-hearted explanation of why they were stood outside his home that evening.

"We - that's Jess and me - are doing our first trade. It's a used window type air-con unit. Mr. McKendrick's selling it for us in the store, but we need a qualified electrician to fit it when it's finally sold. Jess thought of you and that's why we're here sir, to offer you the job?"

Ali shuffled his feet uncomfortably; his lips curled back from his teeth in a grotesque snarl: his shoulders sagged and his eyes flickered backwards and forwards between Greg and Jess, but he avoided looking directly into their eyes. The duo stood quietly waiting for the electrician to speak.

Ali made a sudden, almost violent movement with his right arm, as if he was throwing something away; the whites of his eyes appeared to be bursting out of his head as he exploded into speech.

"Is this some kind of sick joke? I don't do that shit no more."

Jess stepped backwards. The unexpected outburst unnerved him, but Greg stood his ground and maintained the smile on his face. Very quietly he replied, taking care to avoid giving further offense to the enraged man.

"I am sorry to hear that Mr. Ali. It seems we have wasted our time and our expectations. I was told you were an excellent electrician who rewired this whole building. A man that can do that work could surely do a small electrical fitting job?"

Ali thrust his face forward, almost touching Greg's nose, spittle flew from his mouth as he bellowed. "It ain't a question of if I can or if I cain't. I told you I don't do that shit no more."

Jess had recovered his composure and stepped forward once more, to raise his voice in protest.

"Aw Shucks Mr. Ali, you're the best! You know you are. You told me so, that's not changed. Can't you use a few extra bucks?"

Ali turned to face Jess and bawled, "That was then and this is now. Nice of you to think of me. The answer's still no. So go home, or back from where you come from."

The three stood facing each other; none spoke, looking at each other in a standoff for what seemed a long time. Greg saw tears forming in the corners of Ali's eyes, but the man's determination did not falter.

The deadlock broke when they heard a woman's voice coming from the doorway.

"Whatever is all the commotion out here for goodness sakes? Is that you Jess?'

Jasper beat Jess to making a reply.

"Yeah and he's got a job for Pa who don't want to do it and so he won't let Jess play in our farm."

It was a David and Goliath moment Greg and Jess witnessed next. Ali's hugely powerful belligerence and aggression wilted instantly in the face of the aggrieved defiance of his small son. Jasper stood upright, challenging his father, his young face puckered in outrage, daring his dad to argue. Ali held his hands above his head as if in surrender and said quietly.

"Now that's not how it was Jasper and well you know it."

"Yes it was," Jasper cried, almost in tears and stamped his foot hard on the ground, throwing up a small cloud of dust around his ankles. "Jess got a job for you and you don't wanna do it, so you got angry and won't let him play with us."

Greg covered his mouth with his hand to hide his smile. As big and strong as he was, Mr. Ali was no match for young Jasper.

His mother came over to put her arm around her son to placate him, "Well I'm sure your daddy didn't mean to get angry."

Her hazel eyes turned to Jess and then to Greg, who saw a once pretty woman aging prematurely. Greg judged her to be in her early thirties, with swept black hair graying slightly at the temples. Close up, the worry lines around her eyes were visible, but laughter lines were also there. This was a trim and good-looking lady getting old before her time. She wore sturdy black leather shoes; the type Greg's grandmother used to call 'sensible shoes.' They matched her long woolen dress, but was it gray or was it blue or even green? After so many washings, it was no longer possible to determine precisely. Her clothes heralded Good Will; all except for the white apron she wore over the dress, which was clean and neatly pressed.

She pushed Jasper gently back towards his playmates, wiped her hands on the apron and approached the men folk, uncertain whether to smile or keep a straight face.

"Hello," she said pleasantly, holding out her hand to Greg, "I'm Martha Allissandros." A smile came to her lips, but her eyes were asking questions. She looked over at Ali who stood grim faced, with his arms folded across his chest.

Greg took her hand; it surprised him to find her skin so rough, with a touch akin to holding a laborer's hand. "Hello Ma'am, I'm Greg Mitchell and you know Jess already. We thought we had an electrical job for Mr. Ali, but it seems that we were wrong."

She now looked at Ali. "Augustus, what is this about? You can do electrical work. It's what you're trained for when all's said and done?"

Jess looked around in surprise, he thought she was talking to somebody else. He had never before heard Ali called by any other name.

Ali shook his head angrily, stamping his feet and raising dust.

"You know I don't like that name woman and you knows I c'aint do that work no more. They want INS'RANCE these days and we AIN'T GOT NONE! I cain't do that work no more. They won't give me any work without INS'RANCE."

Ali turned away to stand with his back to them like a spoiled child reaching the end of his sweetie bag and wanting more.

Mrs. Ali wiped her already dry hands nervously once more on her apron; her expression pained, but apologetic.

"I'm so sorry Mr. Mitchell. Like my husband just said, seems he can't do the type of work you want anymore. He doesn't have the necessary insurance."

Greg straightened himself to stand tall on the balls of his feet and took control of the meeting.

"Can we discuss this some more ma'am? If I get the insurance, will he do it then Mrs. Ali?" Greg began negotiating with his wife, ignoring Ali, who turned on them in disbelief.

"Hold on there, just hold on," he prodded his chest with his finger while he spoke, "What's goin' on here? You folks're talkin' about me like I'm not here."

"Sorry Mr. Ali," Greg said with his best corporate smile, "we thought you had left us, are you rejoining our conversation?"

"Well, yes, I am." He spoke defiantly and took a step nearer to Greg.

Mrs. Ali put her hand up to her mouth to cover her amusement at Greg's novel way of snapping Ali out of his bad mood: Jess turned away to hide his mirth. Martha took over.

"Let's go inside," she said, "it's getting cool out here now the sun's gone in." Before her husband could remonstrate she called out to her son. "Jasper, five minutes and inside."

"Aww Mom!"

"Five minutes and not a second longer do you hear me now?" She wagged a warning finger at her boy and led the way inside. Jess and Greg walked behind her with Ali following them in a sulk;

spluttering something that nobody heard; or if they did, paid no attention to what he said.

Greg wasn't sure what to expect when he walked through the door into the Ali's living room. Spartan was the first word that came to mind as he glanced around the single, downstairs room with its fireplace at one end and an open, rough timber staircase at the other. A toddler and babe played together on a rug made from scraps of rags sewn on canvas in front of the unlit fire.

His nostrils picked up the savory aroma of a stew bubbling in a large pot blackened with long usage; simmering away on an old wood fired iron range up against the far wall, adjacent to the staircase. There was another odorous undertone beneath the stew that momentarily perplexed Greg.

It was a whiff from his youth and for a moment he couldn't place it until his memory reached deep into its far recesses to bring out a picture of his grandmother on her knees, scrubbing her steps with a white enamel pail of sudsy water, a hard, bristle scrubbing brush and a large bar of carbolic soap in her hands. That was the smell he remembered: carbolic soap!

"Come on in and sit down Mr. Mitchell," Martha looked embarrassed as she indicated the rough hewn, homemade table and its plain, backless, wooden benches as where he and Jess should sit.

"Thank You, Martha." Greg had not sat on a bench like that since his elementary school days. While the others settled themselves onto the benches Greg glanced around the room. He saw no comfort; in fact there was little furniture, other than an old rocker by the fireplace and what looked like a polished wood sewing box beside it.

There were more home made benches against the front wall. An old sepia toned photograph of a middle aged black couple on their wedding day decorated the otherwise bare wall: the photograph and a small posy of freshly picked wild flowers standing in a jam jar of water in the center of the table were the only ornaments. Martha caught Greg's interest in the old photograph.

"They're my folks on their wedding day," she said with a lilt of pride in her voice, "they married later in life. They're both gone now." Greg didn't know how best to comment in reply and made as if to cough in his hand instead.

"Would you like some coffee Mr. Mitchell?" Martha asked pleasantly, changing the subject and rising from the table.

She walked towards the cooking range against the far wall to take a jar from the homemade shelves fixed to the wall between the two rear windows. Greg noticed there were no drapes or blinds over the windows. The shelves held various boxes and tins spread out over the length of the shelves with even, almost measured, gaps between them to use up the space and hide the fact there were so few tins. Greg looked around for cupboards and saw just one under the staircase next to the range.

Ali stood glaring at them from that end of the room with a soured expression, his arms folded across his chest. His wife prodded him in the stomach as she passed to pull a black kettle onto the hot ring and place some scraps of wood into the stove's firebox.

Greg took care not to look at them, neither did he want to say anything in case it was misunderstood and inflamed Ali again. He looked up above him and saw the single light bulb hanging above the table. An intricate shade surrounded it made out of colored pieces of cardboard. This was a poor household, but a clean and tidy home.

Greg welled up inside with anger at a society that was the richest on earth and let its people live in such poverty. More than anything else Greg now wanted Ali to take this job so he could pay him well for his work and make a positive difference for his family. Glancing quickly at the kids on the floor, he saw they wore threadbare clothes, but were as clean as any youngsters of their age could be.

He recognized a small jar of Maxwell House instant coffee in Martha's hands as she took mugs from another shelf and put them on the range beside the kettle. Greg also noticed the imperceptible glance at her husband, as if she was asking his permission to make coffee. In response to which, he also picked up Ali's slighter nod of approval.

She held up the jar to her husband, Greg could see her hand through the clear glass and realized there could only be traces of coffee powder inside; probably all the coffee they had. They were, perhaps, saving it for use on a special occasion, since they would likely have no money in their budget to buy any more. Greg couldn't bring himself to take it from them.

"Excuse me Martha, could I just have a mug of hot water please. I've a touch of dyspepsia I'm afraid." He rubbed his stomach convincingly for effect.

"Oh sure, do you want a pill or something." Martha was all concern. Greg held up his hands and pleaded, "The hot water will be fine thanks, it's not that bad an attack and I try not to take pills for it. They say antacids give you kidney stones."

Martha held the heavy kettle in both hands and expertly poured the hot water into a mug and raised her eyes to ask, "How about you Jess, coffee?"

"I'll have hot water too please Mrs. Ali. With one sugar if that's okay?"

Jess had understood Greg's real reason to refuse the coffee and was warmed by the man's concern and selflessness; he felt himself drawn closer to this strange Englishman.

"Tell me Mr. Mitchell, what exactly is it you want my husband to do?"

Martha sat on the bench opposite to Greg across the table, holding her own mug of hot water in both hands and blowing gently on to its surface. Greg glanced over at Ali who remained morose and unresponsive. He continued to stand with his arms folded across his chest and at some distance from the table where they sat; but close enough to hear everything they said.

Greg repeated his plans to do trades and build a fund to replace Colonel Stewart's lost contribution towards Jess's schooling.

"I think that's wonderfully generous of you Mr. Mitchell," Martha spoke politely, taking a long draft of water from her mug so she didn't have to say any more. Her sense of politeness required that the question on her lips remained unspoken. But Ali wasn't so bashful. He strode forward and stood over Greg to demand,

"And what's in it for you? Why you doin' this fer him. You don't know him or his folks. This do not smell right to me."

"Augustus!" Martha reprimanded sharply, but Ali ignored her and stood glaring malevolently at Greg.

Greg pressed his upper teeth hard onto his bottom lip. He so badly wanted to verbally tear into Ali, but forced himself to remain calm. He turned to look Ali in the eye, his face set and determined.

"Let me put it to you this way. I abhor unfairness however and wherever it appears, it makes me mad and I want to strike it down. Now it seems to me you know a thing or two about unfairness around here?"

He paused to look slowly around the room. Martha and Ali both lowered their eyes, but said nothing.

Greg continued. "I've had my own share of unfairness with a loose-living wife and her family tricking me out of the business I built up while they rode horses and drank sherry at parties. The damned law supported them, for God's sake, so don't talk to me about justice!"

Greg slammed the flat of his hand on the table, venting his present frustrations by giving away this glimpse into his background.

"…Now when I drove into this town I knocked down this young man on his way to get a job. I cost him the job that was to help him fund his way through school. I owe him a job, otherwise I don't know what unspeakable things he might have to endure to pay his way."

Greg paused again, looking at Jess, who dropped his gaze and held the mug over his reddened face to hide his growing embarrassment. Nobody spoke: their eyes remained fixed on Greg, waiting for the remainder of his discourse.

"…Then I found there're all sorts of people in this town who care only about themselves and don't give a damn about others or their predicaments and that's plainly unfair. And that makes me angry and makes me want to do something about it. Because I can!"

Greg slapped the table again and found he was panting and hot under the collar. He looked up to see Martha's eyes smiling at him. She put her hand over his and said quietly.

"Pardon me for saying so Mr. Mitchell, but you are a strange man. You may be very different from us here on the outside, but you ain't that much diff'rent to us on the insides, where it matters most. Is he Augustus?"

Ali sat down next to his wife and leaned on his elbows on the table.

"I guess not, if you says so, hun." Ali spoke with no rancor in his voice, "but how long're you plannin' to stay here; fer always?"

"If that's as long as it takes to get the job done. There's plenty to do here to keep me here for always. I've a friend coming in tomorrow to set up a bio-diesel plant to start it off."

"Bio-diesel plant?" Ali and Martha asked the question in unison and listened with increasing interest as Greg outlined his plan. Jess watched with growing admiration. The impasse was history, but one small, niggling doubt remained; and it hurt him. For Jess this was the one, small, sour moment in the proceedings. Greg had said he would stay for always if necessary to get the job done. But Felix had told Jess that Greg could stay only until his visa expired in September. That was months away however, and he forced himself to rise above the disappointment of this small anomaly.

The evening had closed in and night had fallen. Jasper arrived in the room and Martha busied herself attending to the three children while she continued to talk and listen to the conversation, in which Ali was now taking a full part.

"What is this insurance you need?" Greg posed the question without preamble.

Ali pursed his lips. "It's a new thing to protect the public. Only trained electricians can get it and you need it to get work. Trouble is it costs fifteen hundred bucks."

"Let me have a word with my people to see what they can come up with," Greg spoke consolingly, "is the insurance the only problem or are there any other obstacles preventing you doing the work?"

Ali waved his open palms across the table. "You might need cable and switches an' stuff, but you c'n get them at Walmart. If it's a frame house we'll need a carpenter. I could do that work, but it's best done by someone who does them sort o' things. If it's a brick or block built house, we'd have to take a look round first. Mostly it'll be a wood frame house in these parts."

"Do you know a suitable carpenter?"

"Sure do, right next door, Senor Tomas Perez Padilla."

"Do we need to get any special tools?" Greg was already assuming Ali would take the job. The big man shook his head and said, "We got all the tools we need, just need a chance to use 'em." This was the right moment for Greg to close the deal; that buzz was tingling through his body again.

"So if I get this insurance thing sorted out, would forty bucks cover the job from your side?"

A hard look came into Ali's eye and the big man chuckled.

"You know Mr. Mitchell, just fer a second there I was beginnin' to think you're not too bad a guy."

Greg looked sideways at Ali and with a wry grin said, "I am a nice guy, you'd better believe it, but I need to know how much this is going to cost me if I have to lay out for insurance."

Ali nodded slowly several times. "I don't know about Tomas, but fer me, you get the insurance fer a month or two an' I'll do it fer no charge."

"Nah, that's no good." Greg slammed the table for emphasis, "I might need you to do more work in the Town Hall stables; setting up the bio-plant. There might be some other work later on; we have to come to a proper agreement. I'm not into slavery Mr. Ali, nobody works for nothing anymore."

"He'll do the job for forty dollars Mr. Mitchell," Martha Ali had come back rocking a baby sucking a rubber teat on her shoulder, "and he'll settle with Tomas out of that."

Greg was taken aback and looked to Ali, who sat still and silent. His wife was in full charge.

"That's good of you Mrs. Ali and thank you, but this has got to be right for everybody, what we call a win-win situation." Greg had not realized he had dropped into his business style of speech, "Mr. McKendrick will sell this to somebody who will have particular problems to overcome to fix this into their home. We don't know what they are; all we can give is a ballpark figure. Is it likely to cost more than a hundred bucks?"

"With a reg'lar electrician it would, they c'n charge fifty an hour. We c'n do it fer much less. It won't cost that much."

"Good, can we tell Mr. McKendrick he can put it up for sale with a price tag for fitting between fifty and a hundred bucks?" Ali was quick to chip in.

"Plus materials, that's plenty; but I'll need to check the unit before we fit it. No good fitting a unit that don't work."

"Good point, when can you do that?"

"Right now if you like?"

Martha interposed again as she rocked the baby on her shoulder. "You'd best check with Tomas first, just to be sure he'll do the job with you?"

Ali grinned for the first time, a big open, friendly grin. "That's why I keep her," he joked. Then he became serious and began stroking his chin. "Just one more thing, how'd I get the thing to where it's got to be fitted and how'd I get me there too?"

Greg laughed and slapped the man's muscular shoulders. "That's easy, you take the truck."

"Your truck?"

"It's the only one we have."

Ali's eyes seemed fit to burst out of his head.

"You have got a license haven't you?" Greg asked slyly.

"I do, but I ain't got no insurance," Everybody in the room spoke the last word at once and they all roared with laughter. They were all on the same page at last.

Greg was choking with laughter as he said, "I'll sort that out as well."

"You're spendin' a lot of yer money on me Mr. Mitchell. How'd you know I'll not let you down? How'd you know you c'n trust me?"

It was a tense moment and Greg knew he would need to give a genuine reply. Everybody looked at Greg who turned to Ali and said sincerely.

"I'll have to make sure I get you enough work to get my money back; and as for trusting you? Well I don't." He paused and heard audible gasps from Martha and Jess. Greg paused for a moment and then said with a broad smile. "Yet! I don't trust you yet! But I do trust your wife and Jasper. And I know you'll not let them down."

The sudden spike of tension collapsed. Ali held out his hand again. "I'll shake on that," he said, turning around as he shook Greg's hand and said. "Best go next door before Honora puts the kids to bed." As an afterthought he explained to Greg. "Honora's Tomas's wife."

24

Greg rose from the table feeling increasingly at ease about the whole enterprise and followed Ali and Jess out of the front door into the glare of the setting sun only to sidestep suddenly to avoid running into one of the oldest, and tiniest, women he had ever seen.

"Oops sorry," Greg exclaimed, twisting away from the woman who held a saucepan in her hand beneath a red and white checkered tea cloth. He was further discomfited when she tapped the cold saucepan against his midriff several times and attacked him verbally.

"You'm the bailiff, be you? We don't want no bailiff's here. Don't need 'em. These'm be all good folks livin' here."

There was no mistaking the passion in her words, delivered in a thin, high-pitched gummy cackle through sunken lips that moved constantly, even when she was not speaking. Greg was taken aback by the near miss, but more so with her verbal attack after mistaking him for a bailiff and which posed the question, why is she expecting bailiffs?

Ali enjoyed the spectacle, chortling heartily before stepping in between them. "Hi Ebonie, relax, this ain't no bailiff, this is Mr. Mitchell, he's from England."

He made the introductions. "Mr. Mitchell this is Mrs. Ebonie Marrs, our neighbor from the other end of the building." Ali pointed a finger away from the direction in which they were heading.

"Hi Mrs. Marrs," Greg chirped, trying to sound casual, while taking care to avoid looking down on her as he stood nearly eighteen inches taller than the pasty faced old lady with her severely swept back hair, not gray, but faded black. She regarded him with steady, green eyes, paled as if the sun had bleached them from a deeper color over the years. Greg could see the alert intelligence active behind them while all the time her lips moved without speaking, seeming to sink ever further into her face as if unrestrained by teeth.

She spoke to Ali, but her gaze remained fixed on Greg.

"Y'all ate a'ready. I got me stew if you'm done eatin' and I c'n put it on the hob"

Martha appeared in the doorway to take charge of Ebonie.

"Oh Hi Ebonie, we ain't ate yet, but no trouble come on inside, there's room on the range for yours."

Martha put her arm across the shoulder of the old lady and ushered her inside. Ali watched her go with an expression of proprietorial pride on his face that puzzled Greg. Ali noticed Greg regarding him quizzically and explained.

"She's a real peach is Ebonie. Nobody knows how old she is, but she did important war work in Washington before she went to College. Now look at her havin' to beg space on a neighbor's range to heat up her supper." Ali shook his head in disbelief and a sharp stab of guilt passed through Greg. He pointed at the front door that Ebonie had closed behind her.

"Are you telling me that old lady has no way of cooking her food for herself?"

Ali chuckled again.

"Welcome to Whitewater Mr. Mitchell. We all look out for each other here in this condo. Ebonie makes a pot o' stewed vegetables ev'ry three days with floaters in it made out of a Bisquick packet. She makes it fresh fer herself on her own hob and fer the next two days uses our fire to heat it up. Saves her lightin' a fire. She's good with the kids and helps out with 'em at times. But we best be gettin' along an' see Tomas afore it gets too late in the day."

Greg was shaken by this revelation and followed Ali mechanically while he absorbed this new knowledge. Unbelievable in this day and age! But who in authority would believe you if you were to tell them?

It appeared to Greg that Ali was striding directly into the solid, wooden wall of the building ahead of them. He didn't see the narrow passage between it and the condo until Ali turned sharp left and squeezed his body through the gap. Greg's mind was still wrestling with the knowledge of Ebonie Marr's poverty and wasn't paying close attention to what he was doing until he bumped into Ali.

"Sorry, was still thinking about Mrs. Marrs."

Ali stood under a horizontal, concrete plinth stretching from the condo above him to the wooden building next door. The plinth then came down to ground level at a sixty-degree angle, forming a barrier to any passage beyond. Ali stood watching sardonically as Greg looked for a way to get around and beyond this mysterious barrier.

"What's that there for," he asked Ali, pointing to the plinth?

Ali laughed before replying; a harsh and rather resigned guffaw than a happy chortle.

"That, my man, is the porch to Tomas's house, and that…" He pointed to the inclined slab rising from the ground to the plinth above. "…is the underside of the stairway leadin' to the apartment above - home of Mr. and Mrs. Esteban Reyes Quinones."

Greg's jaw dropped and he pointed to the two inch gap at the side between the concrete stair and the wooden, Fawley building.

"But…but…how on earth does anybody get around it to the other side to go up the stairs to their front door?"

This elicited another dry chuckle from Ali.

"They has to go 'round the other way, past Ebonie's place and the back o' mine to get to the stairs up to their place." Ali spoke forcefully, the sneer of dissatisfaction clearly defined in his tone.

"Incredible." Was all Greg could think of saying before adding, "They can't do that. There're things like building regulations these days. Blocking this passage like that is a fire safety hazard, there has to be a pathway, surely? Where's the boundary between the condo and that wooden monstrosity?"

Ali laughed more heartily, his jaw opened wide, showing the whiteness of his teeth contrasting against the redness of his throat.

"Welcome to Fawley Grain and Feed." He stabbed his finger towards the wooden building. "Owner Mitt Fawley has big, big plans for this area an' he thinks he's such a big shot he c'n do just as he likes. So the bound'ry's where he says it is. Afore he built that there storehouse we had us a nice white picket fence about four feet that aways." Ali's forefinger jabbed repeatedly towards the wooden building as he spoke.

"That's preposterous," Greg spluttered over his words to get them out, "He can't just help himself to other people's property and get away with it; nobody's above the law these days. This isn't the Wild West anymore." Greg's eyes were popping from his head as he regarded Ali who shrugged, smiled and said.

"But that's the way it is here. Fawley's got money an' money's power. He employs people in his plants so the folks runnin' the town let him take liberties."

"And you let him get away with it? What about your landlord, surely he has something to say about the encroachment of Fawley's Grain plant onto his property?"

Ali rubbed his nose with the back of his knuckle.

"We ain't got no landlord. Not no more. We got us mortgages now, but we ain't got money fer lawyers to take on Fawley and he knows that. He's got big plans for this area. He wants to build a big meat packin' plant at the back of this condo. He's already built that thing…" Ali jerked a thumb towards the wooden building. "It's the storehouse, ready for when he starts buildin' the new plant."

"But he don't need to build over your boundary, he can still do that and respect your property."

"No he cain't. The only way fer him to come in from the I-80 is along this road out front comin' from the Truck Stop an' goin' right through this condo. He cain't get in from behind or any other way. There ain't no other exit from the Interstate that'll work fer him. Fawley has to come in this way an' thru our condo, or not come in at all."

Greg stood deep in thought for a moment while the unsavory

reality of the situation dawned on him.

"If what you are saying is right, he must be doing this to intimidate you to sell your homes to him, so he can knock them down to put his roadway through here."

"You got it." Ali slapped his thigh emphatically with a resounding crack, "he's so sure of gettin' his own way he's already built this storehouse. The mayor's runnin' scared of him in case he pulls out o' Bamptonville altogether and sets hisself up somewhere's else. Fawley gives work to a few folks over that fence an' them's the folks that vote fer the mayor come election day. But Fawley cain't do no more with his big plan unless we sell. An' we ain't sellin'."

Greg felt a spark of encouragement at Ali's resistance and a cold spasm of anger when he thought of the greedy self-aggrandizement of Mitt Fawley and his ilk. Pictures of the old board of director's he served at Bailey's floated through his head as they sat around the board room table with greed oozing out of every pore of their pasty, white skins. The memory made him shudder.

Greg glanced to his right, taking in the tall, interloping building with no windows, built out of rough hewn lumber boards rising upwards for forty feet or more above them, shutting out the light and air from the South. It not only came right up to almost three feet of the doorway where they stood, but stretched down beyond the bottom boundary into the distance to the east. It was an ugly, unfriendly and intimidating construction that seemed to be reaching out to embody the condo into its packing case design. Greg craned his neck backwards to see that the wall appeared to rise and end in the clouds.

Ali followed Greg's eyes and said soberly, "Like I said, Welcome to Fawley Grain and Feed."

Greg pursed his lips and nodded; he could not fail to detect the bitterness encasing the big man's words. Ali knocked heavily on the door three times and Greg asked him about the condo while they waited for someone to respond.

"I take it there're two apartments here and another two at

the other end with you in the middle, only difference is you have two floors: like a townhouse?" The door opened, requiring Ali's attention before he could give Greg more than a cursory nod of agreement.

Tomas' high-pitched, excited greeting distracted Greg's thoughts.

"Ali *mi amigo*, what gives?" A thin-faced Mexican of slight build gripped Ali's forearm in both of his hairy-backed hands and shook it vigorously. His lips parted in a huge grin to confirm their welcome, his thick black mustache rising at each end like a bird extending its wings in welcome to the visitors standing on the door step.

"Hi Tomas, hope we're not too late in the day to talk a little business? Has Honora put the babes to bed yet?" Ali asked with polite concern.

"No, no, not too late. My friend, not too late." Greg noted the Mexican's quickened interest at the mention of 'business' and the gleam that came into the man's coal black eyes. They fixed back on Greg while Ali made the introductions.

"Cool! You've met Jess a'ready. This is Mr. Mitchell. He's over here from England with a job for us to do. Can we come in an' talk about it?"

"Sure, sure, come in, come in, welcome." Tomas threw open the door and bowed obsequiously. "Pleased to meet you Mr. Mee-chell." They followed Tomas into his home as he ushered them to his dining table calling out, "Honora, Ali is here with Jess and Mr. Mee-chell, he's here from Eeng-land."

"Seet down please," Tomas invited. Greg looked around and saw the living room was twice as long as Ali's, but half its breadth. They were in the living area. Where Ali's home had windows on the back wall, here there were three doors in an internal wall instead. He surmised they led to the bathroom and sleeping quarters. Within that design the layout was similar to Ali's with a fireplace at the farside wall and an iron cooking range on the back wall nearest the door. A staircase did not crowd this range as in the Ali's home.

Next to the range stood a modern, bottle gas fired hob and oven. There were more cupboards here than in Ali's house, the shelves in the kitchenette were also better filled with tins, jars, packets and bottles than the Ali's. The shelves were so well filled that Greg could not see the wall behind the tins and jars.

The windows on the roadside of the house were neatly framed by plum colored drapes, headed by matching valances. Ali's kitchen floor was of smooth planed floorboards, but a patterned oilcloth covered the kitchen floor in the Padilla home, which was replaced by a colorful carpet where the living area took over from the kitchen. It was old and worn, but still a good carpet to cover the bare floorboards beneath.

Two cushioned armchairs faced each other either side of the fireplace and against the wall; where Ali had a plain wooden bench, here there was an upholstered couch. It was hardly luxurious, but there was considerably more comfort here than next door. This was a complete home, with furniture, ornaments, photographs and pictures on the walls.

Greg saw plentiful foodstuffs on the shelves and a small white refrigerator promised even more. A color TV in the far corner past the fire was tuned to a children's program and a woman sat on a patterned rug with three young children watching the animal antics; gurgling their enjoyment and clapping their hands at the screen. Happy kids. Lucky kids.

Greg noted that their rug was not homemade out of scraps of old cloth and canvas, but a thick, woolen manufactured item. Under the TV stood a basket of plastic toys: ducks and animals, cars and doll-like figures. The apparent wellbeing in this home perplexed Greg, as he believed that Tomas was also out of work. This home was altogether more prosperous than Ali's and he bit his tongue to stop himself asking, "Why?"

"Seet down please Mr. Mee-chell," Tomas pulled a chair away from the table for him to sit on. Ali and Jess had already seated themselves on the other side of the table without waiting for an invitation.

The woman kept her back to the group. Apart from a brief

glimpse when they first came in she had not looked around or spoken. It was as if she was not there, it may have been a cultural difference, but it irritated Greg that she did not appear to want to meet him. He disliked being ignored. It did not appear to bother Tomas who fluttered around and asked. "Can I get you something Mr. Mee-chell?"

"No thanks Mr. Padilla," Greg replied cheerfully, but kept his eyes on the woman's back. Greg had not met the lady before, but there was something strangely familiar about her slight build and flowing black hair that reached to below her hips as she sat with her long tresses trailing across the rug around her. Tomas thought Greg was watching the TV and called out to his wife "It ees too loud. Turn it down *mi vida*, we're tryin' doin' bizness here."

She did not reply, but stood up in an effortless and graceful motion to glide over to the TV where the remote lay high, and out of the reach of exploratory young hands, to turn down the volume.

Everybody was now watching Honora with appreciative smiles and so did not see the grim disgust flooding across Greg's face. He now remembered where he had seen this woman before. The first and last time was yesterday. He had seen her half running from Felix's car into the hostel block at the Truck Stop. Something in Greg's mouth tasted foul. He drew more saliva into his maw to rinse it around before he swallowed to rid his mouth of the sour taste.

Greg's eyes hardened, fastening onto Honora. She must have sensed the vibrations across the ether and raised her own eyes slowly to meet his. Greg read pleading in them 'Don't tell please?' She knew what he had realized, she must also have recognized him from the brief moment he had stood in the shadows beside his car and watched her running to her customer.

Greg's immediate instinct was to walk out. He wanted to get out of that place and have nothing to do with prostitutes and pimps. In that moment his opinion of Tomas collapsed. He now thought of the man as a whore-master for his own wife and understood why this apartment was better appointed, with more warmth, comfort and food here than in Ali's and Martha's home next door.

Ali and Tomas were joking around, but Greg heard only their noise in the background, not their words or what they spoke about. He shook his head with misgiving and tried thinking this through to arrive at a more agreeable conclusion.

It's impossible for Tomas not to know about her philandering for profit. He had to know he was living off her immoral earnings. The acid taste returned to numb his mouth. Honora's eyes with their tacit plea had not moved from Greg's face. She stood motionless, staring at him and expecting him to say something, to acknowledge he knew what she was doing when darkness took over from daylight.

She stood rigid and unsmiling, as if steeling herself for his denouncement and seemed ready to fend off his accusations, but Greg said nothing. He gathered more spittle into his mouth and swallowed once more. He wondered if Ali was aware of this? Was he a part of it in some way, but the deprivation in which he lived next door provided an immediate and negative answer?

Ali was talking animatedly to Tomas about the air-con deal. Ali's newly found enthusiasm pleased Greg, but he remained doubtful about Tomas; who was listening intently and captured some of Ali's enthusiasm.

"Let's do it," He said with a big grin and slapped Ali's hand in a spirited high five, abruptly pushing back his chair to make it screech in protest on the oil cloth before he rushed into the kitchenette from where he pulled a half-full bottle of Tequila from a bottom cupboard and brought it back with four shot glasses. "Let's drink on it!" Tomas announced with a broad grin and held the bottle and glasses above his head as if they were trophies. His voice fizzed like a cork coming out of a lemonade bottle.

"Yeah man! Ali clapped his hands, ready to match Tomas's party mood.

Greg waved his hands across his chest and declined the invitation. "Not for us sorry, we still have things to do and need to keep a clear head."

Tomas and Ali looked at him with dismay, as if he had pooped the party. Greg fended off their efforts to persuade him to join them in a glass. "Sorry guys, another time perhaps. I think you call it a raincheck over here?"

The two men laughed as Tomas poured enthusiastically, spilling the clear liquid over the tops of two glasses to form small pools on the table top around the glasses. With difficulty Greg joined in the merriment, joking and laughing as he and Jess made for the door.

It was clear the neighbors intended doing some serious damage to that bottle of spirits. Greg caught sight of Honora out of the corner of his eye. She was carrying a baby and shepherding the other two youngsters through the door nearest the kitchenette. He looked beyond her to the white tiles on the walls of the room and guessed this was the bathroom. Her eyes remained fixed on Greg. A wry smile flickered at the corners of her mouth as she coaxed her brood through the door. He read her watchfulness as a challenge to him saying 'I dare you to say anything before you leave.'

Greg felt a heavy lump in his gut, but he tacitly declined to accept her unspoken challenge. He didn't want to do or say anything about what he knew about her - not just then. In his heart he no longer wanted anything to do with these Whitewater people, but in his head realized he had no choice in this first deal. It had gone too far already. It was so important in his plans for Jess that this first trade went off smoothly. Jess needed to see trading could work for him and to build on it as a source of revenue for his future. These people were Jess's friends and he didn't want to alienate the boy by dumping them from the project on what would look like a whim and a possible case of mistaken identity. Ali broke through his train of thought.

"We'll be out to the motel first thing in the morning Mr. Mitchell. To check the unit over." He stood up with his hand extended.

"Sure. Sure thing. See you tomorrow," Greg spoke gruffly, shook the hands of both of them and headed for the door with

Jess following closely behind him.

He stood and breathed deeply several times once outside the door, facing the domineering wall of the Feed and Grain plant storehouse. The cool night breeze gently caressed his face, calming him. He didn't mind the taint of burned feathers that came with the gentle wind and ran his fingertips over his cheeks, feeling their heat while he gathered his thoughts. The acrid taste in his mouth had returned, more noticeable than before.

After his own recent experiences, Greg hated feckless, unfaithful women with a passion. But reason came in with the night breeze and he wondered quietly. If Tomas agreed to her unchaste behavior for money, was she actually being unfaithful to him? Greg didn't know what was best to believe. Jess's tug on his arm was well timed.

"What do you think?" He asked. Greg looked into the boy's round, trusting eyes, refulgent with excitement and expectation. Greg could not bring himself to spoil this project for Jess and tell him what was on his mind or what he really thought about his friends in Whitewater. Neither could he entirely leave it to rest.

"They seem a lot better off than Ali and his family next door. Does Tomas do some work or something to bring home more'n his unemployment benefits?" Greg hoped his question sounded casual and did not give hint of the bitterness he harbored. Jess was not fazed. He shook his head and replied.

"Nah, Tomas gets even less offers of work than Ali does."

"Then how can they afford to live as well as they do? Better than the Ali's."

Greg had stopped to face Jess as he waited for the boy's answer. He realized he had snapped at him when asking his question, which surprised Jess, but the boy shrugged it off.

"They're just lucky, that's all. Honora comes from a well-off family in Sonora. They send them money."

Greg nearly choked, restraining his impulse to blurt out his suspicions about Honora's income. He cleared the foul taste in his mouth onto the ground. So that's how she explains away her

Truck Stop earnings. He mulled it over again as they walked to the truck. Tomas had to be in the know. He would be home when she went out. He would have to look after the children - maybe even put them to bed. How many times a week did that happen? Greg climbed slowly into the truck and buckled up, feeling sick in the pit of his stomach. Jess sat in the truck watching him with a curious, questioning look on his face. Greg smiled at the boy's trusting concern, I suppose it takes all kinds of people with all sorts of reasons for what they do - and after some of the things I've done in my time, who am I to judge them? Greg sighed, smiled at Jess beside him and said pleasantly.

"We've got ourselves an electrician and a carpenter. It's a go! Come on Jess, Let's get back to the motel, we have a whole business to build and get organized; but first off we'd best fix that leg of yours."

Jess's face broke into a huge grin as he buckled up and slammed the door shut with an exuberant, "Let's go!"

THE END
Of
A New Road

The story continues directly in:
Stopover 2: Potholes
Book Two of the:
'The Bamptonville Stories'

Acknowledgements:

Writing a story is a solitary endeavor, but assembling that writing into a plausible book form is very much a team effort. Good fortune has blessed me with a formidable team to produce this first book in a collection of novels comprising The Bamptonville Stories

Let me first thank my amazing editor-in chief, Mandy Thomas, for her persistence, patience and editorial expertise, identifying those errors in language and grammar that we don't know we make. I now have a list of words by my side that I tend to overuse - thanks for that Mandy, and for your encouragement and consolation during those dark periods of the writing cycle.

Carey Saunders, like Mandy, is an accomplished author and I am grateful for his detailed suggestions for improvements to the text. Thank you Carey.

Paul Harris is a recruitment expert who has worked extensively with the long term unemployed. I wish to thank Paul for his detailed advice when writing the scenes with the Whitewater condo dwellers.

Angela Stevens is another talented author who has used her technological prowess to layout the text into a form pleasing to the publishing robots. Thank you Angela.

Rick Taylor, yet another gifted author, poet and graphic designer who produced a magnificent cover and layout. Thank you Rick.

To Dean C Moore, also an imaginative and original author for his close edit and help in negotiating the mysteries of Good Reads, Blogs and review sites; my grateful appreciation.

To my beta readers who also know me as 'Hobnails'—Please

accept my heartfelt gratitude for your encouragement, advices and virtual 'raps on the knuckles' when I got things not quite right.

To you, my reader! Thank you for reading this story. You are the salt of the earth for whom I wrote this book and trust that it has not only entertained you, but at times alarmed and made you think on some of the darker aspects of life prevalent in our modern societies.

To readers on both sides of the Gulf Stream: This story is set in the USA and, as far as possible I have attempted to use the spelling and expressions in common use in Bamptonville. Should there be any errors, please do let me know and I will pass on your comments to Dr. Armstrong at the Community College and make the necessary corrections to subsequent editions of this book.

Last but by no means least comes Janet, my dear, long suffering wife. Thank you sweetheart for your unswerving support, patience, encouragement and proof reading skills. Jan has put up with countless hours of aloneness when I have locked myself away to write this. And yes dear, I can now paint the windows, strip the wallpaper and weed out the flower borders...

Peter Thomson
Limousin

The Publishers art as we know it, goes back to the first Gutenberg bible when the revolution of moveable type replaced the age-old craft of the hand-painted manuscript.

These dedicated pioneers of the modern printing industry ensured that the craft-values developed over millennia were not lost to the new process.

At Signature Proof we believe that the traditional values of the publishing and printing industries should be maintained however a book is produced.

After all, quality is a state of mind rather than a process and whether on-line or off-line the same standards should apply.

Signature proof is therefore your guarantee of quality: in the writing; in the editing; in the proof reading – even down to the cover design and interior layout.

We are a group of self published writers, editors, and designers who work tirelessly to ensure that a book carrying the 'Signature Proof' imprint has been lovingly crafted in all areas of its creation.

This means that we only aim to publish a handful of titles each year.

But you can rest assured that whether download or print, the quality is guaranteed.

For further information on this exciting new venture and for updates on forthcoming titles visit our blog.

http://signatureproof.wordpress.com/

OUT SPRING 2015

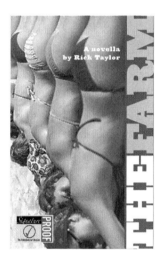

When something seems too good to be true...
it probably is.

When the Travers family win a holiday to Turkey,
all is not as it appears.

As holiday heaven turns to holiday hell,
life becomes a battle for survival.

Welcome to 'The Farm'.
We trust you will enjoy your stay.

Manufactured by Amazon.ca
Bolton, ON

18929661R00144